merciless
HEIR
KOZLOV EMPIRE BOOK ONE
MONICA KAYNE
CW01664145

ISBN 978-1-7782704-0-6

Cover Design by Opulent Design & Swag

Photographer: Emma Jane Photos

Model: Myles Clohessy

Proofreader: Alicia Dean

AUTHOR NOTE

Merciless Heir is a dark mafia romance with mature themes and profanity. Please check my website for trigger and content warnings.

www.monicakayne.com/trigger-warnings

CHAPTER ONE

GEORGIA

"There you are, my little dove."

Cold fear pierces my lungs as Oleg Antonov slithers into the en suite where I'm on my hands and knees scrubbing a Jacuzzi tub. As I stand, his dark gaze tracks the lines of my body like a predator sizing up his next meal. Which is exactly what he is.

Oleg Antonov, head of the Antonov Bratva, is a hunter. And I'm his prey.

"Business kept me away longer than I hoped, but you were never far from my mind." He comes farther into the luxurious bathroom, his eyes lingering over the swell of my breasts. My skin crawls and I tug at the bodice of this ridiculous maid's uniform. A futile attempt at modesty. "I hope you didn't miss me too much."

Miss him? Yeah, right.

I've repeatedly thanked the mafia gods for whatever business called him away from his gaudy New Jersey mansion. I've been here for three weeks now, almost as long as he's been gone. But the first night here was warning enough. His wandering hands and lecherous looks confirmed my worst fear. It would only be a matter of time before Oleg expected more. Much more.

He smirks, leaning his bulky frame against the bathroom vanity. "You work too hard. You deserve some fun."

I straighten my shoulders and offer him a false smile. I sure as hell am not up for the fun he has in mind. "I'm fine. Happy to stay busy."

"You know what they say about all work and no play." He stalks forward. His thick fingers adorned with gold rings come to rest on my jaw. Squeezing. "It makes you dull, and no one likes a dull woman. Even one as beautiful as yourself."

Anger erupts and before I can help it, I push his hand away. "Get off of me," I hiss. Oleg's face contorts into a furious mask as he grabs my arm in a brutal grip.

"Or what? What will you do exactly?" When I don't answer, his lips curl into a cruel sneer. "That's what I thought. Absolutely nothing. I expect you to join me tonight in my suite."

My heart thrashes in my chest, but I don't back down. "I agreed to work for you as a maid. Someone that cleans your home. Nothing more."

His eyes narrow, and he leans forward, his putrid breath hot on my cheek. His grasp, punishing. "Don't be an idiot. I have an army of staff to clean my house and to scrub my bathtub. When you're on your hands and knees, there's only one thing I expect of you. Remember, little dove, it's you underneath me or your father in a grave. Your choice."

My stomach roils. There's a special place in hell for this man.

Just as I'm considering using Windex to blind him, the ping of an incoming text message steals his attention. He yanks away, releasing his hold on me. Taking his cell phone out of his pocket, he checks his message. Whatever he reads causes his lips to thin in distaste.

"*Der'mo.*" I don't speak Russian, but I recognize it as a curse. He throws me one more fierce glare before growling, "You will give me what I want or you will pay the consequences."

He storms out of the room, leaving me to collapse in on myself. My knees hit the marble tile, as I bury my head in my hands. Even though I knew this day was coming, it's still a shock to the system.

How had my life taken such a dramatic turn in such a short amount of time?

Three weeks, but it feels like a lifetime ago.

Three weeks since I traded my freedom for my father's life.

But I've spent my time here wisely. Scheming, planning, eavesdropping. Gathering any information that will help me escape from his heavily guarded estate. Just yesterday, I found the one last thing I need to make a getaway—cash, and lots of it.

My discovery was not a day too soon.

Checking my wristwatch, I realize if I'm going to leave, it has to be now. It's 11 a.m. In an hour, I'm supposed to join the other domestic staff downstairs for lunch. At noon, the guards also change shifts. It'll buy me a few minutes of distraction. It's not much, but it's enough time to slip out unnoticed... if all goes according to plan.

Adrenaline pumping through me, I rise from the floor and leave the room. Not wanting to attract attention, I move through the hallway as I normally would—with a bucket of cleaning supplies in one hand and a duster in the other. I keep my pace steady but efficient; head down, not making eye contact with any of the other staff. Easy to do, considering I haven't made a single friend here. Beelining straight for the back stairs, I'm about to run up to the second floor when a hand shoots out, gripping my wrist.

"What's the rush?" A mocking voice assaults my ears.

Great, now I have to deal with another asshole.

While Oleg was away, Kristian, his second in command, was in charge. Though he never assaulted me, his taunts and creepy stares were enough to sour my stomach. And right now, I definitely don't have time for his crap.

Schooling my face into a neutral expression, I turn towards

him. "I have work to do," I say, lifting the supplies in my free hand. "It's the reason I am here, after all."

Kristian's eyes sharpen to dark points. "The reason you're here is that your father was stupid enough to take a loan from us. One that he had no chance of repaying."

I give him a blistering smile. If I never see Kristian again, it will still be too soon. "If you'll excuse me," I say, ripping my arm from his grasp, "I have tasks to attend to."

"I'm sure you do," he mocks. "Better hurry along. You'll be busy tonight."

It takes everything in me not to knee him in the balls, but I force myself to keep on going, taking the stairs two at a time.

I head straight for Oleg's suite.

It's the last place I want to be, but it's the only room that offers an escape.

I should know. I've cataloged every inch of space in this house. Memorizing the floor plan, camera angles, guard turnover, and noting anything that could be useful to help me escape. That's how I know of a small west-facing window in Oleg's bedroom. There is a Juliet balcony with a drainage pipe running parallel to it.

But the cherry on the sundae—stacks of hundred-dollar bills stuffed under Oleg's mattress. I found it when I was cleaning his room the other day and nearly wept with joy. This money equals freedom for me and my father.

Dad is still at home in the Brighton Beach area of Brooklyn, unharmed, as part of the deal I made with Oleg. But the moment it's realized I'm gone, they'll go after him. That's why I have to act fast. Get Dad, leave town, go somewhere far from here where the Antonov brotherhood can never find us.

Emerging from the stairwell, I knock a few times on the door to his suite to ensure it's empty. When there's no response, I cautiously turn the knob and let myself in.

His cologne hangs heavy in the air, and it's enough to make me lose my breakfast. Or maybe that's just nerves. I'm a regular girl born and raised in Brooklyn. I've never even been out of state! I'm not especially brave or daring, but today I'll have to be in order to make it out of here alive.

Dropping the cleaning supplies, I bend down beside the sprawling California king. The mattress is heavy. It usually takes three of us to change his sheets, but now it's just me, straining with all my might, as I shove my hand between the mattress and box spring, groping wildly.

Footsteps echo past the doorway, and I pull my hand back. A cold sweat breaks out over my skin as two male voices approach, talking in panicked tones. Shit. What would I say if I were caught right now? It certainly wouldn't look good.

When their voices fade in the distance, I release a tight breath. Plunging my hand under the mattress again, I'm more successful this time. It doesn't take long before my fingers collide with something, but it's not cash. It's cold metal. I hesitate for a moment. I've never even held a gun before, and I certainly don't know what to do with one. Indecision tugs at my gut as I drag the pistol out into the light. A weapon would be useful in case I run into trouble, but the chances are I'll shoot myself before I'd use it in self-defense.

I abandon the gun under the bed and dive back in for the cash. I pull out two stacks of bills and shove them into my bra because this teeny tiny uniform—if I can even call it that—has no pockets.

With my heart thumping wildly, I head towards the balcony.

That's when I hear it.

The unmistakable roar of a helicopter—the whirring gets louder and louder until finally not one but several big black choppers come into view. I plaster myself against the wall, inching forward just enough to watch as they land on the back lawn.

Out of nowhere, the air ignites with a massive explosion. My pulse jumps in my throat as I drop flat on my stomach. Gunfire erupts throughout the home, followed by screaming and heavy footsteps.

An icy chill wraps around my skin. The house is under attack.

Outside, all I can see is smoke and chaos. People run in all directions on the lawn below. And like the house, my dream of freedom goes up in smoke.

My best bet is to hide and hope like hell I escape notice.

Scanning the bedroom, my gaze snags on the linen closet discreetly built into the wall on the far side of the room. On unsteady legs, I force myself to move, tucking my body into the closet just as the bedroom door flings open. A predatory presence stalks through the room, moving beyond my little hiding place. I sit frozen in this nightmare, arms wrapped around my legs, stifling the sobs threatening to erupt from my throat.

I don't move. I don’t breathe.

All I can do is pray to the gods above that somehow I get out of here alive.

CHAPTER TWO

ANDREI

He's not here.

That dirty rat fucker abandoned his men at the first sign of trouble. If I wasn't so irate, I'd laugh at Oleg's cowardice.

Shots ring out from downstairs and I know my men are making quick work of clearing the rooms in the palatial compound, rounding up Antonov soldiers that seem more confused and disoriented than anything else.

I don't know what led me to Oleg's bedroom. Maybe I want to see for myself where the monster lays his head at night.

Opening the heavy doors, I enter a room fit for a king, albeit a mafia king. All glitzy gold decor, floor to ceiling marble and chandeliers dripping with crystals. It's tacky, exactly what I would expect from a man without a drop of class.

My fingers are curled tight around my pistol as I clear the room, moving from the walk-in closet to the adjoining bathroom. There's not a paper out of place, not even a discarded suit jacket draped over a chair or a pair of slippers abandoned on the plush white carpet.

But as I move past the giant canopied bed in the center of

the room, something catches my attention. The mattress is askew; the duvet rumpled, and peeking out just underneath the bed is a black pistol.

Bending, I pick up the gleaming metal. After checking that the safety is on, I tuck it into my waistband. The hairs on my neck stand on end as I scan the room again. There's a bucket of cleaning supplies in one corner, but nothing else is out of the ordinary. A maid could have run scared from here when she heard us blow-up the guard tower. It would be enough to make anyone bolt in fear.

Waving my hand over the device to trigger the mic on our comms, I call through to Yulian, my right hand and head of security. "I need an update."

His voice comes through my ear-piece a moment later. "He's not here," he says, confirming what I already knew in my gut.

"And Kira?" I bark.

"Nothing. No sign of her. Your brothers tore apart Oleg's office. They found nothing."

I curse under my breath, frustration pulsing through me. Oleg Antonov should be dead by now, and I should have been the one to slit his throat and watch him bleed out. For what he did to my father. For what he did to my entire family.

"Anything in the bedroom?" Yulian asks.

"No," I say through clenched teeth. "What about the others?"

"The innocents have been released, and we're questioning three of his top lieutenants now."

"Good. Keep them alive until I come down."

"Copy that."

Anger pumps through my veins, and I grab a flower arrangement off a table and hurl it against the wall. Glass shatters into a thousand pieces and water sloshes everywhere, soaking the carpet as flowers scatter across the floor. The destruction quiets the rage inside me, as does the knowledge that my final order today will be to burn this place to the ground. I might not be walking away with Oleg's life, but leaving his beloved estate a pile of smoking ashes will take the edge off. For now.

I turn to leave the room, but a faint noise stops me in my tracks. A muffled sound, like a cough. I stiffen, a shiver of awareness snaking down my spine.

Tightening my hold on the Glock, I go stock still, listening. Years of training kick in. My men are swarming the property and we've taken out all key targets, but it's always possible someone slipped through the cracks. It could explain the gun on the floor.

The sound again, like a stifled sob. Silence falls, but this time as my eyes sweep the room, I find something I overlooked earlier.

Tucked into the far wall is a faint outline of a door. There's no doorknob, but now that I look more closely, it's something.

In five quick strides, I'm in front of the door, listening. I inwardly curse at my sloppiness—if it was Oleg or one of his men hiding in here, I'd be dead already. Gun at the ready, I kick at the door, which pops open with a click. I stand back, out of the line of fire. Prepared for anything.

I don't know what I expect, but it's not this. My pistol is pointed at a woman cowering on the floor of the closet. A pair of gorgeous gray eyes, framed with thick black lashes, stare up at me in alarm.

"Please... please don't hurt me." Her hoarse voice sounds strained. I can almost taste her fear. Her pulse pounds in her delicate throat, and I find it strangely compelling.

My gaze travels lower, and it's then that I notice she's wearing some sort of naughty French maid's costume that leaves nothing to the imagination.

I nearly laugh at my twist of luck. One of Oleg's whores handed to me on a silver fucking platter, with a big, fat, shiny bow.

"Get up," I order. She winces at my sharp tone but follows my direction, unfolding her body from the ground and stepping out of the closet. She's undeniably beautiful, all lush curves and pouty lips, but I can't be thinking with my dick. I motion for her to step forward into the light so I can get a better look at her.

She's even more breathtaking up close. I'm struck by how young she is. Young and vulnerable, but perfect. She's of average height with soft curves, her ample breasts spilling out of her ridiculous outfit. Her skin is smooth and creamy, and even with little make-up, her face is gorgeous with almond-shaped eyes that seem to miss nothing.

My chest twists knowing today won't end well for her.

"Please don't hurt me," she rasps, raising her hands in surrender.

I smile softly. I don't need to threaten her. The gun in my hand is enough of a threat. "I'll be the one making the demands from now on. First off, put your hands down. This isn't a bank robbery." When she complies, I nod. "Now tell me who you are."

"I work here. I'm a maid," she says, fighting to keep her voice steady.

I smirk and gesture at her outfit. "Dressed like that, I find it hard to believe you can do much cleaning."

"This is the uniform he makes us wear." Catching my doubtful expression, she releases a huff of irritation. "I'm not a... a prostitute, if that's what you think."

"That's exactly what I think you are. So how about you tell me the truth? Keep on playing games and you'll join me and my men downstairs. Trust me when I tell you, we have some *fun* ways of getting people to talk."

Her fingers curl into fists by her side and a red flush overtakes her face and travels downward towards her chest. My eyes land on overflowing tits, when a flicker of something catches my attention.

"Don't move." I press my gun against her ribs, while my other hand travels down the front of her dress. I feel soft skin, lush breasts and then something else entirely. She gasps as I pull out a wad of cash from the inside of her bra.

"Interesting." I tilt my head and study her more closely. "Very interesting. I think it's time you started talking, *krasotka*. Start with your name."

"Georgia, my name is Georgia Doukas." Her words come out surprisingly strong. "The money is Oleg's. I took it from under his mattress, but I swear I know nothing. Please, just let me go. I'll walk away and tell no one about this."

"Oh, there's no need to be discreet. I want Oleg to know it was the Kozlovs behind this attack." Recognition lights up her eyes. The Kozlov Bratva is notorious throughout the Tri-State area. My family is just as powerful and connected as the Antonovs. More so since I took over as *pakhan* after my father's assassination. We're not flashy or loud, but we rule with an iron fist.

Silence descends. She blinks up at me but doesn't move a muscle. Whether it's fear or just plain stupidity that keeps her silent, I don't know, but I'm losing patience.

"I don't have time for this shit." I raise my gun to her head. "You're clearly fucking him, which means you know something. So how about you tell me where he is and we get this over with?"

She swallows hard, flinching at the muzzle against her temple. "I have no idea. I really—"

"Don't fucking lie to me," I roar, clicking the safety of my gun.

"Please, I'm not doing anything with him. I'm nothing to Oleg," she gasps, shaking like a leaf. "My father borrowed money from him and wasn't able to repay the loan. I'm working off my family's debt." When I raise my eyebrows she adds, "As a maid. That's what I agreed to at least, but he wanted more. I needed to get out of here."

Pieces of the puzzle fall into place. The money, the gun. "You were trying to escape," I say plainly. Though escape doesn't prove her innocence. I'm sure all of Oleg's lovers attempted to escape him at one point or another.

Georgia's nostrils flare. "Yes. I've only been here for a few weeks. I know nothing, have seen nothing. I'll be of no use to you."

"Oh, I wouldn't say that." I smile wolfishly. "I think you could prove very useful to me."

Her fear gives way to anger as she glares daggers at me. I almost applaud her spirit, standing up to the big bad mobster. There's something about her—the intensity of her gaze, the way she holds her head high, the stubborn angle of her chin—that intrigues me. And it would give me no greater pleasure than to take what Oleg considers his property.

"New plan," I tell her. "You're coming with me."

"What!? No!" Her body tenses in panic. "Why do you want me?"

"I don't know yet. But I have a feeling you're going to be useful."

Despite her fierce expression, tears trail down her cheeks. But I'm immune to tears, as I'm immune to all displays of emotion. My hand is firm on her arm. "You can either come with me, or fold yourself back in that closet while we turn this compound into an inferno. Your choice."

"That's a really shitty choice," she seethes. Again, that feisty spirit. Attraction roars to life. I don't know if I should spank her ass or kiss her. Although both options sound equally compelling.

"Ticktock, sweetheart. What will it be?"

"What will what be?" A voice echoes behind me. Turning, I find Daniil, my younger brother, watching us intently from the doorway. "Well, well, who is this?" The look of carnal interest he gives Georgia tightens my stomach.

"This is Georgia. She was Oleg's maid. Now she's coming with us."

"A maid, huh?" Daniil looks amused as he takes in her barely there uniform. The sneer on Georgia's face tells me she's enjoying my brother's blatant perusal as much as I am—meaning not at all. "As much as I'd love to stay and chat, I came here to tell you we need to wrap up."

"Did you hear that?" I turn to Georgia, standing as rigid as a board. "It's time for us to go."

Daniil cocks an eyebrow when he realizes I'm serious about taking Georgia with us, but he says nothing—he knows better than to question my authority in front of an outsider. When we're alone, it's a different story. With a quick nod, he says, "I'll lead the way."

"I'm not going with you." She rips her arm out of my grip and her eyes dart to the open door behind Daniil, as if she's considering making a run for it. Even if Daniil and I weren't both heavily armed, she wouldn't get far. But it seems she needs a reminder that we're the ones in charge.

"Cover me," I say to my brother as I tuck my pistol into its holster. I reach for Georgia, pulling her flush against my body, allowing her to feel every ounce of male hardness I possess. A blush rushes to her cheeks, and she stops struggling as I wrench her arms behind her, fastening her wrists together with a zip tie.

"You're the same as him. A monster," she spits, venom coating each word.

"No, krasotka, I'm nothing like him." I grip her chin, turning her face up towards mine so she doesn't miss a word. "You'll fucking love it when my hands are on you. You'll beg me for more, for everything that I have to give." My thumb brushes across her cheek, down over her lips as she releases a ragged breath that sounds more like arousal than fear.

"We need to move, Andrei." My brother's impatient voice breaks the charged moment between us. As if his words summoned them, the choppers flare to life.

"What will it be, *printessa*? Stay here as we burn this place down, or join our band of merry men?" Daniil snorts, but I ignore him, watching Georgia as she wrestles with the decision.

"You're insane," she growls, then marches towards the door.

"Seems she's figured you out rather quickly," Daniil quips.

"Fuck off."

I catch up with Georgia in the hallway and take hold of her

arm above the elbow. Even though all of Oleg's men are dead or in our custody, Daniil provides cover as we slip through the long corridors, my hand guiding Georgia towards the landing of the grand staircase. Knowing the view that awaits us below, I stop and turn her to face me.

"Close your eyes. I'll lead you the rest of the way." Her head snaps back as if my suggestion is ludicrous. "It's not a pretty sight," I state.

She shrugs defiantly.

"Suit yourself."

Dead bodies lay haphazardly on the foyer floor in pools of blood. The color drains from her face and Georgia flicks her gaze upwards, avoiding the worst of the carnage. I hope it serves as a stark reminder that Oleg and I are opposite sides of the same sullied coin. I may be nothing like that animal, but we exist in the same underworld.

Several heavy-lift choppers await our arrival on the back lawn of the estate. As we walk across the expanse of green, I bring her in close to me, a protective gesture even if her body goes rigid at my touch.

"I'm perfectly capable of walking without your help." She wriggles her body in an attempt to break free from my grasp, but I just pull her closer.

"Don't fight me," I whisper against her neck. "You're mine now, and you'll do as I say."

"Never," she hisses, attempting to shake off my grasp.

A silent laugh shakes my chest. I'll rather enjoy teaching her how to behave.

I own her. Even if she doesn't know it yet, she will soon.

CHAPTER THREE

ANDREI

An hour after arriving at our estate, I am holed up in my office, nursing my second glass of whisky to calm the adrenaline still working through my veins.

The door to my office swings open and my brothers, Daniil and Leonid file into the room, with Yulian close behind. Leo tosses a file onto my desk with a scowl. “Oleg fled the property a few minutes before we arrived.”

I stare at the manila file but don’t make a move to open it. “I don’t need a report to tell me he was tipped off.” The intel we had confirmed Oleg was on the property fifteen minutes before we landed, which only means one thing. We have a leak.

I grip the glass in my hand so tightly my knuckles turn white. After becoming pakhan six months ago, I’ve worked day and night to clean up our organization. Flushing out members with questionable loyalties. Bringing control of the brotherhood tightly under my leadership, with Yulian, Daniil, and Leo as my trusted *avtoritet*. Captains.

But it never fucking ends.

The lies, betrayal, double-crossing.

This is mafia life.

I rise and walk to the window, folding my arms over my chest and stare out into the cloudless sky. "What did you learn from questioning his men?"

"Not as much as I hoped." Daniil frowns. "The soldiers had information about an incoming arms shipment, but nothing about a mole. And nothing about Kira."

I scrub my hands over my face and release a breath. "You didn't push them hard enough."

"Didn't I?" Daniil gestures to his blood-splattered clothing. "Whatever his reason, Oleg has kept her existence a secret."

"He was careful, methodical," Leo adds. "There's not a clue anywhere in his home."

For fuck's sake. A headache thumps near my temples.

I turn from the window. "We don't have the luxury of time. As soon as Oleg regroups, this will turn into a full on mafia war. We need to flip someone on the inside."

"As if that's easy. Oleg will be on high alert after what we pulled today." Yulian pinches the bridge of his nose, frustration oozing off of him. He hates to lose as much as I do. As the son of my father's most loyal lieutenant, he was raised alongside us. His father died when we were teens, protecting my father in the line of duty. Now that I am the Kozlov pakhan, he guards my life with his own.

Access to an insider would change everything, but Yulian is right, Oleg guards his people closely. Even today, no high-ranking members were on the property. He's skilled at keeping his best men widely dispersed. He even moves between his properties in New Jersey, Chicago, London and Moscow regularly, so we never know where he's going to land. It's what's kept him alive so far.

"There's always a way in," I say. "I need time to think."

A crash from the floor above makes my head snap up.

Yulian shrugs. "It is the girl. She is not happy."

Daniil looks at me curiously. "What do you plan on doing with this little hostage of yours?"

I cross my arms and lean into the window frame. I knew there would be questions. "She's spent time in the Antonov home which means she's seen things, heard things that could be valuable to us."

"Valuable how?" Daniil taunts, an ever-present smirk on his face. "To warm your bed?"

"That's not what this is about," I say, but even as the words leave my mouth, they feel like a lie. My interest in Georgia extends beyond whatever information she may possess. I may not trust my little captive, but my dick has formed its own opinion on the matter. Different scenarios flash before my eyes. My tongue lashing over her clit as she writhes in pleasure. Her plush mouth wrapped around my cock, taking me deep. Her legs draped over my shoulder as I stuff her with my hard cock.

Daniil's voice startles me out of my filthy daydream.

"We don't know who she is, or what she was actually doing in his home. For all we know, she could be a plant Oleg left for us. The way I see it, she's a liability and she needs to go."

Leo, ever the peacemaker, holds up a hand. "Daniil has a point. We need to be cautious. There's already a leak. We don't need another one."

I'd love to tell them to mind their own fucking business but it's their business too. And they are not wrong.

"Fine. Let's do our due diligence. Have your connections look into her. I want to know everything—her family history, when and how she ended up working for Oleg. Let's see if her story checks out." Leo nods. He has a network of top-notch hackers and informants that can do a deep dive into her past. If there's anything suspicious, Leo's guys will get to the bottom of it.

"So it's settled." Daniil stands, straightening his tie. "We keep her locked up until we learn more."

I stroke my jaw thoughtfully, considering Daniil's suggestion.

"No." I tell him. "We'll keep a close eye on her, but we need her to get comfortable, lower her guard. If she has any valuable information, we won't get it by locking her up."

As if waiting for her cue, another loud bang echoes from above us. If Georgia keeps on acting like a brat, I might have to reconsider my stance on not putting her behind lock and key.

Daniil rolls his eyes and mumbles something about me thinking with my brain below the belt.

"I know what's at stake, *brats*," I assure them, using the Russian word for brother. "This is our family's future, and I will not mess with it. Trust me."

I just wish I could trust myself.

CHAPTER FOUR

GEORGIA

I WAKE UP FROM A NAP WITH A DRY MOUTH, A SPLITTING headache and a lingering sense of dread. It feels like I've lived three lives in this one day. The last thing I remember is falling asleep on top of the bed shortly after I smashed every single valuable looking artifact I could find in the room. Room is not even the right word. This place is more like a suite in a five-star hotel. Gorgeously decorated, done in shades of dark gray and white, with teakwood furniture and colorful accents. It's easily twice the size of the apartment Dad and I shared above our restaurant.

I rise from the bed to get a better view of the outside to figure out where I am. From what I can see from the window, I am on the second floor of a secluded house. Below is a giant infinity pool and gardens. The background is lush trees and woods as far as the eye can see.

Judging by the brief helicopter journey, we couldn't be too far from New Jersey, but I have little else to go on. Andrei blindfolded me and placed noise-canceling headphones over my ears the moment we got into the helicopter. It was discombobulating to have my senses cut off like that... and also eye-opening. My face heats remembering how my remaining senses lasered in on the press of his powerful thigh against my own, the smell of his smokey after-shave and the light as a feather touch as he trailed a seductive finger down my bare arm.

It only reinforced what I already knew about him.

Andrei Kozlov is a monster.

A cold-blooded killer.

I should know. I eavesdropped on Oleg's guards every chance I got, and my, my, they were a gossipy bunch.

Word is at age thirty-two, Andrei is the youngest bratva boss, and the only head to be U.S.-born. Like Oleg, he's powerful and ruthless, yet the two families are enemies. I don't know why, but after today's attack, it's clear that there is no love lost between them.

I leave my space by the window and flop down on the bed, taking in the cool, silky-smooth feel of the satin sheets beneath me. I still don't know why I'm here. The only thing I am certain of is that I'm a pawn in a game that's being played by two powerful families. I'll never forget the gruesome sight of dead bodies and blood splayed over the Italian marble floor of the foyer. All at the hands of Andrei and his men. He may have spared my life today, but I know he will make impossible demands judging by the dark look in his amber eyes.

Heavy footsteps in the hallway interrupt my thoughts. The door swings open and Andrei stands in the doorway, looking menacing, and god help me, bloody sexy. Dark blond hair curls just below his ears, softening his angular cheekbones and roman nose. Stubble covers his strong jaw and the cleft in his chin. Damn, that cleft. I'll never understand why a little indent is attractive, but on Andrei it most definitely is.

He is—in one word—striking. Especially now, with his dress shirt rolled up to reveal thick-veiny forearms covered in dark snaking tattoos that continue down over his knuckles.

A cold, shivery sensation moves through me, but I won't let

him see my intimidation. I rise from the bed, squaring my shoulders and force a bland expression on my face—one that I hope says I won't be pushed around.

Or worse, seduced.

"Have you finally come to your senses and realized that I'm not worth the trouble?" I point to the shards of vase on the gleaming hardwood floor.

"Nice to see you too, krasotka," he says, a lazy smile playing on his lips. I don't know what krasotka means, but I have a feeling I won't like it. He eyes the smashed antiques, his face unreadable. "And no, that's not why I'm here. I brought you proper clothes and food," he says, holding up a shopping bag in one hand and a White Castle bag in the other.

"Burgers. Really?" Where did he even get takeout? As far as I can tell, we're nowhere near civilization. I don't bother asking, since I don't imagine he'd tell me the truth.

His jaw tenses. "You need to eat. And everyone likes White Castle."

"I'm not hungry, and I don't like White Castle," I lie. I fucking love White Castle. "No need for pretty clothes, either. I won't be here long enough to make use of them. Even if you haven't come to your senses yet, you will when you realize I know nothing of Oleg's business. Other than telling you what brand of laundry detergent he prefers, I really can't provide you with any valuable information."

An amused grin touches his lips, and he steps forward, thrusting the White Castle bag into my hands. When the smell of deliciousness hits my nostrils, my will to argue disappears.

"You know more than you think you do," Andrei says. His deep voice wraps around me, sending a shiver down my spine. "But that's not the only reason you're here, Georgia. You intrigue me. And the fact that I took you from Oleg brings me great pleasure."

Oh fuck. I never meant to be intriguing. A hot flush crawls up my neck and spreads over my face. Of course, I want nothing to do with this man, with this monster. Except, he sure doesn't look like a monster. I would salivate over him if we met under different circumstances. If I didn't know he inhabits the same despicable world that Oleg does, the same world of corruption and lies that hurt my father. That hurt me.

Yet, unlike Oleg, Andrei doesn't repulse me. I find his attention fascinating.

And that's what scares me the most.

Needing to put an end to this charged moment, I put down the food and clothes and glare up at him.

"You can't be serious. Oleg won't know and certainly won't care that I am gone. He has bigger fish to fry now that you burned down his estate." Pausing for a breath, I soften my tone. An attempt to appeal to his human side, assuming he has one. "I have a life back in Brooklyn. My father needs me. It's just the two of us. Please. I don't belong here."

Only half of that statement is true. My life is not my own. While my high school friends moved on to college, and relationships and fun, my only focus was working to keep the restaurant open and food on our table.

There's no mercy in Andrei's eyes, just a hard stare that lingers too long on my mouth. "It's true. You don't belong in this foul underworld, but unfortunately, you got tangled up with some very bad men, me included. Now here you are."

A sick sensation spreads through me. There is no soft side to this man and I don't know why I thought there was. He's as frigid as they come.

Andrei approaches, his imposing form crowding me back against the wall, caging me between his powerful arms. Waves of danger ripple over his skin, his broad shoulders tight beneath his dress shirt, his golden eyes intense. My traitorous body responds to his proximity; a buzz in my veins that only seems to grow the closer he comes.

"Get away from me," I spit. "I don't want this and I don't want you."

"What is it you don't want?" he whispers. His breath ghosts over my ear.

"You. Anything to do with you or your brotherhood." My cheeks burn and my heart hammers.

Grasping both hands above my head, he pins me to the wall, assessing me with a long look.

"I don't believe you. I think you like it when I'm close. Your body betrays you. I see your pulse pounding... right here." Leaning down he runs his tongue over the vein pulsing in my neck. "Mmm. You taste good, krasotka."

Holy shit. I should recoil from this beast, fight to escape him, yet my body sparks in a way that has nothing to do with fear. I'm frozen in place, captive in more ways than one, to this powerful man.

As if reading my thoughts, Andrei pulls back. A satisfied smirk plays on his lips, as he runs a gentle finger from my neck downwards, stopping when he encounters the bruise on my arm. The place where Oleg grabbed me earlier.

"Did Oleg do this?" His voice is low and lethal.

I consider denying it, but what's the point? "Yes."

"That fucking animal," he growls.

"And you're different?" I challenge, shaking off the spell he cast earlier. His eyes go dark, fixing on me with a devilish gleam.

"I am nothing like that animal. I have my own particular tastes, but I only take what's given. Are we clear?" He's hauled me up against his chest, a large hand holding the back of my neck. I swear I can hear the blood pounding through my veins, my poor heart working overtime.

"We are clear." My whispered words push against his mouth, drawing his beautiful lips into a satisfied grin.

It's at this moment I realize how dangerous Andrei really is. Not because he's a soulless killer, he's dangerous because I'm drawn to him. And nothing good can come from it.

My focus needs to be getting out of here and protecting my dad. No more falling under Andrei's spell. It's time to think rationally and logically. To do that, I need to keep him at a distance.

I lay a hand on his chest and attempt to push him away. He gives me one final lingering look before saying, "I like it when you see things my way." His fingers skim my cheeks, a gentle touch before he steps away. "One more thing. Does the name Kira mean anything to you?"

"No," I answer honestly. "Who is she?"

"That's a story for another day." Andrei heads for the door, then stops and turns around. "The moment you got tangled up with the Antonovs is the moment you signed away your freedom. Get a goodnight's sleep, krasotka."

Before my mind can register everything he's said, he leaves the room, closing the door behind him. I don't hear the catch of a lock, but I know I am a prisoner—his prisoner. And despite his promises of safety, things are only going to get more dangerous from here.

CHAPTER FIVE

GEORGIA

"RISE AND SHINE, GEORGIA," A FEMALE VOICE SINGSONGS above me. Light floods the room, assaulting my eyes before I'm even fully awake. I groan and press my face into the pillow, an attempt to block out reality for a little longer. I slept fitfully last night. Every time I closed my eyes, the stress of the day would wash over me, jolting me awake. Sleep only came in the wee hours of the morning.

But alas, this overly cheerful creature standing by the bed will not be dissuaded. "Come on, there's coffee. You Americans love your coffee first thing in the morning."

I roll over to get a good look at my tormentor. Standing over me is a petite woman in her early sixties, by the looks of it. She's not wearing a uniform, but she definitely has a professional air about her, with stylish glasses, and silver hair pulled back into a chignon.

If I close my eyes and pray hard enough, I wonder if she'll go away.

"I'm afraid not." She chuckles and I realize I spoke that last thought out loud. "I'm Natalia Kashin and I work for the Kozlovs. Andrei has requested that I help you get settled in."

Settled in? As if I am enjoying a stay at a high-end resort. These people are too much.

I sit up, curiosity chasing away the worst of my drowsiness. Settling in is precisely the last thing I plan on doing. I've woke with a newfound determination to get the hell out of here.

"Is Andrei, er, Mr. Kozlov available this morning?" I ask.

She smiles. "You can call him Andrei. He's not one for formalities." She checks her watch and as she does, another member of the household staff opens the door and wheels in a platter of food. Breakfast, I assume, from the delicious smells wafting towards me. "Andrei is attending to business matters today, but I'll let him know you want a word when he's back." Another bright smile. I'd like to know why she is so damn happy working for a bunch of lethal mobsters?

"I am here to assist you with anything you may need," she continues. "I've taken the liberty of having breakfast delivered. I imagine you are hungry."

My rumbling tummy is answer enough. Natalia claps her hands together, redirecting my attention back to her. "I didn't know what you like, so I made sure we have a bit of everything." At the foot of the bed, stainless steel plates lift to reveal a selection of delicacies. Natalia waves her hand over the spread. "We have smoked fish served on potato pancakes; Russian black bread and fresh butter; *syrniki*, which is a pancake made with cheese and fruit preserves; and my very favorite, *sharlotka*, a simple apple cake."

The strangeness of this situation hits me in the gut. Why does it feel like I am on vacation at some luxury resort, rather than being held captive? Gorgeous surroundings, plush bedding, a new wardrobe, and breakfast delivered to my room. With coffee!

I shake my head. The accommodation might be five-stars,

but I'm still a prisoner here, and I won't be dazzled into complacency.

Emerging from the bed, I wrap myself in a robe that Natalia is holding out for me. She motions for me to sit in a chair at a small table in the corner. Loading up a plate on my behalf, she places it in front of me along with the promised cup of coffee, then goes back to make one for herself.

Everything looks incredible. I don't even bother trying to make small talk. I dive right in, savoring every bite.

Natalia grins at me. "What do you think?"

"It's amazing," I say between mouthfuls. I've never tried Russian food before, even when I lived at Oleg's house, and I'm pleasantly surprised, but I don't want Natalia to think a tasty meal is enough to make me stick around. "But I miss cooking for myself and my dad. I really miss my father."

"Of course," she responds sympathetically, but says nothing else, making me wonder how much she knows.

"So," I ask carefully, "what kind of work do you do here?"

She bites into a piece of pancake and chews thoughtfully. "A bit of everything. I take care of administrative work for the Kozlov family and help to run the household. And now Andrei asked me to take care of you."

"Why? I won't be here long, and I don't need to be taken care of."

She tilts her head. "We'll see."

I don't waste my breath arguing with her. It's Andrei that I need to convince... or more likely, escape from.

"Fine," I say, crumpling my napkin and pushing my plate away. "So what's your deal? How did you come to work for a deadly gang of mobsters?"

She gives me a patient smile as she regards me through the steam of her tea. "After their mother died, I was brought on as the boys' governess, helping to raise them. Now that they are older, they've kept me on to serve in another way. Their business dealings are no concern of mine, and neither should they be yours," she says, with a pointed look.

A million questions dance on the tip of my tongue: What happened to their mother? What was it like to raise future mafia kings? What led to the Kozlov/Antonov feud? But she heads me off at the pass, placing her cutlery down beside her, and saying, "If you're finished with breakfast, I can show you around the property, and then—"

"What!?" I shake my head, unsure if I've heard her properly. "I'm not being chained up in this room?"

She shrugs. "That depends on you. Act like a guest, and we'll treat you like a guest. Act like a captive, and we'll treat you like one. Andrei was clear that we are to make you comfortable."

Comfortable! What the hell does that mean?

Freedom is comfortable. Being kept against my will, not so much.

But Natalia reeks of loyalty, and if she's known the Kozlovs most of their life, she's immune to the darkness of this world. She's sure as hell not going to help me, so I am going to have to help myself.

"In that case, sure, I'd love to look around." Figuring out where we are is the first step towards making a run for it.

Because it went so well the first time.

"Great." Natalia looks pleased. "I'll let you get ready for the day. A maid has put away your clothes and you'll find a fully stocked bathroom at your disposal." Natalia delicately folds her napkin in front of her and stands before heading for the door.

This should be interesting.

I SPEND the morning alone with Natalia, roaming around the incredible property. Well, not entirely on our own. Two guards trail behind us from a polite distance, their presence inconspicuous, but never forgotten. We start outside, where the sprawling property is surrounded by woodland. Beyond the pool and grand terrace, there are tennis courts, a hot tub, a vegetable garden, and a flower garden.

In the early June warmth, the gardens and trees have come alive, and the grounds have a magical quality. I swear I can smell the tang of salt in the air, as if we are by the ocean, but when I ask Natalia about it, she ignores me and continues the tour.

Beyond the greenery is a helicopter landing pad and a tower that I imagine comes with heavily armed security guards—a stark reminder that this isn't some peaceful wonderland. I wonder if this is to keep prisoners like me in or intruders out. Likely both.

Inside is equally impressive. Natalia shows me the private movie theater with leather floors and plush couches and a state-of-the-art gym, which certainly explains why Andrei is built like a Navy Seal.

Natalia looks at me expectantly as we come to a stop in front of giant oak doors. "Are you ready for this?"

"Sure, as long as it's not where you stash the weapons or a freaky sex room, I'm fine."

Natalia rolls her eyes. "Nothing like that. It's the library." She opens the door to reveal a room even more opulent than the rest of the house. Onyx marble shines at my feet, flowing to countless bookshelves stretched to the ceiling. Despite the size of the space, cozy reading nooks abound.

"Andrei had it renovated recently. Designed it himself. What do you think?"

I'm literally too stunned to speak.

Original fine art covers the walls. Bold abstract pieces beside classical paintings, and a few pop art pieces thrown in for whimsy. The walls are an art historian's dream and I should know. Art is my obsession. It was what I wanted to study—what I wanted to be—before life got in the way.

As Natalia draws me farther into the room, I can smell *his* scent, faint wood smoke and sandalwood. My body reacts on its own accord, heat surging through my core.

"Are you all right?" Natalia lays a hand on my shoulder.

"Yes, all good." I flash her a smile. "This room is incredible. I'm a big fan of libraries... and art."

She nods. "So is Andrei. Feel free to borrow any books of interest. It's stocked as well as the New York Public Library."

While I would love nothing more than to take her up on her offer, I can't let myself get seduced by my surroundings. Natalia might be gracious, but I'm still a prisoner here and I should be actively trying to escape—starting with figuring out where we are. I make my way over to the picture window near the far side of the room, but the view doesn't tell me much more than we are somewhere secluded.

"Are we still in New York State?" I ask point blank.

"So many questions," she clucks. "All you need to know is that you are safe here."

"Safe!" I wonder for a moment if she's a bit off her rocker. "We must have very different definitions of the word safe." Being locked up in the home of a menacing mob boss is *way* outside of my definition. "Don't you think it's messed up that I'm being kept here against my will?"

"My job is not to question," she says, her voice tinged with steel. "If Andrei wants you here, there's a reason."

"If you say so." I roll my eyes. She's drunk on the Kozlov Kool-Aid.

She looks down at the phone in her hand. "Andrei just messaged. He's on his way back to the estate and he wants to see you. He'll meet you here."

My body flushes cold and hot, unable to settle on a reaction —nerves and excitement warring inside me. I seem to have developed a warped fascination with his smell, magnetic smile, and golden eyes.

This is not good.

As she leaves the room, I swallow to get rid of the sudden dryness in my throat.

I knew what Oleg wanted from me, but Andrei is a different beast. His dark pull is all-encompassing and I can already feel myself drowning.

CHAPTER SIX

ANDREI

I SPEND THE NEXT DAY IN TENSE MEETINGS WITH MY MEN evaluating the fall-out from the Antonov attack. Oleg has gone underground for now—licking his wounds and planning a counter-attack—but we need to be ready when he emerges. We only have a few weeks at most before shit hits the fan. We are on the verge of a mafia war, and that's always bad for business.

After I give everyone their marching orders, my men file out of the office, everyone except for Daniil and Leo. Leo takes the chair across from me, while Daniil stays planted on the couch against the wall, resting his ankle casually across his opposite knee like a spoiled prince, a retractable pen between his fingers that he's mindlessly clicking. If it was anyone else, I would have shot him by now.

"Would you cut that out?" I lean my elbows on the table and rub my pounding temples.

"What? I'm thinking. This is how I think," he says, all fake innocence. Daniil is the middle brother and he fucking acts like it, always vying for attention. Unlike Leonid, the youngest of us brothers. He's the low-key one, keeping his cards close to his chest until he's ready to throw down.

I grit my teeth and flick my gaze towards Daniil. "By being annoying as hell?"

He stops for a second and looks up at me. "I'd ask what crawled up your ass, but I know the answer to that."

I lift my eyebrows. "Care to explain?"

He makes a humming noise. "Oh, I don't think that's necessary."

Georgia. The woman that haunted my dreams last night.

The way my brothers eye me makes it clear they know exactly what I'm thinking. My suspicion is confirmed when Leo clears his throat and says, "About that. I have information about the girl. Georgia."

My head snaps up from my computer screen. "That was quick."

"My hackers worked through the night." He takes his phone out of his pocket and pulls up the report. "Her full name is Georgia Doukas. She was born and raised in Brighton Beach, just her and her father, Maurice Doukas. Her mother died of cancer when she was four. Her father runs a small restaurant four blocks up from the beach. It was a popular local spot for a long-time, before the neighborhood turned." My upper lip curls in disdain. Two years ago my father lost his hold on the Brighton Beach area of Brooklyn, and it became Antonov territory. Oleg is the reason that the drugs and street thugs moved in. He takes the protection money that local businesses are forced to pay him, rather than keep his streets clean. "Since then, their business has struggled," Leo continues. "Georgia was studying visual art at Brooklyn College, but dropped out of school to help her father at the restaurant."

A bitter taste fills my mouth. Losing her mother, and then having to sacrifice her future for the family business, is no easy pill to swallow. I should know. I've experienced some of the same disappointments.

"The Antonovs were regulars at the restaurant. They'd take meetings there, swing by for an espresso, dinner. Maurice knew they were bratva, but he tolerated them. What else could he do? When things got bad, Oleg offered Maurice a loan. Seems Maurice put off accepting as long as he could, but about three months ago, with the creditors banging down the door, he finally accepted."

I drum my fingers across the desk. "I know where this story is going."

"You do." Leo shakes his head in disgust. "Dad got behind on his payments, and that's when Oleg's guys paid him a not so friendly visit. They gave him a couple of warnings, one of which resulted in a broken leg. Finally, Antonov's goons hung him out a window. And that's when Georgia stepped in. She made a deal with Oleg to work for him as a maid for the next two years. In exchange, Oleg forgave the loan and allowed her father to live."

"A raw deal, if you ask me." My blood pumps hard and fast. The desire to pummel Oleg's face thrums through my veins. He didn't take Georgia to work as a maid. He wanted her for very different reasons. Oleg's dark appetite for young, vulnerable women is no secret—he had twisted plans for Georgia that had nothing to do with her dusting and polishing. I'm no saint, but I don't believe in forcing women to spread their legs for me—they'll come willingly or not at all.

Daniil's brows knit together, betraying his doubt. "So her story checks out. She is who she says she is. That doesn't mean we can trust her."

If it were anyone else, I might agree that she's a liability, a loose end that knows too much. Just the fact that I've used Kira's name around her could be a problem, but I saw for myself the hatred burning in her eyes, and I know in my gut she's not loyal to him.

"She was willing to risk her life in order to escape Oleg. That's all the assurance I need." I don't have to explain myself to anyone, but I need to be smart. I run a multi-million-dollar international empire. I can't be thinking with my dick.

Leo leans forward propping his elbows on my desk. "She lived inside the Antonov compound, she must know things, you even said so yourself. It's time that we question her... properly."

My vision turns black. I don't like the idea of torturing my little captive.

"Or," I say, my brain churning with a new idea that doesn't include whipping her feet with an electrical cable. "We use her as our insider. We send her back to work for Oleg."

As soon as the words spill from my mouth, I question my sanity. Is sending her back to Oleg any better? Maybe not, but it's smart business.

"Well, shit." Daniil's head snaps my way, his eyebrows raised as the pen in his hand clatters to the floor. "How does that work?"

My foot beats an anxious tempo beneath the desk. "Once he's out of hiding, Oleg will expect his loyal staff to come back to him—Georgia included. No one knows we have her now. If we send her back, she could truly be our eyes and ears on the ground to help us find Kira." I pause, holding eye contact with my brothers. "Oleg lusted after her—she can use that to her advantage to get close to him."

My plan makes sense. It's what any other pakhan would suggest; it's the best way to infiltrate Oleg's empire, and find out where he's hiding Kira. So why does my stomach sour at the thought of sending Georgia back into the viper's nest?

Daniil shakes his head as a humorless laugh escapes from his lips. "You think that little wisp of a girl can play Oleg Antonov? He might be a nightmare, but he's no dummy. He'll know something is off when she offers to spread her legs for him."

"I wouldn't be so sure of that." Leo tilts his head in thought. "Oleg is a drunk who can't think straight when it comes to pussy. She just needs to lead him on long enough to get him talking.

Anyhow," he adds with a heavy sigh, "Mama would have wanted us to find Kira... at all costs."

I rise to my feet, pacing the room as I think through this plan in more detail. "Here are the ground rules. We don't send her in until we've trained her as well as any other operative. She has to know how to protect herself with a gun, in hand to hand combat and in any other way necessary. If this plan fails, Oleg Antonov will exact his revenge on a young woman—and that responsibility will weigh on our heads."

Daniil shakes his head. "You better be damn sure you can trust her."

"I trust my instincts. That's what matters." I snatch my blazer off the back of my office chair, buttoning it up and slipping my phone into my pocket. "I'll go talk to Georgia."

My brothers exchange a look. "Now?" Daniil asks. "We have other matters to discuss. Yulian can talk to her."

"She'll argue with Yulian," I point out. "She needs to know who is in charge, and that we're not fucking around. I plan on setting her straight before she gets any more fantastic ideas about escaping."

The truth is I need to see my little captive again.

The thought of tossing Georgia to the wolves—or to one big bad wolf in particular— causes my chest to tighten. But it's the price of doing business in the underworld, and whether or not Georgia likes it, this is where she's landed.

CHAPTER SEVEN

ANDREI

I SPY HER BEFORE SHE SEES ME. GEORGIA IS IN A RED SUNDRESS, curled up in one of the oversized armchairs by the window, basking in the afternoon sunlight. She looks so peaceful and innocent, her nose buried in a book, as if she's found a moment of respite in the storm. I hate to be the one to ruin it for her, but I will anyway.

Georgia's eyes go wide when she finds me watching her. She swallows hard before composing herself.

"I see you've settled in." I remark, pushing away from the door towards her.

"Define settled in," she says icily.

"You're curled up like a cat in the sun enjoying a good book. Looks pretty cozy to me."

"Looks can be deceiving. This is not my idea of a good time."

I stand above her, close enough to watch her pulse feather in her throat. "I'm sure I could help make it a good time. If that's what you'd like." My shadowed gaze communicates everything I don't say, and while she holds eye contact, a blush creeps across her face. I know she is thinking back to yesterday in her room and how close I was to devouring her.

She's not used to men like me—brutal, scary, dangerous. And yet the way she's fighting to keep her face blank tells me I've intrigued her.

"I need to talk to you."

"Fine." She puts her book down on her lap and crosses her arms in front of her body. "Talk."

My hand twitches to discipline her for running her mouth, to see her draped over my knee. I clench my fists, fighting those primal urges.

"I give the orders here, krasotka. It will serve you well to remember that. Join me." I motion to two plush reading chairs situated beside the tall marble fireplace. Obeying for once, she crosses the room and lowers herself into the seat beside me.

"I suppose you're not here to tell me I'm free to go." She fidgets with a thin gold necklace, running her fingers back and forth over the chain.

"If only it were that easy, but it's not." My eyes crash into hers. I want her full attention. "I'm here to offer you a deal. Oleg is still alive and well, and once he emerges from whatever rock he is hiding under, he's going to come looking for you. And if he can't find you, he'll exact his revenge on your father." She looks doubtful for a moment, but continues to listen. "I can offer your father protection, but I need your help."

She swallows hard. "What kind of help?"

"I need you to go back to work for Oleg. There's information he has that we need—the type of information that only someone close to him would be privy to."

She shakes her head in disbelief. "You are insane if you think I would willingly go back to that madman. And you are even crazier if you think he'd share anything of importance with me. I was nothing to Oleg, a mere plaything. There's only one thing he wanted from me, and it wasn't to sit around braiding each other's hair and swapping life stories."

I smile, knowing this would be her initial reaction. Strangely, I'm looking forward to sparring with her. Convincing her that this is really her best option. "Let's run through your choices together, shall we? Say I let you go. Then what?"

Her chin lifts. "I can take care of myself and my father. If we're in danger, as you say, we can leave the city, or—"

"And go where? With what money?" Her face falls, and it's strangely satisfying. She needs to understand the shittiness of her situation. "Did you think Oleg would just forget your father's debt? That's not how the bratva works. You made a deal with Oleg and if you don't return to him, it won't be just you paying the price. He'll go after your father and it will be ugly."

Reality sinks in and I clock the moment she's heard enough. Her chair tumbles back—not an easy feat considering it's an armchair—and she makes a break towards the door. But I'm fast, too fast for her. She's restrained in my arms before she's made it six steps.

"I need you to listen to me, Georgia. It won't be pleasant if you don't." My voice is soft, but carries a deadly note. I've given her fair warning. What she does now is up to her. I can feel her quaking in my grasp, her body rigid against mine.

Her breath mingles with my own, and I fight the urge to crush my lips against hers. A current crackles between us and my body reacts as if struck by lightning.

"Get off of me," she explodes. I pull away but keep a hand locked around her wrist. We stand there for a silent moment, faces inches apart, hearts pounding, breaths coming fast. She licks her lips and looks up at me with a steely expression.

"If Oleg believes you're loyal to him, he'll accept you back into his home, back into his life. It won't be easy, but we will train you and ensure you are ready to take on what we ask. I see the strength in your eyes, and I know that you have it in you."

She shudders at my words. Unshed tears shine in her eyes, but by sheer force of will, they don't fall. "I never want to see that man again. He was a nightmare." A hot flush spreads from her neck, up to her cheeks. "Why are you doing this, forcing me to go back to him?"

"I'm not doing anything. Your father got you into this mess the day he accepted a loan from Oleg Antonov."

"He had no choice," she spits, her scowl full of accusation. "*You* have a choice."

"Yes, I do. And I've made my choice." I lean down so my lips are an inch from hers. "You will help us and in return, I will keep you and your father safe. Understand, krasotka, once you dance with the bratva, it's for life."

Her eyes meet mine, stormy gray and wary. She shakes her head like she can't believe what a dick I am. Good. It's better to act like the beast, then pretend to be a prince.

I don't hold my position because I care about being liked. I care about getting my way. And the sooner Georgia falls in line, the better for everyone.

CHAPTER EIGHT

GEORGIA

I HATE THIS MAN WITH A BURNING RAGE. IT BOILS UP FROM A place deep in my soul.

In theory, I hate Oleg more, but Andrei is almost worse because he knows better. He knows what this will cost me. Now he's acting like he's my savior, when really, he could just let me go, and help my father and I get to safety with no strings attached. He's a gazillionaire. It would be nothing to him. And yet, he's using me in the most heartless way possible.

But when he's this close—so close I can feel the heat emanating off of him, every hard line of his pressed against me—my body misinterprets lust for hate. I'd dance on his grave if given the chance, yet I have to fight the urge to lean into him and press my face into his corded neck. I'm seriously messed up.

My nipples tighten beneath my dress, and my eyes keep on falling to his shapely lips. This would be much easier if he was as ugly on the outside as he is on the inside. But no such luck.

I need space from him before I do something I'm going to deeply regret. And the best way to get space is to poke the bear.

"How do you know you can trust me?" I taunt. "I can reveal your dirty little plan to Oleg, and then what? When I'm in his home, you can't control me."

His hand rises and cups the back of my neck, holding me in place. His face draws closer until I can feel his breath on my cheek. So much for space. "I don't think you would do that. You're much too smart to play with fire." He drags a thumb over my lips, making me shiver. "If you think he's a better option than me, you are sorely mistaken. I may be ruthless, but I don't make it my business to hurt innocent women. Oleg deals in human trafficking and prostitution, an ugly world that he'll force you into when he is done with you. And despite that, he'll still kill your father, because killing brings him joy."

I recoil instinctively, trying—and failing—to put distance between us. "You're just saying that to scare me."

"If I wanted to scare you, I could tell you stories that would haunt you for life. I'm leveling with you—I need your help, and you need mine." His fingers trail down my throat, stopping just under my collarbone, brushing his thumb over the bone with a barely there touch. I clench my legs together, but refuse to show him my desire.

"You leave me with no choice," I spit.

"I'm glad you see it my way." At my acquiescence, he finally steps back, giving me room to breathe. "I am your best option. Unlike Oleg, I make good on my word and I don't hurt women and children. I will protect you and your father, but I expect you to keep up your part of the deal."

"This is insane," I mumble under my breath, but deep inside, I know this is a losing battle. My father's safety is all that really matters.

My chest tightens at the thought of my father and how worried he must be about me. How worried he's been for weeks.

That's when I came home to find Oleg's henchmen dangling my father out of our apartment window. It was their third visit, and we still couldn't pay back the loan. The first two visits left

Dad's legs mangled. This visit would see him pay with his life. Until I stepped in. I pleaded. I begged for mercy for my only living relative, the man who raised me single-handedly. Oleg sensed my desperation. He had me where he wanted me.

For so long, it was just me and my father against the world. He did the best he could to raise me when my mother died. Pulling double-duty as mother and father—attending every dance recital and school play that I was involved with. He was the one that had to take me bra shopping and figure out how to French braid my hair. It couldn't have been easy, but Dad did his best, trying to keep the restaurant going while raising a child on his own.

He may not have been perfect, but he's always put me first, and that's why when he needed my help to run the restaurant, I put my dreams aside and dropped out of school. It's why I agreed to work for Oleg. Dad begged and pleaded for me not to do it, but it was either pay with my freedom, or Dad pays with his life. The choice was clear.

Now I'm back in the clutches of a powerful man—a powerful gangster, no less—and I'm still bargaining for my dad's life. So be it.

My lungs feel so tight I can barely breathe. "What if I fail?" I voice the terrible thought that has been stewing in the back of my mind this whole time.

His mouth flattens into a straight line and his eyes glint with ice. "Failure is not an option."

With that, he turns and heads for the door, putting an end to our discussion.

If I thought I was in danger by simply working for Oleg, I'm in a much worse position now. One Bratva leader is using me as a pawn to play another. I have a horrible feeling that his plan won't end well.

Which is why I can't let myself go through with this suicide mission. I have to find another way to save my father and myself.

I'll play his games for now and let Andrei think I'm willing to go back to Oleg's house of horrors. But the first chance of escape, I am out of here.

CHAPTER NINE

GEORGIA

The next morning, I'm woken early by the sounds of someone moving through my room. I crack an eye open to find a staff member laying out coffee and pastries for me. It's a weird sight, someone in my space tending to me as if I'm royalty or something. I've never experienced luxury like this, and although I don't hate it, I'll gladly leave it all behind when the time comes.

Before leaving, the maid informs me Natalia will be here in fifteen minutes to escort me to a meeting. She doesn't say it, but I assume it's with the Kozlov brothers. I shower and then head to the walk-in closet stuffed with designer clothes. Bypassing all the Prada and Gucci I choose a simple white linen peasant dress.

After dressing, I brush my hair but don't bother with makeup. I want to look young and innocent. I'm twenty-two, so it's not all that hard. These men are hardened bratva and they probably don't have beating hearts in their chests, but I want them to have to face reality. They're asking a young woman to risk her life.

I meet Natalia by the door to my bedroom. She gives me a

once over, taking in my flat strappy sandals, simple dress, and hair still damp from the shower. Her lips curl into a subtle smile as if she understands my intentions, but she doesn't comment.

Natalia leads me through the sprawling home. I don't bother asking her what's going on because I know she won't tell me. After my meeting with Andrei yesterday, I have a pretty good sense of what we'll be discussing this morning—the plan to send me back to Oleg.

As if that's happening.

Natalia delivers me to the ground-floor terrace where four hulking men sit around a table under the shade of a trellis dripping with bright pink bougainvillea. It's quite a picture. A mafia meeting in paradise.

Andrei is the first to spot me, the intensity of his gaze warming me from the inside out. Even in the June heat, he's wearing a dark suit. His dark blond hair is swept back from his face, a hint of a five o'clock shadow across his jaw. The sight of him hits me like a blow to the chest, and I need to look away to break the spell.

He certainly didn't get any less attractive overnight. I remind myself he's a monster on the inside.

A beast of a man rises and pulls out a chair for me. As I take a seat, Andrei introduces me to his head of security, Yulian, and his two brothers, Daniil and Leo. I remember Daniil from the attack on Oleg's, but we certainly weren't properly introduced.

Good looks clearly run in this family. While Daniil and Andrei share the same coloring and height, Leo is no slouch. Dressed more casually than the rest in ripped jeans, white t-shirt and a leather vest, he's even bigger than his brothers, as if that's possible, with darker, shaggier hair and clear blue eyes. They are all inked up the wazoo. I guess that's a gangster thing.

"We need to talk about the details of our plan," Andrei says, getting down to business. "We have a security detail watching your father's home and restaurant."

"Really?" My head whips up. "Is he okay? Can I see him? Speak to him?"

I had a restless sleep worrying about my father—and to be honest, worrying about myself—but I do feel marginally better knowing he's protected. Even if he's being protected by the bratva that I'm trying to escape. This complicates my plan, but I can't think of that now.

"Soon. We can't risk communication at this point, and we have to focus on the job at hand. You have a part to play, *kra*—" He nearly calls me by that Russian pet name he has for me, but seems to think better of it with the others at the table.

His slip of the tongue doesn't go unnoticed. Daniil grins, Yulian cocks an eyebrow, while Leo eyes him curiously.

"Georgia, you know why you're here, but you don't know the entire story." Andrei pauses, as if he's choosing his words carefully. "Six months ago, Oleg assassinated our father, Sergei Kozlov, head of the Kozlov Bratva. After a decades-long feud, it was an attempt to destroy our family once and for all."

"I remember reading about that in the newspaper," I say. "I thought they didn't catch his killer."

"Not by the authorities. We handle our own business," Daniil says with a smile and a wink. Is he flirting with me? Judging by Andrei's thunderous expression, maybe.

"I'm sorry about your father," I say and mean it. Even hardened criminals love their parents. "I don't understand the world of the bratva, but I understand why you would want revenge. I just don't see how I can help with that."

"We'll take down Oleg when the time is right," Andrei says, his expression hard as stone. "But first, we need you to help find Oleg's daughter. Kira Antonov."

"I'm sorry... Did you just say Oleg has a daughter?"

"He does."

I sit in stunned silence for a moment. "I certainly never saw her, or heard that name mentioned. By anyone. And trust me, all I did was eavesdrop when I was in his home."

Andrei's face darkens. "Think harder. There must be something of relevance that you picked up."

Memories flood my mind as I mentally catalog every overheard conversation, every exchange I had with one of the other maids or guards. But try as I might, I keep on coming up blank. "Oleg was gone for most of the time I was at his home, along with most of his top lieutenants. I was completely focused on escaping, but I would have definitely noted if Oleg had a daughter, or if I heard the name Kira. I assumed Oleg had no family."

"Well he does," Andrei says, irritation creeping into his voice. As if it's somehow my fault I've never heard of her.

"What do you want with Oleg's daughter? Isn't she the enemy?"

"Don't worry about the details," Daniil advises. "All you need to know is that we want to find her, and we think you can help."

I frown, crossing my arms over my chest. "I won't be part of this if you are going to hurt her. Even if she's Oleg's daughter."

"This is not about hurting her," Andrei says, his voice dark ice. Judging by the intensity in his expression, Kira must be someone important to him. Like a girlfriend or a lover. Then again, maybe he wants to use her to get back at Oleg. Either way, I have no intention of helping them.

"You overestimate me," I snap, heat creeping up the back of my neck. "I'm not crafty. I'm a terrible liar. Oleg will know it's a set-up the moment I land on his doorstep."

Yulian leans back in his chair, crossing his arms over his beefy chest. "We've planted spies in the home of our enemies before. We will train you as well as we train any of our other operatives. By the time Oleg emerges, you'll be more than ready to take him on."

"What kind of training are we talking about?"

"Hand to hand combat, firearms, psychological manipulation, cracking computer encryption."

I snort. These mafia guys are truly out of their minds if they think they can turn me into a super-spy. I love art and theater and baking. I won't kill a spider for chrissake, forget handling a gun. But what's the point of arguing further? I don't plan on sticking around long enough to actually see this plan through. And some bad-ass spy training can only help me break out of here.

I lean forward and take a slow sip from my glass of water, as if I'm considering what they're saying.

"He'll want more than just information," I shrug. "You're aware that Oleg's a vile pig, right?"

Andrei's mouth twists in distaste. "His weakness is alcohol. Get him drunk enough to loosen his lips. When he wants more from you, slip Rohypnol into his drink. His guards won't think anything of it. Most nights he passes out on the bottle."

"So let me get this straight," I say, holding up a finger. "You want me to slip him a date rape drug?"

A hint of a smile pulls at the edges of Andrei's mouth. I'm glad he can at least see the humor in what he's saying. "Yes. You'll flirt with him. Let him think that you're willing to bed him. But the moment he expects more, you slip him a roofie."

"We don't expect you to fuck him," Daniil adds, with a teasing lilt. "Unless you want to."

I make a gagging sound just as Andrei throws his brother a look that could peel paint. His hands clench to fists on the table, and for a moment I think he's going to deck his brother.

Daniil holds up his hands in defense. "I was kidding. She knows I'm kidding, right?"

A muscle tics in Andrei's jaw, and I wonder if this is how the brothers normally act or if there is something more. Daniil doesn't seem bothered by the interaction, and Yulian and Leo are already distracted by their phones.

Andrei rises from his seat. "Your training starts today. I'll walk you back to your suite to prepare."

Under his breath, I hear Daniil mutter, "Well, this just got interesting."

Andrei pushes by him and comes to stand beside me. As I

rise, his firm hand lands on my lower back, guiding me towards the door.

I don't bother looking back or saying goodbye. My entire focus is on the place where Andrei's hand meets my body. His touch burning with heat, a live wire between us.

Good god. What have I got myself into?

CHAPTER TEN

ANDREI

Her footsteps echo behind me as I lead her through the hallway towards her room. I can't look at her in that fucking *white* dress for another minute. All long legs and rounded hips, with waves of dark hair spilling over her shoulders. She's temptation wrapped into one perfect package and nothing good can come out of my desire for her.

"Natalia has your training itinerary," I say, as I forge ahead of her. "She'll make sure you get where you need to go. Listen to her."

"Uh-huh." Georgia sounds distracted. I turn around to see what's caught her attention. Her eyes are glued to a painting on the wall, as if the world's secrets are held in its brushstrokes. "This painting. Is this a Kazimir Malevich?"

I nod. "It's called *Morning in the Village after Snowstorm*."

"It's amazing to see up close," she says, taking it in with the reverence of a church parishioner. "You must have had a top-notch curator."

I can't help but move towards her. My curiosity piqued. "Why do you say that?"

She shifts her attention to the painting beside the Kazimir. It's Picasso's *Nature Morte.*

"Your collection is..." she shakes her head, "impressive."

Most people say shit like that just to sound cultured, but they don't give a shit about the art. With Georgia, I can tell she means it.

"I'm glad you think so."

"God, I sound pretentious." She cringes. "I'm no expert, but art is my passion. I hoped to study it, but..." Her words die in her throat.

"Do you paint?" I don't know what compels me to ask, but I'm strangely curious to learn more about her.

She shakes her head, her delicate features framed by loose waves. "A little when I was younger. As I got older, it was hard to find the time." I think back to what Leo told us about her having to drop out of school to work in her father's restaurant. "Anyhow, it's really cool to see a Picasso in person."

She continues walking when I blurt out. "I curated this collection. These are mostly pieces I choose."

"Oh." She turns to face me, biting her bottom lip in a way that makes my cock twitch. "I'm impressed, and maybe a little surprised."

Pride fills my chest. For a moment, I consider taking her to the top floor gallery where I house my most prized and rare pieces of art, but I stop myself before I unravel like some pubescent kid with hearts in my eyes and a boner in my pants.

"How did you learn about collecting?"

"My mother loved art. Some of this collection is hers, and I expanded on it as I got older." Despite myself, I keep on talking. "After she was gone, it felt like a way for me to connect with her." What I don't add is that collecting art might have been one of the few things that made her truly happy.

Understanding washes over her face, her gaze full of sympathy, and worse, pity. I can handle hatred, scorn, rage, but not fucking pity. I experienced enough of it to last a lifetime after my mother's suicide. Coming from Georgia, it's like a hot brand on my skin.

"Let's go," I snap, annoyed with myself for caring what she thinks of me. A flash of hurt passes over her face, but I ignore it and continue to walk towards her room. Georgia trails close behind.

Upstairs, I stop in front of her door. Mikhael, one of my loyal guards, is patrolling the hallway. I give him a quick nod to let him know we need a minute and he wanders out of sight.

"Natalia is waiting inside to help prepare you. Listen to her. I will get daily reports about your training, and I expect to be impressed."

She narrows her eyes. "Are you always so bossy?"

"Are you always such a brat?" My hand twitches to teach her some manners.

"I guess you just bring out the best in me."

My patience snaps. I advance on her, pressing her back against the wall. I restrain her with a hand on her collarbone. "I hope I do, because if you disappoint me, I'll punish you."

Her eyes go wide. "If you hurt me, I won't help you."

"Yes, you will. You have no choice. You don't help me, and I pull my protection from your father."

She sucks in a sharp breath. "I hate you." She meets my gaze head-on, daring me to react.

My desire to touch her overrules my good sense. My fingers dance up from her collarbone until I'm cupping her jaw, holding her firmly in place. I don't know what I'm doing, I just know that I can't resist her anymore.

Frozen, she stares at my mouth. "Who is Kira to you? Is she your girlfriend?"

My lips twitch. "Is that jealousy I detect?"

"As if," she scoffs, her nostrils flaring.

I make an amused sound from the back of my throat. "No, krasotka, it's not like that."

Our verbal sparring is practically foreplay. The air between us is thick and weighted. Her eyes carve a path to my lips, and the way she looks at them makes it clear she wants a taste. And I really want to give her one.

Before she can respond, I dip my head, capturing her mouth with mine. She's slow to respond, but after a moment her lips part for me, allowing my tongue to sweep in and lay claim to her mouth. She tastes like cinnamon and spice, her flavor as addictive as I feared. I can't stop. I kiss her until she's flushed and burning, arching against me, desperate for more.

My hands grope her everywhere; her tits, waist, cupping her luscious ass while I grind my erection into her body. I need to feel all of her. When she moans, I lift her dress and rub her pussy through the silky material of her panties, creating a friction that has her throwing her head back in pleasure. Wetness seeps through the thin material. My little captive is a whore for me.

"More," she whimpers, her eyes closed.

And fuck, there's nothing I want more right now than to push aside her panties and stuff her with my fingers, my tongue, and god, my cock, but reality intrudes. Messing with her could put our entire plan at risk, and nothing is worth that.

I yank away abruptly and without explanation. Dropping my hand from her body, Georgia whimpers at the loss of my touch. I'm just as pained by the loss of her heat, needing to adjust the painful hard-on in my pants.

Her eyes flutter open, and she looks at me with a horrified expression. "What did we do?" She throws her hands over her face. "That should never have happened."

"Call it a momentary lapse of judgment." My voice is icy as I straighten my tie. I may have put a stop to things, but does she need to act so disgusted? "From now on, just follow my orders. And never, ever wear white in front of me again."

Then, before I do anything really fucking stupid like drop to my knees and taste her cunt, I turn and leave, praying an ice-cold shower will calm the beast raging in my pants.

CHAPTER ELEVEN

GEORGIA

I don't see Andrei for the next week, but he's never far from my thoughts. Memories of his hands roaming my body play on repeat in my mind. How ironic is it that this man I despise also turns me on like no one's business?

Ironic and disturbing.

Where Andrei is concerned, my body is not in-synch with my head. The pure want I feel when I am near him is unsettling. He oozes danger, ferocity, dominance, and he collects art. Apparently that makes me very, very wet.

What kind of twisted person craves their captor's touch? It's just that compared to my experiences with boys, he's all man. Andrei, with his unforgiving eyes and lush, stern mouth, knew exactly how to coax maximum pleasure from my body.

And then he rejected me. Gah! I let myself get carried away in the moment, but I won't make that same mistake again. Ever.

Before I double over in shame, Natalia's voice breaks through my spiraling thoughts. She's currently leading me down the byzantium hallways in the manor's basement for my next training session.

"How do you think your training is going so far?" she asks, while still maintaining her efficient gait.

"Fine, I guess." I've been learning Krav Maga, an Israeli self-defense and fighting system, which is surprisingly fun and a great workout. The computer hacking stuff is challenging, but pretty cool. What hasn't been going quite as smoothly is the firearm lessons.

Natalia makes a noise that sounds like a harrumph before turning to face me. "And the firearms training?"

I blow out a frustrated breath. Every day, my training starts at the gun range where I refuse to hold a pistol because those killing machines terrify me. Instead, I watch as Boris, my trainer, shows me the basics of how to hold a gun and make it safe. He insisted that I have to at least pick up the gun in my next session. Despite his intimidating frown, I just smile vaguely at him. Me and guns don't mix, and I have no intention of learning how to use one.

"Boris has been showing me what I need to know," I say defensively. "I think that's a good start."

"If you don't listen to Boris, we'll have to replace him with someone that you will listen to."

"What do you mean by that?"

Natalia just shakes her head and continues walking down the long hallway. I think about asking her who Kira is to the brothers, but she's unlikely to tell me. Andrei also warned me never to mention her to anyone, and never to reveal the true reason for my training. I suspect Natalia knows, but I won't push it. Nothing matters other than getting out of here and rescuing Dad. Somehow. I still don't have much of a plan.

As we round a corner, I hear grunts and heavy breathing, followed by rough male voices.

"What is that?" I ask, as unease drips down my spine. What if we're going to the dungeons? I don't know for a fact that they have a dungeon in this home, but I assume every Bratva compound has one. Oleg did.

Natalia stops in front of an open door on our right and waves me close. I peek around the door to find a fully furnished gym complete with punching bags, speed balls, and a boxing ring in the center of the room.

Shirtless, sweaty and all male, Andrei spars in the ring with Yulian.

"You call that a jab?" Andrei taunts Yulian, who grunts in response and attempts another hit. His square jaw is tight, eyes focused as Andrei deftly moves out of reach.

Fuck me.

My mouth goes dry and my heart rate accelerates to a full on gallop as I watch sweat drip down his muscular form. Intricate tattoos grace his back and chest, leaving his forearms bare, save for the corded veins underneath his skin. Andrei is fit, that much is obvious through clothes, but with his shirt off he's smoking hot. Lean, taut muscle in all the right places, a smattering of hair on his chest, and that little V that leads down to *there*.

I look back up to find Andrei's eyes on me. He winks and gives me a cocky grin that suggests he knows exactly what I was thinking a moment ago. This man needs no more ego-stroking, so I offer him a bored look instead, but I doubt he's fooled by my suddenly cool demeanor.

"Just to be clear, that's not part of my training, right?" My voice is a hoarse croak.

Natalia snorts. "Not unless you want it to be."

"Definitely not," I gulp. Although I certainly don't mind the view, I have no desire to be that close to Andrei while he's sweaty and leaking hot male pheromones, and likely itching to discipline me for any misstep on my part.

Why that turns me on is something I am going to have to further examine in therapy.

A smile plays around Natalia's mouth. "Ready to move on?"

"To where?" I shake my head, trying to clear my head.

She motions for me to follow her as she continues walking past several more nondescript doors. The basement is like a maze. I can imagine getting lost down here. Natalia stops in front of the very last door at the end of the hallway.

"Are you ready to meet your acting coach? He's very French and very eccentric," she says with no small amount of sarcasm.

Monsieur Coset is a small-boned French man dressed all in black, with drama oozing out of his pores. He introduces himself to me, shaking my hand with a simple *"enchantée,"* and then waves off Natalia. She just rolls her eyes and shows herself out.

"No offense, but what's the deal with these acting lessons?" I ask.

He definitely looks offended. "Acting is key to the success of your mission, my dear. You'll need to be observant, you'll need to immerse yourself in a persona, and think quickly in a pinch. I'm here to teach you how to do all of that."

"Great," I mumble. I'll take this over firearms lessons any day.

Monsieur Coset explains he teaches the Stanislavski System for acting, developed by a famous Russian actor and director, Constantin Stanislavski. It's sort of like method acting, where the actor—me in this case—uses their emotional memory and experience to immerse themselves in a role.

Well, good luck to my French friend here, because no experience in my life has prepared me to seduce an ugly toad like Oleg, extract secret information from him and then drug him before he demands I get naked. The more that I think about it, the crazier this all sounds.

Sitting in the middle of a bare bones room, he asks me to recall the last time I felt powerful and confident, in a new or difficult circumstance.

"How is this relevant?" I ask, drawing a blank.

"You need to access that feeling," he says in heavily accented English. "Intelligence gathering is all about confidence. Nerves betray ulterior motives."

Is this man serious? I was always nervous around Oleg Antonov and no amount of training can change that.

Noticing my reluctance, Monsieur Coset places a reassuring hand on my shoulder. "Close your eyes, Georgia. Get comfortable. We're going to try a different tack."

After he leads me through a series of breathing and relaxation exercises, I feel more calm and grounded, so when Monsieur Coset asks me again to conjure the feelings of power and confidence, a vision of Andrei kissing me outside of my room springs to mind, the delicious friction of his hand rubbing my pussy over my dress.

What the... ?

This is not the image I expected, yet, as I hold on to the vision for a moment longer, I'm suffused with the feeling of... rightness. Even though I was not the one in charge, there was a certain power in driving a man like Andrei crazy. Crazy enough to do something he clearly didn't mean to do.

"Are you picturing the experience?" he asks.

"Yep," I rasp, heat flooding my face.

"Bravo, Georgia. Now hold on to that feeling while you envisage a few scenarios that you may experience when infiltrating the enemy."

Infiltrating? Damn, he makes it sound so impressive.

He takes me through a series of exercises—acting out intimidating scenarios I may find myself in when I am back in the Antonov household. Monsieur Coset plays Oleg, and while he's no physical match for the brute, he does a good job of embodying his general boorishness. None of the scenarios we act out are sexual, but they are intimidating—like being questioned about what I saw during the Kozlov attack on Oleg's home. Every time my voice shakes, or my breathing speeds up, I conjure up the image of Andrei and me in the hallway. He may have been the one exercising control, but in that moment, I knew he was captive to me. As I replay the scenario, my nerves transform into something that feels like power.

Monsieur Coset must be happy with my efforts because he gives me a little round of applause, and an air kiss on each cheek before he sends me on my way with some exercises to practice on my own. I've never had an interest in acting before, but today might have actually inspired something new.

CHAPTER TWELVE

GEORGIA

I wake with a start in the middle of the night. My heart beats wildly, a thin sheen of sweat covering my forehead and body. Images from the nightmare I had are still close at hand. Images of Oleg tying me up, forcing my legs open and demanding entry into my body. Just reliving the dream makes me dry heave, and I run to the bathroom before I am sick all over the floor. Nothing comes up. Just fear, which I attempt to douse with cold water splashed all over my face.

The dream only serves to remind me I need to find a way out of here before I am back in Oleg's clutches. The Kozlovs might believe their training is enough to save me, but I know the truth. Once I'm in Oleg's home, there'll be no salvation. He'll bend me, break me, take what he wants from me and then discard me like yesterday's trash.

And then there is Andrei.

Andrei may be the most dangerous of all. The way my body reacted to him in the hallway, holding back nothing, wanting him to take more than he did. He's my captor, not my lover, and the sooner I'm gone, the better.

That's why I need to get far away, and that planning needs to start now.

Wrapping a silk robe around me, I head for the door of my room and step out into the hallway. Miraculously, there are no guards standing watch. I imagine it has more to do with the elaborate security system throughout the mansion, rather than any trust in me, but I still say a silent prayer of thanks.

Moving through the quiet halls, I retrace my steps towards the library. I'm hoping I will find a clue to tell me where we are. I'm sure I've smelled the tang of salt in the air, as if we're near the ocean, but not the busy Brighton Beach shoreline that I'm used to. This air is cleaner here. Considering the brief flight from Oleg's estate, I'm confident we're somewhere on Long Island, likely in the Hamptons, which means it's possible for me to escape by foot. As isolated as this place seems, Long Island is tiny. If I could just find a map of the area, or blueprints of the house—something, anything to help orient myself, it would make a big difference.

My slippers are soundless as I carefully pick my way through the halls to find myself in front of the tall doors to the library. I'm surprised I haven't bumped into a guard roaming around, but even if I did, who could fault me for needing a book to help me sleep? It's a rock solid excuse.

As I enter the library, my gaze is pulled to the solid wood writing desk in the corner. I know this is not Andrei's main office, but Natalia has mentioned he enjoys working here occasionally. Swallowing the ball of fear in my throat, I walk towards the desk and try the top drawer. As expected, it's locked. I hurriedly check the bottom drawers of the desk, and they are all locked as well.

I pull my robe tighter around me, casting a searching look around the room. I approach the shelves, scanning to see if I can find a book that might hold a clue to where we are. The books are meticulously organized by subject. There is a section for literary classics, art guides, even cookbooks, and then on a lower shelf under the picture window is a section for outdoor and recreation. One guidebook in particular catches my eye. Pulling it from the shelf, I find it's a sailing guide to Long Island Sound.

I drop to my haunches and nearly laugh out loud with giddiness. I was right! We are on Long Island and this guide might be the key to finding out exactly where. Flipping through the pages, I search for any pencil markings or notes in the margins that could provide clues.

"Krasotka." The vibration of Andrei's low voice washes over me. "What are you doing here?"

I freeze, my blood solidifying in my veins as his shadow dances along the floor.

Fuck. Of all the people who had to find me...

"I couldn't sleep," I gulp. "Bad dream."

My mouth goes dry when I get a glimpse of him. Moonlight leaks through the soaring windows, illuminating his muscular chest peeking through his open dress shirt. He's abandoned his blazer, his tie loose around his neck, a whisky glass in his hand.

"Is this how you relax after having a bad dream? Reading sailing guides."

I stand to meet his gaze head on. "Yes. I happen to enjoy sailing."

He laughs heartily at that. "I'm sure you do." He bends, bringing his lips against my ear. His voice is practically a sensual purr. "What were you hoping to find in the library, krasotka? Are you looking for a way to escape from me?"

"Of course not."

"Don't lie to me. It will only make it worse when I punish you."

Heat floods my core. Logically, I know he's the enemy—he abducted me, demanded my obedience, and much worse—yet the sight of him overwhelms my senses, awakening a dormant need inside me.

He lifts his head, and I see an answering hunger in his amber gaze. His eyes rake down my body, hot and possessive, admiring my every curve hugged in silk.

"I suppose it's normal to think of escape. Even when it's impossible." He looks like he almost feels bad for me, but I know better than to believe his false sympathy. "What should I do with you?"

"Let me go."

"Make me."

Anger becomes my best friend, exploding in my chest. I back-up, desperate to get away from him, but he reaches out and grabs my wrist. His hand is a shackle, holding me in place. I struggle to get him to release my arm, but his grip remains as strong as iron.

A slow, evil smile builds on his face. "Enough talk of freedom. What do you really want?" He looks down at my sheer night-dress. "The other day, you wanted more from me. You craved it. The proof was all over my fingers."

He's right, and I can't fight him anymore. I'm dying for him, and he knows it. His eyes darken, and he pulls me towards him, his tongue gliding over the seam of my mouth, sucking at my sensitive lower lip. Heat washes through me and my lips part for him. He releases a low moan of satisfaction, plunging his tongue into my mouth, tasting me, conquering me.

His taste is intoxicating, and nothing else matters right now. It's just him and me, and that crackle of white hot electricity that snaps between us.

My insides go liquid as my nipples harden. Every cell in my body is attuned to him and what's going to happen next.

ANDREI

Before I give in to Georgia, I need to know what she's thinking.

Because the last time this happened between us, she was soaked in regret afterwards.

I pull away from her, and she releases an annoyed groan.

"*Ty krasivaya*," I say. Her intense eyes study my face, as she attempts to make sense of my words. "Beautiful." I tell her, brushing her hair behind her back, so I have an unimpeded view of her creamy skin. She doesn't react to my words, just continues to study me, her eyes hooded with lust. "Is this what you want, Georgia? My hands on your body?"

In place of words, her fingers creep into my hair and pull me towards her. Standing on her tiptoes, she leans in and runs her tongue along my jawline. Jesus, that's all the answer I need.

I spin her around and push her up against the wall. She doesn't move a muscle, breath caught in her throat as she waits to see what I have planned for her.

"You naughty, naughty girl," I breathe into her ear. "Trying to escape. Let this serve as a lesson."

I slide my hand under her nightgown to find her bare. No panties, good lord. Caressing her full cheeks, my touch is deceptively tender before it turns rough. Her body stiffens in shock when I deliver a hard smack to her beautiful ass.

"What the—" she cries out.

"Careful," I threaten. "You don't want to finish that sentence."

I slap her other cheek, gloating when she releases a cry of pleasure, not pain. Her excitement is confirmed when I stuff her with my fingers and find her dripping wet. I can hear the moisture with every pump inside of her. Her head falls back against my shoulder as she releases a deep moan that goes straight to my cock. I bury my face in her neck, inhaling her, needing to consume more of her.

I know this is wrong. It's what I said I wouldn't do. But after lusting over her for days on end and two shots of Macallan, I find I just don't care anymore.

"Better keep it down. Others might hear you. One of my guards could come running in here and catch us."

The threat of being heard only drags her closer to the edge. I turn her around, needing to see her face when I touch her. A shiver works through her body, and I press myself against her perfect curves. One hand works her pussy, the other hand lands on her breast. Seeking her nipple, I pinch and roll the little bud between my fingers. Her core tightens around my insistent fingers and I know she's on the verge of release. I bring her close to the edge, and then, in a blink, I pull my fingers out of her.

Her eyes snap open. "Andrei," she gasps. "Please... I need more."

I chuckle low against her throat. "It's your punishment for snooping around the library. You don't get to come until you tell me what you were looking for. A secret exit, perhaps?"

It takes her a moment to understand me, still lost in the fog of sexual desire. When it clears, a low growl rises in her throat.

"You are a real ass," she says boldly, but she doesn't make a move. My hand is still cupping her bare pussy, moving just the tiniest fraction, a tease to keep her in place.

"I've been accused of worse," I say with an arrogant wink. "Now tell me and I'll let you come."

Georgia attempts to pull away from me, but my grip on her is tight. She looks perfect like this. A flush of arousal colors her high cheekbones, while her eyes burn bright with anger.

She's not making this easy, but I know how to make her talk. Without warning, I sink to my knees in front of her, lifting her nightgown and wrapping one long leg over my shoulder. She's forced to grip the back of my head to keep her balance, and as she does, I spread her pussy lips and dive in. A few hard pulls on her sweet little clit with my mouth and she's babbling incoherently. This time when I pull back, the loss is even more pronounced.

"Why are you doing this?"

"Admit you were trying to escape," I say, my warm breath sliding over her drenched pussy.

She fists my hair with one hand as I run my tongue once through her slit. She groans.

"I just want to know where we are."

"To escape?"

"Yes, to fucking escape," she cries. "I never asked for any of this."

A few gentle flicks of my tongue, and then I say, "It's useless, krasotka. There is no escape. From here or from me."

I don't make her promise not to try to escape again, because I know it would be a lie. I just wanted her to admit it.

Attacking her with my mouth, I tongue fuck her with the ferocity of a starved man. And I am starved. For her, her taste, her little breathless moans. All of it.

The addition of two fingers pumped inside of her, along with my tongue flicking her clit, makes her explode.

"Oh god," she cries out as her cunt spasms, milking my fingers deep inside of her. My tongue and fingers working in tandem, wring every last drop of the orgasm out of her.

She's still breathing heavy as she untangles herself from me, closing her eyes, refusing to acknowledge my presence. She's hiding from me, probably filled with shame about what just happened.

My cock twitches, eager for its turn, but that's not happening. Not tonight. Not ever.

I step back and release her from my grasp. Georgia turns to reach for her discarded robe. Tension ripples along her back, but she says nothing. Something has changed between us and I know she can feel it too.

I don't comfort her. I don't bother with any soothing words. It would just be false.

I turn and leave like smoke in the wind.

CHAPTER THIRTEEN

ANDREI

I TAKE GREAT PAINS TO AVOID GEORGIA FOR THE NEXT FEW days and it's a goddamn relief. When I'm near her, the temptation to touch her, to possess her, is overwhelming. Not that staying away from her is doing much to quell my obsession.

When at home, I'm either sleeping, or cloistered in my office, working. I even eat in here, wanting to avoid a possible run-in. But try as I might to avoid her, she is constantly on my mind. After I lapped at her sweet pussy, there is no going back. She tasted like nectar from the gods, her flavor forever branded on my tongue.

I know I was harsh with her the night in the library, disappearing without a word, but I had to be. Tenderness would leave the door open for more to develop between us. Just because we have off the charts chemistry doesn't mean we can act on it. We can't.

But it's a struggle.

Business should be my priority—end of story. As pakhan, I don't get my hands dirty, not like I used to. Now it's about directing an army and staying two steps—no, fuck that—a mile ahead of our competition. And competition is breathing down our neck. Everyone from the South American cartels to the Vietnamese mafia all want a piece of our street trade. We have most of Brooklyn and surrounding areas locked down, but for how long? Every day, a new threat comes out of hiding, and we have to put them back in their place. Not to mention the Antonov Bratva. They still have Brighton Beach, though not for long. They're like a snake slithering in the grass—I can't see them now, but they'll rear up at any moment and we have to be ready.

"We're here, boss." Yulian says from the front-seat. As I step out of the car, I take in the industrial building on the outskirts of Brooklyn, where we conduct our less than savory business.

Bloody business.

Nothing good comes from being taken to this nondescript cement block on the wrong side of town. But those that we bring here deserve it.

Entering through the backdoor, I'm hit with the familiar sounds of machines whirring. A cacophony of sewing and fabric cutting equipment echoes off the walls. We operate a garment factory on the main floor of the building—a way to wash our money clean and distract from our other activities. The third floor, high above the ruckus of honest business, is where we get answers to all of our burning questions.

Grunt. As I turn the corner, the sound of a punch landing on soft human flesh fills my ears. I open the door to the interrogation room to find Daniil is holding our long-time accountant, Pavel Kalashnik, by his collar, as he lands a hard jab to his face. Blood sprays and spittle flies. Leaning into the doorframe, I watch the show as if it's a boxing match that I paid top dollar to attend.

"Seems like everything is under control here," I say cheerfully. Daniil's eyes flick my way as he wipes down his bloody knuckles with an already soiled rag he flings back on the floor when done with.

"Turns out this half-wit has been on Antonov's payroll for months."

Red flares in my vision. I knew we had a mole in our organization, but it's a punch to the gut when you find the person who betrayed you so brazenly—and it's particularly sickening when the traitor is one of your father's oldest confidantes.

"Mr. Kalashnik was just about to tell us what information he leaked to Oleg." Pavel is doubled up on the ground in the fetal position, the smell of piss wafting off him. The least loyal are also the easiest to break.

"Tell me what I want to know," Daniil hisses, delivering a kick to Pavel's stomach. He twists in pain on the floor. "You don't walk out of here alive either way. But it's up to you how painful your last hours will be. And trust me, I can make them very painful if I want to."

When the moron stays silent. Daniil's fist flies again, this time a blow to the face. A sickening crack as blood pours from Pavel's nose. He coughs and sputters, moaning pitifully as he processes the pain.

But until Pavel talks, there is no mercy.

I remove my dress shirt and hang it over a chair in the corner. Daniil doesn't get to have all the fun. Naked from the waist up, I crack my knuckles, deciding how to best motivate him.

I don't like assholes who play me, especially not in the most important battle of my life. With all the pent-up sexual energy I am carrying around, there's nothing more that I'd like to do than use this buffoon's face as a punching bag.

I lean down and whisper in the now sobbing man's ear. "Listen, you traitorous fucker. There is no hope for you, but if you want your precious wife and daughters to live another day, you better start talking." Sometimes words are more savage than fists, especially for a coddled suit like Pavel. Violence is far from his stock in trade. This little pig just got greedy.

"I... I'm sorry." First with the tears. Then more piss.

"Of course you are," I say, my words dripping with mock understanding. I deliver another kick to his gut. "Get talking."

"I didn't want to, I swear it, but Oleg, he wanted information. That's all. He threatened me, threatened my fam—"

"Likely fucking story," Daniil scoffs. "The bank records tell us everything we need to know. Oleg paid you a shitload of money to rat on us. Starting, oh, about nine months ago."

Ice shoots through my veins. Oleg killed my father six months ago. Hard to believe there's not a connection here. That Pavel didn't feed information to Oleg, so he knew exactly when my father would be most vulnerable.

"Stick to the truth," I seethe into his ear. "You lose a hand next time bullshit comes out of your mouth." Another kick, this blow delivered by Daniil.

Curled into the saddest ball I've ever seen on the wooden plank floor, his words coming out in weak pants. "Oleg approached me in Moscow when I was back home visiting my mother. He took me out, wined and dined me, got me stinking drunk and then dumped me in a brothel. He blackmailed me. That *mu'dak*, got pictures of me and this whore." Pavel stops for a moment and coughs up blood. "If I didn't do what he said, he was going to publish photos of me tied up and being whipped. It would be the end of me. I had no choice."

I heave him up by his collar, now soaked with blood and spittle, so he has to look me in the eye. "Did he force you to take his millions as well? If you had a brain and an ounce of loyalty in your little worm body, you would know that dancing with the enemy would end very, very badly."

I slam his head into the ground, and he weeps like a baby. I take pleasure in his pain. "It's because of you Oleg knew we'd be at that airport hangar in Berlin. It's because of you a rogue sniper bullet nearly killed me, along with my father. He bled out in my arms. I held my father as he fucking died," I roar.

Anger and grief are a live wire in my chest, but I shove them aside, trying to erase one of the worst days of my life. I slam my pistol down across his skull, pulling my arm back, ready to deliver another blow, but a warm hand on my back stops me.

"Don't finish him yet," Daniil says to me, aiming his gun at Pavel, curled up in the fetal position. "Tell us what you know about Kira and we'll end your suffering."

"Kira? I don't know an Kira, I swear it," he rasps, "but I heard Oleg say that name once. He was fighting on the phone and told someone named Kira to stay away from Brooklyn. I assumed it was a mistress." He coughs again, and a wet gurgling sound echoes in his chest.

Daniil looms over him. "Where is he hiding?" A man like Oleg can't stay underground for long. He's too important. He's lying low now because we are on the attack; knowing where he is gives us the benefit of surprise. And I'm all about surprises.

"I don't know where, no one knows where," Pavel sobs. Another wheezy breath. "I'm sorry, I did wrong by you and your papa. I take that to the grave."

BANG BANG.

Daniil stands behind me, the gun still smoking in his hand. "Too late for apologies, *blyad*."

Drip drip drip.

"We really need to get that thing fixed." Daniil eyes the offending leaky pipe above him. We're congregated in our office. It's on the other side of the building from the interrogation room. This space is as bare-bones as it comes, a complete departure from the opulence of our home.

"That's the least of our worries," I say, buttoning up my dress shirt after washing off Pavel's dried blood in the corner sink.

Leo, seated on the couch in the far corner of the room, is brooding after absorbing the news that Pavel was the mole. As the man responsible for our organization's intelligence, he blames himself for not discovering Pavel's betrayal earlier. I shoulder just as much responsibility for that oversight. One that I won't forgive myself for any time soon.

But this moment isn't about me, it's about Leo. I give his shoulder a quick squeeze as I pass him on the way to my desk. "Don't blame yourself. Pavel knew all the tricks of the trade. He covered his tracks like a pro. And Papa trusted him implicitly."

Leo shakes his head. "But for a whole fucking year. We need to assume Oleg knows way more about our organization than we can imagine."

"God, I should have ripped out his heart and fed it to the dogs." Daniil's hands form into fists on the table in front of him. "I'll need to install a whole new firewall system, update all passwords, new shell companies, everything. And vet every soldier like it's their first day."

I nod. "I want to see all the communication between Pavel and the Antonovs. Ransack his house, computers, cell phones, cars, anything that can tell us how far his betrayal actually went. We'll also need to question his family."

Leo leans forward, dark hair falling around his face. "What did he say about Kira?"

"He confirmed she exists, and that Oleg is in contact with her," I say through clenched teeth. "He overheard an argument they had on the phone. Oleg wanted Kira to stay away, and it sounds like she was fighting him about it."

"This is good news." Leo sits up taller and rubs his hands together. "She's alive and Oleg is in contact with her. Now it's up to Georgia to figure out the rest."

"Speaking of which," Daniil says, his lips curled upward. "How's her training coming along?"

Jerk.

He got Yulian's report just the same as I did. He's making a point.

"Fine," I grit out.

"That's not what I heard."

According to the detailed reports that land on our desk every morning, Georgia has made great strides in everything but firearms. She's refused to pick up a gun, even once. Boris may not know what to do with her, but I sure do.

"She'll be more than capable when I'm done with her," I say. "If Boris can't teach her to fire a gun, I will."

"I'm sure the head of the Kozlov Bratva has better things to do than target practice with a noob. Unless you think you're the only one she'll listen to." Daniil gives me a slow, evil smile.

I grunt in annoyance. "She's integral to finding Kira, therefore teaching her to use a gun is worth my time. Now, can we just drop this?"

But he can't. Daniil is nothing if not persistent. "She won't be off-limits forever. When this business is done—"

"Yeah, then what?" I run an agitated hand through my hair. "You know the life that we live, the danger any woman involved with us is exposed to. If you don't have the seed of darkness planted firmly in your DNA, and Georgia most definitely does not, there's no surviving this world. Mama didn't."

Daniil and Leo both flinch. I shouldn't have mentioned our mother. It's a sore spot, but it's also the truth. Our mother married into the world of the bratva, but never got used to the ugliness of this life. Papa did his best to keep his terrible deeds quiet but when he came home with dried blood underneath his fingernails and stacks of cash hidden in a briefcase, there was no mistaking the world in which he operated.

"I think you underestimate Georgia." Leo takes me in with those sharp eyes of his. "She's tough. There's fire in her blood. She'll survive Oleg, and she might just survive you."

"Why would she have to survive me?"

"I think we all know why. You look at her like she's your next meal, and you haven't eaten in weeks." Leo and Daniil exchange an amused look as I shoot daggers their way.

I stand and stretch out my body, sore from another night of restless sleep. Another night of restraining myself from going to

Georgia's room and waking her up with my head between her legs.

I grit my teeth and do the best to ignore my suddenly hard as steel dick.

Leo leans back in his seat, resting his head in his hands. "You need to work out some of this restless energy. Go to the club. You can always exorcize some of your demons out on the many willing females that will be overjoyed at your presence." The Dark Side. A sex club staple in the bratva for men like me who love control and crave a certain kind of release. It's true. I haven't been there in ages, the responsibility of being pakhan bleeding into my every waking hour.

Before Papa's death, I was a regular at Dark Side, unleashing my sexual urges on any willing female under the cloak of anonymity. My brothers may be onto something—I have to be proactive to get Georgia off my mind.

"I think you're right." I crack my knuckles. "After this shit-storm of a week, a little fun is called for."

"I'd offer to join," Daniil says, "but after this garbage with Pavel, I have my work cut out for me." Daniil is a womanizer through and through. I'm not much better, I suppose, but for him to turn down a night of mindless, kinky as hell sex... I guess we're all off our game.

"I'll stay and help," I offer.

"Nah, we've got it covered." Leo shoos me off with his hand. "Go work out your demons tonight. Maybe you'll stop being such a grumpy asshole."

"Hilarious," I grunt, although maybe he's onto something. I've had an even shorter fuse than usual since a bratty captive with a plush mouth and fuckable body landed in my home.

I need the release that only a gorgeous woman—or three—tied up and spread before me can provide. Tonight I'll fuck her out of my system, and tomorrow I'll get back to work, with Georgia far from my thoughts.

CHAPTER FOURTEEN

ANDREI

If anyone from the outside world stumbled into Dark Side, they would think they traveled back in time to a nineteen-thirties speakeasy, all secret doors and passwords, low booths and dark velvet. Then again, no one from the outside world would ever just stumble in here—it's an invitation-only private club for the city's elite with kinky tastes.

Sliding into a seat at the large circular glass bar smack-dab in the middle of the main room, I take in the sight in front of me. Immaculately dressed men and women mingle, just like at any other high-end bar. The difference here is that soon most of the party will move on to the next act—the private rooms in the basement, or in the case of those that like to be watched, the not so private rooms.

Here, surrounded by the kinky VIPs, subtle electronic beats creating a sexy lounge-like atmosphere, it doesn't matter if I'm a bratva pakhan or another high-roller, if you're granted access to Dark Side, it's because you belong.

Yulian has joined me tonight with his wife, Rowan. He fell hard and fast for her after he took her as collateral while he hunted down Rowan's brother for selling intel about us to another mob. He and Rowan are about as unlikely as Georgia and I, but somehow they are making it work. More than just making it work, judging by the way they are eye banging each other, eager to get to a private room.

As Yulian and I put in our order with the bartender, a luscious little redhead sidles up beside me and whispers in my ear, "Are you looking for company?" From the looks of her latex dress and the dog collar around her neck, she appears to be the kind of company that I would usually be interested in. A natural submissive who would give it all to me on her hands and knees. Yet, the thought of playing with her elicits no response in me. Nothing.

When I shake my head, Yulian flashes me a worried look.

"What?" I say, exasperated.

"She looked fun and willing. What's the problem?"

"I don't have a taste for gingers," I say dryly, taking a sip of my martini. "Apologies Rowan," I add because of her own flaming red hair.

"No need to apologize," Rowan smiles. "We're not for everybody, just a select few." Her eyes collide with Yulian's and he looks ready to drag her into the nearest available playroom and maul her.

Turning my attention back to the crowd, I scan the room looking for someone, anyone, that might get my heart rate pumping. Truth be told, before Georgia, I had no preference at all. Blondes, brunettes, redheads, or any shade in between. I just liked a good nameless fuck with a submissive woman, but somehow, my thirst is now focused on one woman with a curtain of raven hair and haunting gray eyes.

I am so fucked.

I gulp down the rest of my martini, hoping a little buzz might loosen me up. The point of tonight is to fuck away the craving for Georgia. I can't do that unless I choose a partner and go for it, not sit on the sidelines like some wallflower.

"What about her?" With a flick of his head, Yulian gestures to a curvy woman with a waterfall of braids down her back, watching us coyly from across the bar. "She seems interested."

"Fine," I relent, feeling like this is more of a business transaction than anything pleasurable. "I'll take her to the playroom."

Yulian chuckles and shakes his head. "I'm not trying to force this on you. It's been a tense couple of weeks. You deserve the release."

Rowan leans against Yulian's arm, her voice teasing. "Unless there's something—or someone—holding you back?"

I roll my eyes. It's good to know Rowan doesn't find my pakhan status intimidating.

"Et tu, Brute? Have you two been talking to my brothers?"

"I always talk to your brothers," Yulian says dryly. "It's my job. And we all agree that you need to loosen up."

"*Mu'dak*," I curse at him, which only seems to amuse him further, but I'm already rising from the stool, fixing my cufflinks and straightening my tie. As I approach my target, sipping on some horrible blue concoction through a straw, her eyes light up at my attention. I know I'm just going through the motions. My cock should be painfully hard right now. Weeks of no sex, yet here I am completely dead inside.

Standing in front of her, I don't need to say anything. My intentions are apparent when I lift a brow and cock my head. I am asking her if she wants to play. Her eyes light up and she rises from her stool, sliding her hand in mine. She looks like a goth Playboy bunny and I'd be into it if it wasn't for the hot little captive burning a hole in my head twenty-four hours a day.

"Private room, or do you prefer to be watched?" Goth girl asks as we head down the stairs to the lower level.

"Private," I bark, leading her to the room that I rent only for my personal use. Once inside the ornate room, decorated as lavishly as the rest of the club, she sways to the music, performing an impromptu strip tease. I shake my head for her to stop. This feels awkward as fuck.

If she's annoyed with me she doesn't say. "Fine, I get it," she purrs. "Let's get right down to business." She lowers herself onto the circular bed in the center of the room. Propped up on her elbows in order to gauge my reaction, she spreads her legs wide so I can see the goods on offer. No panties, naturally.

"How do you want me?" she asks, her voice low and husky.

She crooks her finger, beckoning me forward. I don't like to be summoned, but tonight will not happen unless I make a move. I walk to the edge of the bed.

"That's more like it," she smiles, reaching out and unzipping me, reaching into my pants to cup my still soft cock.

An unpleasant tension thins the air in the room. My collar feels too tight, my suit constricting as if the walls are closing in on me. Nothing feels right about this moment.

Nothing.

And so I take the cowards way out.

"This isn't going to work." Her face drops in disappointment, but I don't even give her time to argue. Stepping back, I zip myself back up and rush up the stairs and out the front door of Dark Side.

CHAPTER FIFTEEN

GEORGIA

Drops of sweat trail between my shoulders and down my back as I head towards my bedroom, exhausted after another Krav Maga session. As usual, Natalia is my escort, ensuring I don't wander on my own. I wonder if I could take down the older lady, especially after these butt-kicking workouts, but I know just behind her is an armed guard. And just around the corner, there are ten more mean-looking Russians.

The truth is, I like Natalia. We've spent a good deal of time together now, and while I still know nothing about her personally—like most connected to the bratva, she keeps her cards pretty close to her chest—but she has kind eyes and she feeds me well.

Wow. That's pretty sad. Talk about Stockholm Syndrome.

She's my jailer, not my friend.

As if she can hear my thoughts, Natalia turns towards me before opening the door to my room. "I have a surprise for you," she says, looking pleased with herself.

"Oh really. What is it?" I'm not sure how I feel about surprises under this roof.

"See for yourself." She opens the door to my suite, where a petite dark-haired young woman stands wearing the black uniform that all domestic staff in the Kozlovs' home wear. At least it's tasteful and flattering, nothing like the atrocity that Oleg had his all-female domestic staff wear.

"This is Piper," Natalia says by way of introduction.

Piper holds out her hand for me to shake. "Very nice to meet you. I'm here to help you get ready for this evening."

My eyebrows pull together. "This evening? What do I have going on this evening?" I usually just scarf down dinner in my room, exhausted after a long day, and then watch TV until thoughts of Andrei invade my brain. Let's just say that I've become very familiar with the shower massage in the connecting en suite.

I'm still looking for a way to escape, but now that Andrei is on to me, there is always a guard posted outside my door at night. I am going to have to be a lot craftier from now on.

"The Kozlovs have invited you to join them for dinner tonight. Piper is part of our domestic staff and was kind enough to offer to do your hair and make-up." Natalia explains.

My insides clench with something that feels an awful lot like excitement. Pushing the feeling away, I cross my arms in front of my chest. I haven't seen Andrei since he turned ice cold after he went down on me in the library. While that dismissal still burns, I know why he did it. He wants me to focus on finding this Kira person, whoever she is, not getting my rocks off. And for that, I am going to make him pay in the most evil way possible.

"Ready for me to work my magic?" Piper tilts her head to the side, taking me in—probably gauging how much work she has cut out for her.

"You bet I am," I say, a thrum of excitement building in my veins. "I'll jump in the shower and we can get started."

Nerves get the better of me as I take a last look in the vanity mirror. Piper is, in fact, a miracle worker. My hair is down in soft waves, pinned back on one side. My gray eyes are done up soft and smoky, with a feline edge, and my lips shimmer with the slightest hint of color. As promised, it's a natural sultry look that screams sexy, but not overdone. Exactly what I wanted.

"What do you think?" Piper asks, standing back to admire her handiwork in the mirror.

"I'm kind of speechless," I say, running a hand down the length of the sparkling off-the-shoulder minidress. "I've never been spoiled like this."

She tilts her head curiously. "Never?"

"Not really." I sigh. "I spent most of my free time helping my dad at his restaurant. Going to the prom or even hanging out at the mall with my friends was never really a priority."

"That sounds tough." Her tone is gentle, sympathetic even.

"Oh, it wasn't too bad." I smile softly. "It was nice to help my dad, to be honest." A sadness settles over me at the thought of my father. I'm grateful he's protected, but I hope he's doing okay and taking care of himself—eating well and taking his heart medication now that I'm not around to remind him.

"And what about you?" I ask in an attempt to lighten the mood. "How did you learn to do make-up and hair like a professional?"

She beams at the compliment. "YouTube videos and practicing on my friends."

"Do you work here full time? I don't recall seeing you around before." I'd notice someone around here that's close to my age, and I definitely haven't noticed Piper before.

"I'm a new hire," she says, heading towards the door. "I'm glad I could help you out tonight. Ask for my help anytime."

I nod and wish her a goodnight. As I gaze at myself in the mirror, I have to admit that I'm having a total Cinderella moment which is messed up; Natalia is no fairy godmother and Andrei is the furthest thing from Prince Charming that I can think of. Even so, that won't stop me from the making the best of tonight.

DANIIL AND LEO sit at the end of the long mahogany table in the dining room, dressed to the nines in form-fitting dark suits. Although that seems to be the prescribed dress of the Kozlovs, Leo usually has more of a motorcycle club look. Ripped jeans and lots of leather. Tonight might be special for him to dress up in Armani. Daniil reclines in his high-back chair like royalty, while Leo sits beside him, slowly sipping a glass of red wine. Both men stand as I enter the room.

"If it isn't the guest of honor." Daniil winks and offers me a playful smile. "Wow. You look… just wow."

Damn right.

I get the impression Daniil flirts with all women in a twenty-mile radius, and more so when it irks Andrei. I throw a subtle glance around the room, hoping to see Andrei. But there's no sign of him.

Leo pulls out the chair across from him and motions for me to take a seat. His cool gaze follows my every movement.

"I'm the guest of honor? I'm sure you have much more important people to attend to," I reply, ignoring his compliment.

"Not tonight," Daniil says, unbuttoning his suit jacket and taking a seat at the head of the table. The one usually reserved for Andrei. "I'll level with you, Georgia. We just want to get to know you. We're going to be working closely together to fulfill a very important mission. And here you are now, living under our roof. It seems like we should get to know each other better. Bond, as the kids say."

"Taking someone captive is not usually the best way to kick off a *trusting* relationship."

Leo smirks, pouring me a glass of champagne. "Agreed, but here we are."

Taking a sip of champagne, I take in the two brothers. One brash and cocky, with the face of an Adonis. The other, quieter, more reserved, sitting back and taking everything in before offering his two-cents.

Before I can get my bearings, a team of waitstaff filter into the room, carrying platter after platter. Leo explains that we're having borscht, caviar over blini with Creme Fraiche, herring in dill sauce, smoked oysters and picked cucumbers. It's way over the top, and I've never eaten this indulgently in my life—not to mention that all this Russian food is new to my palate, though so far it's been undeniably delicious.

"What is it?" Daniil asks, noticing my reluctance, fork midway to his mouth.

"Shouldn't we wait for Andrei?"

"He won't be joining us." Daniil's attention slips back to the food on his plate.

"Oh." The word seems to echo in the big room, and I fight the instinct to slump in disappointment. Two sets of eyes regard me with interest.

Flashing a bright smile, I say, "Great. Just us."

Daniil barks out a laugh. "Andrei sucks the fun out of the room with his big-dick energy. This is much more enjoyable."

I chuckle at Daniil's attempt to make light of this situation, and I certainly can't deny that Andrei is a force to be reckoned with, but this entire set-up feels strange. It seems to me Andrei is being purposefully kept away tonight, and I don't know how I feel about that. The brothers are obviously assessing my every move, sizing me up to decide if they can trust me to help find their precious Kira, or if they need to cut me loose.

Which, in the world of the bratva, means death.

I take in a steadying breath, attempting to chase away the nerves bubbling in my stomach. This is the moment to put Monsieur Coset's lessons to good use. Charming the brothers, gaining their trust and favor, is in my best interest. Andrei may choose to freeze me out, but I can snake my way into the heart of the other Kozlovs. Not that I expect they'll abandon their plan of sending me back to Oleg, but if I play my cards right, they'll lower their guard around me. Best-case scenario, they'll get sloppy and I'll find a moment to escape or at least find a phone or computer to email for help.

Worst-case scenario? Fuck, I can't even go there. It probably ends with my body floating face down in a river.

A shiver works through me as I take a bite of the blini, moaning at the pop of caviar filling my mouth. "This is incredible," I enthuse. Daniil grins, and Leo grunts in agreement. "And the champagne," I say, tipping back a sip of the luscious bubbles sliding down my throat. "I've never tasted champagne this creamy and smooth."

Leo raises his eyebrows. "This is Louis Roederer, Cristal Brut. Twenty thousand dollars bottle."

I cough into my flute. Crime certainly pays well.

"Well, cheers to that." I hold up my flute, and after a moment of hesitancy, they clink their glass with mine. I'm determined to make this dinner as enjoyable as possible; they *will* adore me when we're through with this meal.

Leo throws me a cool, curious gaze, as if trying to figure out what's behind my enthusiasm. "Tell us about training today."

"What? You don't get a full progress report on me every day?"

"Of course we do," he confirms, "but we're asking for your thoughts."

All right then. I choose to be honest. "I'm not interested in picking up a gun. They scare me and I honestly don't think I'll ever be able to use one. But I do like Krav Maga, though it's a hell of a workout and I can barely sit down to pee because I'm so sore. And Monsieur Coset is great." I shrug. "But I'm not yet a super-spy, and I don't know if I ever will be."

"Yes, we heard you're not very fond of guns." Leo sighs heavily. "But it's an essential part of your training. You need to use a pistol."

My brows pull together. "Why?"

Daniil pauses mid-bite, then lowers his fork. "Anything can happen when you're at the Antonov compound. You need to be prepared."

"Right." I swallow heavily and change the subject before they can push me further. "Any word on my father? I'd really like to speak with him soon."

Leo sits back and folds his arms across his enormous chest. "Your father is safe under our protection. You should be relieved."

"Yeah, relieved," I mutter. "Relieved I'm being held captive by the Russian mafia or relieved they are forcing me to work for them? Please be clear which part is supposed to bring me comfort."

For a moment the air is static between us with no one saying a word.

Way to go and run your mouth.

But after a moment, Daniil chuckles and Leo smiles his secretive smile, and I can't help but join in. Even big bad mobsters have a sense of humor, I guess.

"Touché. Point made. Don't think about all of that tonight." Daniil waves his fork in the air. "We're not here to talk business, we're here to enjoy ourselves."

"In that case." I straighten in my seat. "Since I'm sure you've researched the heck out of me, how about you tell me more about your family?"

Leo's lips twist in distaste. "What is it you'd like to know?"

"I get it. No secret mafia stuff. But I'm curious. Where did you all grow up?

"Here in the U.S.," Daniil says, chewing thoughtfully. "Unlike most of the bratva families, my father built his empire in the States."

"So this feud with the Antonovs, how did it start?"

The brothers exchange a look, before Daniil shrugs and says to Leo, "It's only fair. This feud, as you call it, goes back to

Russia. My father was a member of the Antonov Bratva when Oleg's father, Alek, was pakhan. Without getting into details, when Alek was killed, my father was no longer welcome to stay in the brotherhood. He came to Brighton Beach and established his own empire." Daniil smiles, but it doesn't quite reach his eyes.

"Glad we are finally building some trust." I hope his talkative mood continues; I am bursting with questions. "Speaking of which, have you located Oleg yet?"

A member of the waitstaff moves forward as if to refill all of our glasses, but Leo stops him with a hand. "We'll switch to the white Burgundy."

If I didn't know better, I'd think they were trying to get me drunk.

"Not yet," Leo replies vaguely.

"Are you going to share any more details?" I ask sweetly, cutting into a piece of fish.

"As soon as there's something worth sharing." A muscle in Leo's jaw ticks. He's the least assuming of the brothers, happy to sit back in the shadows and observe everyone else. Though I don't expect him to open up, I push a little more.

"Is that what Andrei's dealing with right now? Finding Oleg?" I ask casually. Maybe not casually enough because both brothers look up at me in amusement. "It's Friday night. Seems weird to be working."

Smooth, Georgia, smooth.

"Hard to say." Daniil pops a piece of potato in his mouth, mischief dancing in his eyes. "Probably out on a date."

"A date!? How nice for him." I gulp down the remaining champagne in my glass. "I'm glad dating is his priority during a time like this." Liquid steam must pour out of my ears. After teasing me, then treating me like I'm nothing more than a piece of gum on his shoe, he's out on the dating scene.

Whatever.

Shrugging casually, I accept the server's offer of the fancy new wine that Leo requested. "It doesn't matter to me." I give both of them a sharp smile and then take a deep drink of wine. "I could use something stronger than this," I say to one in particular.

Daniil cocks an eyebrow. "Is it vodka time?"

Leo shakes his head, eyebrows raised. "That's a terrible idea."

"But it is Friday," I reason. "And I've had a pretty rough few weeks. No offense. I mean, your estate is beautiful, and I haven't been mistreated exactly, but this isn't really my idea of a good time."

"She has a point," Daniil says, grinning. "Two against one."

"You're insufferable." Leo sighs, like arguing with his brother is the most exhausting task in the world.

Daniil heads to the bar cart in the corner and grabs a bottle of clear liquid, pouring out three shots.

The vodka goes down smoother than expected, tasteless but without the nasty after burn that cheap brands have. One shot turns into two, then three. An hour later, I'm way beyond counting anything. The room is spinning softly, and I'm actually enjoying myself.

"So Georgia," Daniil says, leaning heavily on the arm-rest of his chair. "What do you like to do for fun?"

I don't know why but I think his question is hilarious. "Shouldn't this have been in my background report?" I tease. "I don't have time for fun."

"You're so young. What do you mean, you don't have time for fun?"

"I watch movies and read books. Does that count?"

Daniil says, "No," at the same moment that Leo says, "Sure."

"No, fuck that," Daniil says, standing. "I mean real fun. Partying with your friends."

I shrug. I don't remember the last time I went dancing or had carefree fun. Not when there was a business to run, creditors to fend off, a father in poor health.

"That is unacceptable. Come with me," Daniil commands in

a way that reminds me so much of Andrei. Bossy pants. Still, I follow him. He leads us to the great room, with its soaring overhead wooden beams and wall of windows.

I'm a bit sad and a bit drunk and I just want to forget about everything. Music pours from speakers, and suddenly dancing seems like a really great idea. Daniil thinks so, too. The music is something sultry and electronic, and I let loose, swaying my hips and throwing my head back as I get lost in the beat.

Leo refuses to join us. Instead, he watches from the couch, a hint of a smile playing on his lips, as he throws back more vodka. I do not know how he's still drinking and I tell him as much, but he just shrugs and says, "I'm Russian. They practically put vodka in our baby bottles."

I think he's kidding, but I can't tell.

Daniil moves his body in sync with mine. He's not touching me, just allowing me to let loose and doing the same himself. I'm sure we look like drunk, crazy people, but we sure are having fun.

Until Andrei walks into the room and ruins everything.

CHAPTER SIXTEEN

ANDREI

"What the hell is going on here?" My words are low and deadly as I try to absorb the picture in front of me. Daniil and Georgia dance around drunk out of their skulls, and Leo happily watching them act like fools.

My anger cuts through their alcohol induced haze. They all stare at me as I move to turn off the music and grab the drink from Leo's hand.

"I think you've had enough of this," I seethe. Leo just flicks me a bored look.

On the other side of the room, Georgia is still swaying to the non-existent beat. A giggle escapes her mouth when she looks at my thunderous expression. "So serious," she stage whispers to Daniil.

"He is, isn't he?" Daniil grins at me. "You're home early."

"What's going on?" I demand, even though I know the answer to that question. My brothers played me. Sent me on some fool's errand so they could get close to Georgia.

"Loosen up, will you? We're just having some fun." Daniil continues to sway like he doesn't have a care in the world.

"Georgia's had a really, really rough few weeks, you may have heard."

"He knows all about it," she grumbles.

"Enough." I take her face in my hands. "Just how drunk are you?"

"I'm fine. We just had a few drinks. I was just getting to know your brothers," she says, poking my chest with her finger. "And I'm going to let you in on a little secret; they're a lot more fun than you. By the way, how was your date?" she taunts. "Is she here? Could we meet her?" She glances behind me, swaying a little on her feet, and I reach out a hand to steady her waist.

"A date?"

"Your brothers told me." She hiccups. "I hope you had fun." There's a note of hurt in her voice that twists my insides. Jesus. My brothers couldn't leave well enough alone.

I send Daniil a lethal look. "You're a dick."

Leo just chuckles, sitting back and watching the drama play out, and as usual, staying out of my line of fire. I now understand the kind of 'work' my brothers had planned tonight. Scrutinizing Georgia. They still don't trust her, and they thought getting her drunk would lower her guard. Maybe spill all her secrets.

Georgia stands in front of me, confusion written all over her face.

"Time for sleep." I take hold of her elbow, but she shakes me off and stomps her foot.

"Not until you tell me what's going on."

She's drunk, and I won't have this conversation here. Not in her state, not with my brothers watching, but I'm done arguing. She should know by now that my word is law.

Without another word, I pick her up and throw her over my shoulder.

"What the hell!?" Georgia yells, but I'm already walking out of the room, Daniil's howl of laughter behind us. "Put me down, I can walk."

"Not in a straight line, you can't." I continue towards Georgia's bedroom, right beside my own. She struggles in my arms, but I have her in a tight grip, ass in the air. I am sorely tempted to punish her for everything. All of it. Except, other than her smart mouth, tonight is all my fault.

I throw open the door to her bedroom and release her down on the bed while I lean over her, making sure that she's actually all right. Her throat bobs, color rising to her cheeks.

"Whoa, two women in one night," she seethes. "That's even rich for you, bratva kingpin. Or maybe that's how you usually roll."

Gently gripping the side of her neck, my voice is low and soft when I finally respond. "There was no one else. No date. Nothing happened. You think I can touch another woman, no less think of anyone else? You consume all of my waking thoughts, krasotka, and it's driving me fucking mad."

Her face lights up at my words, seeming to sober her up faster than a double espresso. She grabs my shirt and brings her mouth to mine.

For a heartbeat, time comes to a standstill. My world shrinks to this moment— the feel of Georgia's shapely body pressed to mine, how she opens her mouth on a moan, allowing my tongue to sweep in and taste her—like vodka and sunshine.

Like perfection.

Her fingers curl into my hair, digging into my scalp as she wraps her legs around my waist, moaning when I slide my hands around her, grabbing her ass, and grinding myself into her core.

I would do anything to bury myself deep inside her right now.

Anything.

But a niggling voice stops me. She's drunk, and I'm leading her on. Exactly what I said I wouldn't do.

I pull back to find her eyes hazy, her breathing harsh.

I shake my head. "We can't..."

"Why not?" Her gray eyes spit fire. "Fuck you and all your rules when you know we both need this."

She dares me to contradict her, but I hold my tongue. She's not wrong, but I can't be weak. The fate of my family rests on my ability to be strong. Make the right decisions for us as an organization. It's not just about me anymore.

"This thing between us." I hold her face in my hands, desperate for her to understand. "It's never going to end well."

She pushes me away. "Because I'm just a pawn and nothing more."

I clamp my jaw shut. It's better for her to believe that, than to learn the truth that I can never give my heart away. The woman who I marry will stand by me out of duty, nothing more. And I won't feel a quarter of what I feel for Georgia, for my future wife. And that's the way it needs to be.

Her eyes blaze. "Fine. You've made yourself clear. Just go." She points at the door, her lip quivering as she does so.

"Krasotka—"

"I'm tired, and drunk, and I need you to go."

"I'll go when I make sure you are all right," I say, channeling pakhan authority. "Get under the covers."

"Oh, now you're making demands of me." She turns away from me.

I go to the bathroom to get her a glass of water and a Tylenol. When I come back, she's tucked herself in, eyes closed. I can't tell if she's actually asleep or just pretending, but her breathing is steady and she looks at peace.

Leaning over her still body, I drop a kiss on her cheek. "Sweet dreams, *dusha moya.*"

My soul.

CHAPTER SEVENTEEN

GEORGIA

THE MORNING AFTER VODKA SHOTS AND ILLICIT DANCE parties with Russian mobsters, I lie splayed out on my bed feeling like something the cat dragged in. Then chewed up and spit out.

At eight on the dot, the door opens, and Piper enters my room pushing a cart.

"Good morning," she announces cheerily. "Natalia has other things to attend to, so she asked me to help today." When she spies me flat out on the bed, she chuckles. "Rough night?"

"That obvious," I say, pushing myself up to a sitting position. I warily eye the plate of eggs and toast that she places on the table. "I don't think I can stomach solid food at the moment."

"Hope you at least had fun," she says with a teasing smile.

"I'm not sure fun is the word. It was *something*, though."

Something, indeed.

My heart stumbles a beat when I think of Andrei, all menacing and growly, when he caught us wasted and dancing up a storm in the living room. Was he jealous that I was dancing with Daniil? His brother is a flirt, but it's not like we were grinding all over each other. At least I don't think that's what we were doing, but it's all a blur now.

Perhaps the Kozlov brothers had ulterior motives for getting me drunk.

I shouldn't have let my guard down around them. Though if I hadn't believed that Andrei was out on a date with another woman, I probably wouldn't have needed those ten thousand shots to drown my sorrows.

His words from last night come back to me, flooding my insides with warmth.

He can't stay away from me.

Did he really say that, or did I dream it in my drunken haze? In the cold reality of morning, his words mean nothing. Or at least they shouldn't. No matter the heat that lies between us, Andrei's made it clear he's not interested.

Why I'm torturing myself, lusting after a man that I should run far away from, is beyond me. I must be a glutton for punishment.

Andrei is my enemy. My captor. I won't forget that next time.

"The Russians have a great hangover cure," Piper says, intruding into my spiraling thoughts. "Come here and I'll show you." She beckons me to the small breakfast table. As I take a seat, Piper offers me a glass of a suspicious-looking liquid. I take a sniff and nearly lose my lunch, or more accurately, yesterday's dinner.

"I'm sorry, but I can't drink that." I grimace and push the vinegary smelling substance to the far end of the table. She pushes it right back at me.

"It's pickle juice," she says. I give her a questioning look, expecting her to yell out that I'm being punked, but she doesn't. She's dead serious. "A few shots of this and you'll feel good as new, trust me."

"You've been working for these Russians for too long if you've already picked up their disgusting hangover remedies."

"Must be," she says, not quite meeting my eyes.

I'm sure the pickle brine shooter will have the opposite effect than Piper is promising, but what do I have to lose? Well, except the contents of my stomach. I plug my nose and down the shooter, much like those smooth vodka shots from last night.

"Ugh," I roar, slamming my glass down as the vinegary brine stings my throat.

"Well done." She pats my hand and hands me a pastry. "To wash the taste away."

"Thanks." I take a huge bite, grateful for the rich carby pastry. Just what the doctor ordered. Looking up, I watch as Piper tidies up the room, making my bed and picking up the dress I discarded on the floor at some point last night.

"I can do that." I stand, chagrined that someone else would have to clean up after me.

She just smiles and shakes her head. "It's my job. You need to worry about curing that hangover. I'm sure you have a busy day ahead of you."

"Don't remind me," I whine, sipping my coffee.

She stops for a moment and sits on the bed, watching me closely. "What are you training for?"

Shifting in my seat, I recall Andrei's warning to keep details of my mission quiet. "Nothing in particular. Andrei thinks I could be an asset at some point in the future." I shrug. She nods, but intense eyes keep their focus on me.

Memories of the conversation we had yesterday come back to me. She's new here. Which means she may not be as loyal to the Kozlovs as Natalia, and maybe, just maybe, I can rely on her to help me escape. During my time here it's become abundantly clear that Andrei runs a tight ship, and that includes the armed guards, cameras and god knows what other security measures that I don't know about.

Time is slipping and if I am going to escape and find my father, it has to be soon—before Oleg comes out of hiding and Andrei's plan moves into overdrive.

The next chance I get, even if it means resorting to something out of character, I'll take it.

I push back my half eaten breakfast and turn to face Piper. "You said you're new here, huh? How did you come to work for the Kozlovs?" I can't imagine one of the most powerful bratva families hires through the usual household staffing agencies.

"I worked for a royal household in Luxembourg for the last year. Natalia found me through a connection there. Monarch royalty and mafia royalty aren't so different. They demand the same thing from the people that work for them: complete discretion and absolute loyalty."

Loyalty—that tricky word.

I take a last sip of coffee and rise from my seat to stretch my sore limbs. The training over the last few days has finally caught up with me. Soreness imbues every step. My thighs burn as I step into yoga pants, my arms so stiff that I abandon a sports bra, and choose to wear a tight fitting tank top instead. With my hair pulled up in a messy bun, I slip my feet into trainers and wish Piper a good day, heading out the door for a punishing day of training.

As usual, Mikhail is my ever present guard shadowing me, accompanying me through my day, but rarely speaking. Today I joke with him it's like I'm enrolled in bad-ass spy school, but his face remains stony as he ushers me through the basement doors of the house to a small clearing in the woods.

"What's going on?" I ask, but of course get no response. In the distance, I can see some makeshift target practice set up against a tree.

I'm not sure why they think being in the great outdoors might convince me to pick up a gun, but it won't.

Probably not.

Ok, the thing is, I've reconsidered my no-gun stance. I still think they are evil, but I have to be smart. If I find a chance to escape, a gun might come in handy, but only if I know how to use it. I've reluctantly come to the realization it's time for me to suck-it-up buttercup and learn how to use a death ray.

I square my shoulders, ready to surprise Boris with my newfound willingness, but instead I am greeted by the wide shoulders and powerful muscles of a very familiar back.

Shit.

He turns and gives me a slow, seductive smile.

"Good morning, krasotka, I'll be your firearms instructor today."

ANDREI

Georgia stands frozen in place as if she's just stumbled face first into the villain in a James Bond movie. Not a surprise considering I have more in common with a movie villain than Mr. Bond.

"Come closer. I won't bite." I may not make good on that promise, but I offer nonetheless. A Cheshire grin overtakes my face as she shuffles forward like a lamb towards slaughter.

Her gray eyes are chips of ice as she stares at me. "I'm not scared, just wasn't expecting you this morning, that's all. What happened to Boris?"

"I gave him the day off." I flick my gaze up at her from the Glock that I'm polishing. "I thought it would be more effective if you had a more dominant instructor. You don't seem inclined to follow Boris's rules, but you'll follow mine."

Heat momentarily flares in her eyes, but just as quickly as it appears, it's gone, replaced by an eye roll. "I'm surprised that a big, important mob boss like yourself has nothing better to do than to teach me how to hold a gun, oh, and to break up dance parties."

Ah, she's still sore about last night. I wondered how much she remembered. I guess this is my answer.

She remembers everything.

And so do I. The way she smelled, the way she looked, damn, the way she danced. How she swayed her hips to the rhythm of the music last night—lost to the beat, and looking so happy—it was nearly my undoing. Maybe that's what crawled under my skin—she looked *happy*, and it wasn't because of me.

Daniil earned himself a black eye in the boxing ring this morning for the shit he pulled last night. Not only getting Georgia drunk—though I'm pissed about that—but also scheming behind my back. My brothers think my attraction to her clouds my head, and maybe that's true, but fuck them. They're not the boss, I am.

My gaze locks with Georgia's, and something unreadable stirs in her remarkable eyes. The edge of my lips curl up into a smile. "I don't make a habit of breaking up dance parties, no, but then again, it hasn't really been an issue until you showed up." She huffs a small laugh, her eyes crinkling in the corners. "And as for your training, I think my help is more than necessary."

She purses her lips. "I was doing just fine with Boris."

I grab the back of her neck and bring her face towards mine. "You weren't. And I think you like it when I'm in charge. When I tell you what to do."

"Maybe." Her body quivers, but it's not with fear. It's with anticipation. The air hangs heavy between us, and once again, a zing of chemistry flies between us, becoming harder and harder to ignore.

"Are you feeling up to this today?"

"I'm fine," she says, her spine straight, her chin high. "I was introduced to your Russian hangover cure. Pickle juice. Disgusting, but effective."

Despite not wearing a lick of make-up and her hair piled high on her head, she still looks stunning. Yoga clothes fit her perfectly, every lush curve on display. A black spaghetti strap tank-top bares her slender shoulders and does little to hide the soft bounce of her breasts with every movement. It's enough to bring a hungry man to his knees—and I happen to be starving.

"So, are we going to do this or are you going to stand there polishing that death ray in your hand?"

My head snaps up to meet her eyes, and I see the naughty glint. Georgia knows she's pushing me and if that's the game she wants to play, fine.

"Put on protection and get into position," I order. All playfulness between us disappears, replaced by something much heavier. Her nipples tighten beneath her tank-top, and I'm aware of how much she likes this game we're playing. Perhaps I shouldn't be tempting her when I have no plans of following through, but I just can't fucking help it where she's concerned.

Georgia follows my command, putting on the eye and ear protection I have laid out for her, and steps into position on the firing point.

Maneuvering myself behind her, her firm backside presses against my front and it's all I can do to keep in a tortured groan. After last night, my resolve is dangerously low, aching to push her down head first and thrust inside my little captive.

"What now?" Her voice is a husky whisper.

"I am going to put a gun in your hand and you are going to take it. Understand?"

"Yes, sir."

Fuck, is she trying to kill me?

I reach both of my arms around her body, holding up the Smith & Wesson and checking the clip before pointing it at the target. Her body shudders at my nearness and a deep sense of male satisfaction settles in my chest. "Relax," I say into her ear. "It won't hurt you if you know how to handle it properly."

With my arms still in front of her, I show her how to hold the gun with her right hand as I guide her left hand up to wrap her fingers around the handle. "This pistol has no recoil. Perfect to build your confidence."

"It's not a confidence issue," she replies, giving her hips a little shimmy against my quickly hardening cock. "It's an anti-gun issue." I contain a groan at the contact between our two bodies. We're definitely playing a dangerous game.

"You don't have the luxury of being anti-gun. Oleg uses guns. His men use guns. Knowing how to use one could save your life."

I feel, rather than hear, her shaky exhale. "All right, show me."

"Let's talk about grip. First time you grip any handgun you want to grab as high on the back strap as possible. This allows you better control." When her grip is satisfactory, I move on to talk about stance.

"You want to make sure that you're leaning forward a bit, feet shoulder-width apart and your weight is on your toes, slightly bent forward at the waist to keep from being pushed back when a gun has a strong recoil." I adjust her hips and help her swing a leg back until she's in the proper position.

Stepping back a little so she doesn't feel my semi-hard cock pressed against her ass—I'm pretty sure that would be against all safety recommendations—I give her some time to get used to the feel of the pistol in her hand.

"You ready to shoot that thing?"

"As ready as I'll ever be." She swallows hard, tucking a fly-away strand into her bun high on top of her hair.

I instruct her to, "Line up the barrel with the target." She focuses on the silhouette with a target on its chest eight feet away. "Now, steady your aim, exhale, and pull the trigger."

Her first shot is way off target, somewhere above the paper silhouette's shoulder. It lands deep in the wilderness surrounding my property. She frowns, and I tell her to get back into position, and try again.

With a deep breath, she steadies her shaking hands, gripping the gun like I taught her, and pulls the trigger. This bullet lands much closer to that center target, and she releases a whoop of joy. And then she's off to the races. She lets off three shots in a row. The last shot hits the bullseye, and it's damn beautiful. Her face lights up with a smile after she realizes she released the perfect shot.

"You're a natural." My attention goes right to the pulse point at the base of her neck. Shooting for the first time can be a scary thing, invoking the flight or fight response, but after the feeling of danger has passed, there's often a rush of serotonin—the feel good chemical. And if I were to guess, Georgia is in the grips of happy chemicals.

She turns around and the look she gives me is nothing less than hungry. No longer the reluctant gun-totter of ten minutes ago, her dilated pupils reveal she's still on a high.

"That was fun," she breathes. "Show me how to reload. I wanna do that again."

I fold my arms across my chest, amusement turning into pride as I admire Georgia holding a pistol like she was born with it in her hands. "Does this mean you're reconsidering your anti-gun stance?"

"No. Obviously. I still hate guns that kill real people, but I can make an exception for shooting at little paper men." She tosses a smirk my way.

"I can work with that." I show her how to reload the pistol and stand back as she lets off another round. For a woman who is admittedly anti-gun, she's a naturally great shot, pumping lead into the hearts of at least ten paper silhouettes.

I whistle my appreciation when she releases her last bullet and turns around to give me the thumbs up. She's sexy as hell holding a gun—even sexier rejoicing in her success.

"Tomorrow we move on to something a little bigger. How do you feel about that?" Her eyes open wide in surprise. I'm playing with her. I shouldn't be, but playing with her is just so damn satisfying. Relishing her body while I fucked her into oblivion would be a hell of a lot more satisfying, but just being around her makes me feel good. She banishes the dark shadows—my near constant companion—with her light.

Fuck. Thinking like this is only going to get me in trouble.

"I can handle something bigger." Her cheeky tone makes it clear that we're playing the same treacherous game.

Leaning back, I watch as Georgia takes off her ear and eye protection, and puts away the gun safely, like Boris must have shown her. "I'll walk you to lunch," I offer.

She shrugs. "I'm not hungry. I want to keep on going."

"Too bad. Food is essential for training."

She makes a frustrated noise in the back of her throat, but then turns towards me, batting her pretty eyes. "A little more time?"

I have a million things to attend to right now, but when she looks up at me with those soulful gray eyes, my mouth can't form the words no.

Dermo, I'm going soft.

"You ready for another round?" I ask, grinning as her eyes light up.

CHAPTER EIGHTEEN

GEORGIA

FOR A PERSON WHO HATES GUNS, I'M KIND OF KICKING ASS right now.

The piece in my hand is heavy, a solid weight like an extension of my arm. Andrei is standing behind me, watching as I unload a round into the poor silhouette man, but my mind is elsewhere. Invading every thought is the fact that we are alone on the edge of the Kozlovs' property line. Woodland surrounds us, and I am in possession of the lone gun between us.

This is my chance to escape.

Andrei always wears his weapon in a side-holster, or tucked into the back of his pants, but not today. Today, he's wearing a thin t-shirt and a pair of worn-in jeans; I don't even see a cell phone in his pocket.

For this brief moment in time, I have all the power, though Andrei doesn't realize it. He's smiling, looking as carefree and as relaxed as I've ever seen him. I'm working hard to give the impression that I am just as relaxed as him, but the truth is I'm as tense as a violin string, because the only way to escape him is to shoot him, or at least threaten to shoot him. I definitely don't want to kill him, just to stop him from coming after me.

But what if I sever an artery?

Could I just leave him to bleed out on the grass?

Horror ices my blood at the thought of Andrei dying by my hand. He's asking me to risk my life, but he's not doing it haphazardly. Or at least he doesn't think so.

Andrei releases a low-whistle as my last shot finds the target spot on. He's still standing behind me, leaning against a tree, his pose casual, unguarded—as if we are two friends hanging out for the day. "You're going to be giving Boris lessons at this rate," he exclaims.

My mouth is as dry as the Sahara desert at the realization that it's now or never.

Do it, Georgia, it's your life or his.

My knees shake as I turn slowly towards him, gun gripped in both hands.

His eyes meet mine, surprised and wary. Confusion turns to understanding in moments. "What the fuck are you doing?"

My throat is so thick, I can barely swallow. But the thought of my father, the thought of me at Oleg's mercy, hardens my resolve.

I aim the gun straight at his chest with enough room between us he can't easily lunge for the piece of metal. If he was paying closer attention, he might have realized that I held one more bullet back in the barrel. One chance to get this right.

"I don't want to hurt you. I just want you to let me go."

Andrei's body tenses like a tiger about to pounce, but he doesn't actually move a muscle. His face is pale and haunted, his eyes dark pools of fury.

"I will let you go when you serve your purpose."

That's the first mention he's ever made of releasing me after this is all said and done. But that's not really the point. The point is, going back to Oleg will destroy me. If not physically, it will destroy what's left of my soul.

"You don't get it," I say, frustration bubbling up hot and heavy. "You think a few weeks of training can transform me into some femme fatale who can coax secrets from your enemy?" I shake my head sadly. "That's not me."

His narrowed gaze drops to the gun in my hands before sliding back up to mine. "You fucking underestimate yourself. I just witnessed what you are capable of—an hour ago you didn't want to look at that gun, and now look at you." His voice is tinged with a lethal edge. He points to the bullseye that I hit several times in a row, but his eyes stay glued on me.

My arms are shaking from the weight of the metal in my grasp. Is he trying to tire me out? But he doesn't need to. All powerful muscles and coiled-up energy, deep inside, I know he could take me down if he wanted to. It's why I have to finish this now.

"Put the gun down." The raw command in his voice has me nearly acting on instinct, but I block out his words and focus my attention on where to shoot to maim, not kill. Trying to think back to human biology class, I have a vague recollection of a major artery supplying blood to the legs. Probably best to aim elsewhere.

"You might need to work on your response time." His voice is a menacing growl.

Block him out, block him out, block him out.

"Thighs and upper arms both feature important arteries—the femoral and brachial arteries. If a bullet severs either of these, the blood loss will cause death in just a few minutes. If you're just trying to injure me, I suggest the hands or feet. Painful, but it would pose little deadly threat."

He holds his hands up helpfully to give me a clear shot. An internal battle consumes me, stealing the air from my lungs and suffocating me. Why is this so hard?

"Fuck you." Tears of agony run down my face, but I can't move my hand to wipe them away.

"Get it over with, krasotka. Don't you want your freedom?" he taunts.

"I can't." How pathetic do I sound? Andrei steps forward, a muscle pulses in his jaw. I raise the barrel to his chest and even though my arms shake with the weight of the gun, I stand my ground. "I want my freedom, but I don't want to hurt you for it."

He remains uncompromising. "No."

He doesn't rush, just takes one commanding step towards me, and then another, hands still out, daring me to shoot. My heart pounds in my ears, frantic energy coursing through me as my finger tightens on the trigger and I suck in a wild breath.

BANG.

A tense, unnerving silence follows the blast. Holy fuck! It was an accident, my finger just pressed a little too hard on the trigger, but I don't think I'm going to be able to sell that to Andrei. My stomach twists at the sight of red blooming on his shoulder, but he doesn't flinch. Frozen not from shock, but savoring the moment before he exacts his revenge on me.

"Not your best shot," he growls. The gleam in his eyes is predatory. The gun drops from my hands, though I don't hear it land on the soft grass. "You really, really shouldn't have done that."

Andrei reaches for me. On instinct, I turn and run.

Terror spikes my heart rate and makes my limbs pump ferociously. Running is delaying the inevitable, but I'm acting on pure instinct as I dash farther into the wilderness. A rock catches my foot, and I stumble forward, landing hard on my hands and knees.

Andrei closes in on me, one big hand wrapping around my arm. Throwing my other elbow back, I hit something hard, and he grunts in pain. His grip loosens enough for me to escape his grasp. Struggling to my feet, I continue my mad dash to nowhere. I don't have a direction, other than aiming towards a more densely wooded area.

His footsteps follow at a distant pace. He's either losing

steam or losing blood, the thought of which I find unsettling. My lungs burn, but I can't turn around. There's no point now. I'm in too deep, and the only way out is to move forward.

When I think I've lost him, I scoot behind a boulder and hold my breath. Staying stock still. Listening for any signs of an angry mob boss hot on my heels. A bird squawking, the wind rustling through the leaves, a woodland critter scampering through bushes—those are the sounds that fill my ears and give me momentary peace.

A terrible, false sense of peace.

A hand reaches out and collars me around my throat, pushing my back hard against the boulder. Then his face comes into view. He looks wild; like a beast unleashed. I vaguely register the pressure of his hand against my neck, the jagged edges pressed into my back—my only focus is on the rage contorting his face, and beyond that, the look of molten heat in his golden eyes.

"You think that I'm a fair man because I haven't hurt you so far? You think I can control myself?" He laughs cruelly. "I am not a good man, krasotka." The pressure on my throat doesn't let up, and it's all I can do to suck in a shallow breath, my heart pounding in my ears. "You are going to pay for what you did, and you are going to pay with your dignity."

CHAPTER NINETEEN

GEORGIA

TERROR IS A FERAL BEAST UNLEASHED INSIDE OF ME. BUT behind the terror is something different all together. Something unexpected. Arousal.

Andrei leans forward, his lips brushing the shell of my ear as he whispers in a disarmingly gentle voice, "How should I punish you, my little captive? Are you going to suck me off, or is it time I claimed that sweet pussy for my own? Or if you feel like getting kinky, I could start with your ass."

A shiver scatters through my body, but I manage to choke out, "You're... you're bleeding," His eyes flash a shade darker and I realize my error in pointing out my transgression.

"And whose fault is that?" He slips a finger under my chin and raises my head. His thumb toys with my bottom lip, rubbing it suggestively. A harsh promise of what's to come. "Lucky for you, the bullet just grazed my shoulder. I'm alive and well and ready to dole out your punishment."

His words create a heavy ache in my core, molten heat pulsating deep inside me. With one hand still around my throat,

Andrei's other hand caresses my shoulder for a moment before brutally ripping my right tank-top strap straight off. Before I can blink, he's done the same with the other side, pulling down my tank top, exposing my breasts completely. My pants are the next to come off, leaving me only in a thong.

"Better," he observes darkly.

"I'm sorry." I don't know why I bother apologizing. It will not buy his forgiveness, but I need to appease him because his heavy-lidded gaze is beyond menacing—promising terrible things to come.

"Your words mean nothing." His powerful thigh settles between my legs. Releasing my throat, his thumb invades my mouth. "Show me how sorry you are?"

I reach for the fly on his pants, but he stills my hand, pressing his leg hard against my core. "Debase yourself, krasotka. Show me how desperate you are for my forgiveness."

Understanding blooms. Andrei will not be satisfied with an apologetic blowjob underneath the oaks and maples. He means to make me pay. To make me feel ashamed. The most painful punishment there is.

I shake my head furiously as his thumb continues to twist in my mouth. But with every tense moment, my shame transforms into something else. Something hungrier, something dark and pulsating with need.

"Come on me," he commands. "Show me what a good little whore you are."

The top of his thigh nudges between my legs. It's horrible to think of coming like this, rubbing against him like an animal. Humiliating. And yet my hips move against him as if by their own volition. His eyes come alive, watching me rub wantonly against his leg like a dog.

"Good girl. Look at what a slut you are... just for me," he hisses, his hand fisting in my hair.

Desire courses through me. Grinding against him, every glance of my clit against the rough material of his jeans is sweet relief. My body craves this release as much as it does my next breath. He pulls back, his gaze zeroing in on where I am taking my pleasure against his leg.

"Beg me to come," he says, voice tight.

"I can't... "

"Beg me!"

"Please, Andrei, please let me come on you."

Even through the material of my thong, a wave of pleasure builds with every undulation of my hips, the mounting pressure of release close at hand. Andrei presses his leg harder against me, and I'm like a bomb about to detonate. I bury my face into his shoulder, crying out as the orgasm overtakes me—pleasure blasting through me in scorching waves as every muscle in my body contracts and then releases.

I don't know how long I stay hovering in this strange otherworldly space, but when I finally lift my head from Andrei's shoulder, he tips my face up to his, searching my eyes. "You want out of here so badly you'd be willing to kill me?"

"I never meant to shoot. My finger slipped," I say, cringing at my stupidity. I step back to assess his injuries, but I can barely make out the spot of blood on his dark t-shirt. Either it really is a graze wound or he's made of titanium and can't be killed like the Terminator.

"I..." The words get caught in my throat. I want to tell him yes, I really want out of here, and far from the world of the bratva. "I want my freedom."

His finger brushes down my cheek, eyes solemn. "Freedom is such an objective word. If I let you go, are you really free? Or are you shackled to your fears, to family obligations, to making others happy? What do you really want, Georgia?" His eyes burn into mine, his face dark and inscrutable.

I shake my head, at a loss. I've never spent a lot of time thinking about what I want, because it never mattered. My life has been more about what I've had to do than what I desired.

"I want to paint." The words fall out of my mouth before I

can process them, but Andrei doesn't laugh at me. He doesn't move a muscle. "I've never really had the chance. I would just like to try it. I'm sure I'd be terrible—"

"Stop. You'd be wonderful, krasotka. Like you are at everything. Even shooting a gun." His lips twist up and amusement dances in his eyes. I wonder why he's being so nice to me. I can handle the beast, but this gentle version of Andrei destroys me. "You underestimate yourself time and time again. Do you really think I'd allow you to work for me if I didn't think you could do it? I've trained hundreds of soldiers in my life—after fifteen minutes in their presence I know who is capable of what, and who I can trust. And I know you are capable of anything." My heart beats frantically in my chest and I feel a pull of pleasure at his words. "If you want to run and hide in the woods, I'll grant you your freedom. But if you're only running because you don't think you are capable, I want you to think again."

Did I just hear him correctly? He'll give me my freedom if I just ask?

But his offer gives me pause.

I want my freedom more than anything, but where will that leave me? Oleg won't stop hunting us. My dad and I will have to leave our whole life behind and live on the run, always looking over our shoulders. It's not truly a life.

I look up at Andrei, his handsome face almost blinding in the early summer light. I can't believe what I'm about to say.

"I'll see this mission through with you. I'll try my best, I will. If I'm successful, I want freedom for me and my father. And when you destroy Oleg Antonov, I want to dance on his grave."

His jaw flexes, a momentary shadow crossing in front of his face before he nods once. "I promise you, but Georgia," he reaches out, his hands blazing a trail from my neck down to my waist, where he grabs me and pulls me against him. "Enough games. While you're here, you are all mine. I own every inch of you."

A shiver coasts down my spine. I can't fucking resist this man any longer, so I'm just gonna have to stop trying.

ANDREI

She crashes her lips against mine, her tongue sliding into my mouth. I guess that means she's onboard.

Thank fuck.

I almost have to laugh at the situation. That sly little devil. Turning a gun on me. I'm fucking furious—not with her, but with myself. I underestimated this crafty creature, and she proved me wrong. Georgia has more fire and cunning in one little bone than half of my men. And that realization makes me so fucking hard for her.

I've tried the other way—resisting her, avoiding her, staying away—and it's futile. Change of plan.

Maneuvering her away from the boulder, I push her up against the closest tree I can find. I breathe her in slowly, taking my time with her. My attention snags on the area between her ear and her neck. Such a perfect place, soft and warm, and she smells like peaches. I nip at her, my cock hard as granite in my pants, desperate to be inside of her, to feel her hot pussy squeezing me tight.

"What's it gonna be?" I purr into her ear. "Does this gorgeous body belong to me?"

She moans in response, but that's not enough. I want to hear her say it. Delivering a hard smack between her legs, I press her again. "Say it."

"Yes." Her voice is throaty and smooth, like syrup. "I belong to you, Andrei."

That's my girl. I don't give her time to say more. Ripping off her thong, Georgia stares at me, cheeks flushed from her recent orgasm and the knowledge of what I'm going to do next.

My hand slides down her belly, landing on her neatly trimmed pussy. I rub my fingers between her folds, seeking her swollen clit, massaging the sensitive bundle of nerves before plunging two fingers deep into her cunt. I groan at the heavy slickness that meets my digits.

"Look how wet you are for me, baby. Does this mean you're ready for my cock?"

Her answer is a strangled sound of pleasure, and I take that as my cue to fuck her hard. I push down my pants and free my cock, but I'm no match for Georgia. Her delicate fingers wrap around my length, squeezing my already dripping dick.

Desire bubbles inside of me, spinning around like a tornado, as I grind my cock against the length of her slit. So hotShe throws an arm around my neck, while her other hand guides my cock into her hot, wet opening. Wrapping her legs around my waist, I slide deep inside of her, bottoming out on the first thrust. She's incredibly tight, but I don't have it in me to be gentle. I need her hard and fast, and judging by the way her arms clamp around my neck, and her sweat-soaked body grinds against mine, she is as desperate as I am.

Her hot pussy clenches around my cock. Squeezing me. Destroying me. I did not know Georgia could let go like this. A new woman has been unleashed; wanton and crazed. *Free*.

I bounce her hard on my length, and she grunts, taking every thrust, her eyes rolling up to the back of her head. She gives me everything she has and as she gets close to the edge; she grinds into me like her life depends on it.

It's the most intense fuck of my life, and I never want it to end. I press her back up against the tree and rail her, desperate to give her the same heady pleasure that's ripping me up inside. She clutches the back of my neck, her nails digging into my skin as she pants against my ear that she's going to come.

"Come all over my dick, baby," I coax her.

When she quivers around me, I lick her neck and then bring my mouth down to suck and nip at her breasts.

"Fuck... " She releases a long, desperate moan before letting go. Every hard stroke of my dick draws her climax out. She's no longer in control. Her legs shake as she closes her eyes and submits to the pleasure surging through her body.

I am going to explode soon, but I want to mark her with my cum. Make her mine. When I've wrung every morsel of pleasure from her body, I pull out and force her to her knees on the soft grass. Before I can jack myself off all over her face, she eases forward, swiping her tongue along my tip. It's such an erotic and unexpected vision, my dick swells in my hand, pulsing with need.

"Allow me," Georgia says, before opening up and swallowing my cock until it hits the back of her throat.

Jesus, I didn't see that coming.

"My dirty little girl," I praise her. "You like my cock in your mouth?"

She looks up at me, her eyes wide and hungry. My hips buck and roll, dragging my veined length in and out of her hot mouth. She may be the one kneeling at my feet, but right now, she's the one in charge. I'm merely along for the ride.

When she stiffens her tongue, delving the tip into the center of my sensitive crown, I can't hold off any longer. My orgasm goes off like a bright flash, a guttural sound breaks free from my chest, but she keeps me firmly planted in her mouth, swallowing every drop I have to give.

When Georgia finally releases me, she looks up at me with the hottest expression of self- satisfaction. I haul her up and press her against my chest, my body still quivering with the aftershock of my release.

Georgia shakes her head and lets out a contented sigh. "Shit," she groans. "That was... unexpected."

I bark out a laugh. "I think the word you're looking for is amazing."

Even after what we just shared, her face reddens and her gaze flicks to my shoulder.

"We should probably go inside and get your shoulder looked at."

Without another word, she moves to retrieve her clothes, leaving me wondering if I just made the best or worst decision of my life.

CHAPTER TWENTY

ANDREI

I FIND YULIAN IN HIS BASEMENT OFFICE SURROUNDED BY A tower of computers and high-tech spyware that keeps the estate safe. He smirks at me the moment I step into the room, which tells me his surveillance tools were put to good use today.

"I'm not in the mood," I grumble. "I just need to get bandaged up and get on with my day."

He nods and directs me to sit in a chair in the corner, while he gathers a first aid-kit from the closet. He's an ace head of security, and our de facto medic.

He gives me a sideways glare while cleaning some of the blood around the wound with alcohol. It stings like a bitch. "Are you generally in the habit of letting your captives pull a gun on you?"

"None of your business." I tense through the pain as Yulian bandages the area. It's more of a burn from the bullet's shock wave, so I don't need stitches, but I'm gonna feel this for days.

I am also going to feel the heat of Georgia's cunt wrapped around my dick for days.

Just the image of Georgia naked in my arms is enough to

reinvigorate my cock. I just had her, yet my body is already craving the feel of her butter-soft skin against my own. If this is how I feel after having her just one time, against a tree no less, I am going to lose my ever-loving mind when I get her naked in bed. Which I hope will be very soon.

"All done." Yulian stands back to admire his handiwork.

I force myself onto my feet and grab the clean suit a member of staff delivered for me. I need to get my head back in the game. There are things that need my immediate attention—arms shipments, cartels moving into our territory, troublesome cops that need to be put in their place—things that I've put off for too long because of my beautiful captive. Well, no more.

I'll fuck her out of my system, and be done with this mad obsession. One day I'll marry because it's a good business decision—some cartel princess or spoiled mafioso daughter to secure a powerful alliance—not because of all these feelings.

With Yulian's keen eyes taking in my movements, I carefully dress, avoiding pressure on my right shoulder. He holds my suit jacket out for me to slip into. The last thing I do is take my pistol off Yulian's desk and tuck it into the back of my waistband. My holster is too uncomfortable to wear today.

Yulian crosses his arms and sits on the edge of his desk, his dark eyes drinking me in. "What happened out there?"

"Firearm training." Yulian continues to scowl at me. "Fine. We both know what happened," I admit. Yulian knows everything that happens on the property. No doubt he watched everything go down between Georgia and I—well, not *everything*.

Yulian's face tightens. "You're playing with fire, letting her think she has power. Fear keeps people in-line. She needs to fear you more than Oleg if she's going to carry out what we need her to do. Yet here you are, giving her one-on-one lessons and letting her pull a gun on you. One more inch to the left and that bullet would have done much more damage."

A growl releases from deep within, and my hands instinctively ball into fists. If he wasn't one hundred percent right, and my oldest friend, I would deck him for insubordination. "Let's be clear. I'm not looking for any unsolicited advice in this matter. Imagine it was Rowan. What would you do?"

His lips press together—he knows he'd do the same. Hell, he lost his head for Rowan. Hiding her in his private residence, personally protecting her from her brother's enemies that were out for revenge.

What happened today happened only because I allowed it.

Letting Georgia pull a gun on me, letting her believe she had power for one tiny moment, was a risk, but it paid off. Trust is earned. But the person Georgia has to trust most is herself, and that's what today accomplished. It showed Georgia what she was capable of with a gun in her hand—certainly a lot more than she ever imagined.

Than I imagined.

Yulian sighs deeply. "I never meant to overstep, you know that. I just want what's best for the family." His tone softens. "I want to help you find Kira. You and your brothers deserve to know her, and so far, Georgia is our best chance at that."

Exhaustion and soreness settle in my limbs and suddenly, this day feels like it's been sixty hours long. He knows my family history better than most, and I know his concern is genuine. We may not be blood, but Yulian would take a bullet for me. In fact, he has taken several.

"I got this. Trust me. And don't go telling my brothers. The last thing I need right now is to hear their opinions on my life."

"I don't gossip with your brothers." He frowns. "But do me a favor and don't let her pull a gun on you again."

"Fine," I agree. "I can promise you that."

CHAPTER TWENTY-ONE

GEORGIA

I've really done it this time.

My heart races like crazy as I throw myself onto the bed. Holy shit! What just happened? The gun, the sex, the deal with the devil, all of it. It's a miracle I'm alive right now.

Turning a gun on Andrei has to be the stupidest thing I've ever done. I cringe at the thought. Way to nearly get myself killed.

But that's not what happened. I know Andrei could have overpowered me, taken and turned the gun on me. Even as I ran away and refused to admit defeat, I knew I was as vulnerable as a butterfly dancing around a snake, but I would not go down without trying.

That's not me, or at least that's not the woman I was when I was brought here over three weeks ago. I've changed and today was the proof. Not just my daring escape attempt, but what came after.

The sex.

Oh my god, the sex.

Squeezing my eyes shut, I turn my face into the pillow, still flushed from the pleasure he gave me. It might just be the shock, but I feel euphoric, still high on everything we just shared.

Andrei broke down my defenses with every kiss, with his fingers, his tongue, his cock and with his declaration that he can no longer fight this pull between us.

Arousal tugs at my core, as visions of Andrei's head thrown back in ecstasy flood my brain. I'm far from sexually experienced, but I know what Andrei and I shared is rare. My first time was with a guy I dated briefly in high school. Our fumbling in his dark bedroom was pleasant at best, but nothing like the feel of Andrei deep inside me, stretching me, making my toes curl and my eyes roll up inside my head.

Our connection is all-consuming. I don't have the strength to turn away from him, even knowing at the end of all this he'll still send me to Oleg. I made a deal with the devil, and I intend to honor it.

Even though it's insane, I feel a misplaced sense of loyalty to Andrei. He's protecting my dad, and weirdly, me too. Once he kills Oleg, I can go back to my life, my father, and start again not indebted to anyone.

A soft knock on the door has me sitting up in bed. Is it Andrei?

"Come in," I say softly, hugging my knees to my chest.

The door inches open and Piper's head peeks around the corner. When she sees me in bed, she steps into the room, gingerly closing the door behind her.

"You okay?" Her eyebrows pull together, and concern pours from her as she makes her way towards me.

My blood freezes. What does she mean?

I tilt my head to the side, trying to get a handle on what she knows. We were well-protected in the trees, but could she have seen something?

When I don't respond, she hurriedly continues. "It's just that I overheard something. Not that I was eavesdropping purposefully!"

"What did you hear?" I say, my insides wound tightly.

"Andrei and Yulian talking. Did you shoot Andrei?"

"I did." I lower my head to my knees. "It was an accident." Sort of.

"Whoa, and he didn't... get angry? Hurt you?"

Good question. I suppose the stunning pleasure that I took on his leg was his form of twisted retaliation. Punishment in the very best form.

"Nah." I shrug like it's all no big deal, hoping I'm not sweating through my t-shirt. "It was an accident while he was teaching me how to shoot a gun."

She nods slowly, still hovering around the bed. She obviously wants to know more. I guess it couldn't hurt to be a little friendly.

"You can sit down," I say, gesturing to a spot beside me on the bed.

She props herself on the edge as if prepared to jump up at any given moment. The way her eyes keep on dancing towards the door, I know she's worried about someone coming in here and seeing us talking. Not that anyone specifically banned us from hanging, but I'd say spending time with the captive is probably an unwritten do-not-cross rule. Then again, am I still a captive anymore?

I have to admit, it's nice getting to talk with someone my age who isn't completely entrenched in the Kozlov world, so I offer her an olive branch.

"How about this," I suggest. "Do my hair, and we can talk while you're technically working. If someone comes into the room, they won't think anything of it." I stand and move towards the vanity on the far side of the room.

She smiles. "Good idea." Piper comes up behind me and releases my dark strands from the messy bun it's been in all day. She divides my hair into sections, meticulously brushing through each segment until it's shiny and soft.

"I know this is not my business," she says, eyes trained on the curling iron twisting a strand of hair, "but why are you here? In this home, I mean. Natalia calls you the Kozlovs' guest, but it doesn't feel that way."

I consider how to answer her question without revealing too much. "Sort of. I don't exactly want to be here, but it's best if I stay for now. I'm safe here."

The truth of my words hits me in the solar plexus—it's ridiculous, but I'm safer here than anywhere else.

"Safe?" She laughs. "In the home of a mafia kingpin. I won't ask who your enemies are."

"It's complicated," I agree, not wanting to divulge anymore.

Her eyebrows shoot up to her dark bangs. "Weird. These guys do not act like normal Russian gangsters."

I giggle at that. "And what do you know about Russian gangsters?" I tease, because there is nothing dark about Piper. She used to work for royalty for chrissake.

"Nothing!" Piper nearly jumps out of her skin, and the curling iron in her hand swings precariously close to my ear. "Sorry," she says, wincing. "I'm all done, anyway. What do you think?"

My hair hangs in soft waves around my shoulders. Princess hair is what I would have called it at one time in my life, but I'll admit it's a huge improvement from my usual messy top knots. I grin at her in the mirror. "I could get used to having you around."

Piper flashes me a warm smile in return. "Anyway, I just came to check on you." She shrugs and lays the curling iron down on the desk in front of me.

"Thanks. That's kind of you, but I'm really okay." And I am, strangely. It doesn't quite make sense. I've literally agreed to work for the Kozlov Bratva and to put myself in a situation which I know will be dangerous. Hell, maybe even life threatening, but if it's that important to Andrei, and it leads to Oleg's demise, I'm in.

Although I do wonder about Andrei's connection to Oleg's

daughter, Kira. What part does she play in all of this? Now that I'm committed to this mission, he owes me some answers.

"I'm glad." Piper's voice cuts through my thoughts. "I didn't mean to cross any lines, I just wanted to make sure you were all right. I'm still finding my footing here, too."

"It's nice to know you have my back." I turn in my seat to face her. "Also, I didn't know you speak Russian. When did you learn it?"

Piper freezes. Her body remains rigid as she shakes her head. "I don't speak Russian."

"Oh. But how did you understand the conversation between Andrei and Yulian? I've never heard them speak anything but Russian together?" Amongst themselves and their closest staff, the brothers often speak their native tongue, perhaps to deter nosy Nellies like Piper.

"They were speaking English."

I shrug. Weird. "Well, thanks for coming by. It's nice to have someone to talk to."

She nods. "For me, too. Oh, and Georgia. Maybe you could not mention the eavesdropping to anyone. It was very unprofessional of me."

"Yeah sure," I say. But as she walks out of the room, I definitely get the feeling something is not as it seems.

CHAPTER TWENTY-TWO

ANDREI

I DON'T SEE GEORGIA THAT NIGHT. AS MUCH AS I WANT HER in my bed—underneath me, on top of me, any which way I can have her—duty calls. A shipment of cocaine went missing in transit and the Sicilians were the likely culprit. Our retaliation is swift and brutal, delivered in one bloody night in the gritty streets of South Brooklyn.

I finally get home as the sun crests the horizon. I'm just out of the shower and ready to collapse into bed when Leo texts me. He found a source that has information about our mother. Information that I'll want to hear directly.

Shit. We've spent the last six months digging for any information we could find that explains How my mother ended up pregnant by Oleg. It's a mystery that eats at me day and night.

Leo's text is vague, but I know with Leo there is always a reason. He wouldn't summon Daniil and I in person unless it's something we need to hear for ourselves.

Now I'm in the backseat of the Land Rover with Yulian driving, my stomach in knots about what I'm about to learn. Memories flood my brain. I can still smell the metallic tang of blood as my father lay bleeding in my arms, revealing the twisted family secret that would come to consume my brothers and I.

After all those years, was it guilt that led him to admit on his death-bed that we have a half-sister? I suppose I'll never know. He didn't live long enough to tell me. The only information he shared was that our mother bore a daughter to Oleg, and Oleg raised her out of the country.

The months following Papa's assassination were chaotic, with me figuring out how to step into the role of pakhan virtually overnight. He hadn't prepared me, and I hadn't ever demanded he did. My mistake. By the end of his reign, Papa was tired, having lived a thousand lives in one lifetime. He had gotten sloppy, which is how Oleg moved into Brooklyn.

But Oleg made one tiny miscalculation in his plans when he killed our father. *Me*.

I strengthened and grew our organization beyond the reach of the Antonovs. I was brutal, merciless in my expansion and ambition. We've thrived. I've taken back most of Brooklyn, and before long, the Kozlovs will rule over all of it.

Understanding what happened to our mother and sister is the last piece of the puzzle before we castrate Oleg and feed him to the pigs. He deserves nothing less.

From the front seat, Yulian tells me we've arrived at our destination. I stare out at a rundown low-rise in a residential area. I expected to be taken to a warehouse or a strip club—where most of our business takes place—but this appears to be the furthest thing from it.

The sign out front reads Shore View Nursing and Rehabilitation.

I exchange a sharp look with Yulian as I step out of the vehicle. Why are we here?

Ignoring the dull pain in my shoulder, we enter the building. A scowling, older woman manning the front-desk greets us. Although perhaps greet is the wrong word.

"Yes?" She glares up at us through thick glasses, her lips

puckering as if she just sucked on a lemon. I can't say we're used to such an obvious dismissal, but maybe they don't get many guests in dark suits and neck tats in this part of town. Just as I am about to tell her to mind her own business, Daniil steps off the elevator and into the front lobby.

"There you are," he booms, announcing his presence. He slaps Yulian and I on the back, and shoots sour-puss a flirty wink. Hearts explode in her eyes and it's all I can do not to gag. "Don't worry, Myrtle, they're with us."

Her expression immediately softens. "Visiting your long-lost aunt after all this time. Can't begrudge you that."

"We love to take care of the women in our life." Daniil bats his whisky eyes at her while she blushes like a schoolgirl. Damn flirt.

Myrtle waves us through, and moments later we're stuffed into a tight dank elevator on the way to the third-floor.

"Care to explain what the hell that was all about?"

"Soon." Daniil's demeanor is serious now. No more Prince Charming. He leads us out of the elevator and stops in front of a nondescript closed door. There's not a soul wandering around the halls—neither nurse nor patient—and I wonder if that's my brother's doing or if this place is always so desolate.

Daniil nervously swipes a hand through his hair, furrowing his brow. "You're about to meet Rosa Menendez. She was a nurse at the hospital Mama was at. She has details about Kira's birth."

A bittersweet ache expands in my chest as it does every time I think back to this time, some of the darkest days of my life. When I was ten years old, our mother was committed to a mental health center for months. We were told she was sick and needed time to rest and recuperate. Mama was never the same when she came back home.

"Shit." I adjust the lapel of my suit and let his words sink in. "I was not expecting you to say that."

"I know," Daniil says solemnly, "Leo's guys tracked her down this morning, and we had to move fast. Rosa doesn't have much longer. We waited for you."

"Let's go in." I nod towards the door. Yulian puts his hand on my arm, telling me he'll wait outside to give us space. Daniil and I step inside a small room that reeks of antiseptic and floor cleaner.

Leo is seated in an armchair beside a rickety hospital bed where a tiny old lady is propped up with several pillows, giggling at something Leo said. He's not exactly a laugh-a-minute kind of guy, but he can be charming when he wants to be. *Wants* being the operative word.

Leo stands. "Rosa, I want to introduce you to my oldest brother. This is Andrei," he says gesturing towards me. Rosa holds a veiny brown hand out to me in greeting. It seems to take all her strength to grasp my hand, but she does anyway, her watery eyes shining with warmth.

Too worked up to sit, I lean against the window frame beside the bed and wait for her to speak.

"Your mama talked about you often, Andrei," she says, her voice straining with effort. "She talked about all of you. She loved you boys greatly." Weight settles heavily on my chest. Grief and anger churn together in a familiar dull ache. "I'm glad that you found me. I thought about reaching out to you many times, but I never did. I suppose you can imagine why." Leo leans forward and squeezes her hand. She was scared for her life. My father would not have been happy to hear from her—family business is to stay just that—in the family.

"It's time you know the truth. Your mother would have wanted you to know." She closes her eyes and takes a deep breath. "Your father sent her to the hospital in order to hide a pregnancy, a child conceived out of wedlock." Even though we know this, the truth of it sends chills down my spine. "See, I was the nurse assigned to your mother's care. Dahlia and I became friendly. From the start, it was clear to me she didn't belong there. She was sad and anxious, yes, but that had to do with the life she was living more than anything, but she was mentally sound."

Rosa pauses, coughs racking her body. Leo pours her a cup of water and offers it to her with a straw. She is struggling, but I don't suggest that she rest her voice. I need to hear what she has to say. Our mother was gone for months with no explanation other than she was sick. We did not know what that meant at the time. We were just scared and confused kids trying to act tough, missing our mother with a father consumed by his own grief, and distracted by the empire he had to run.

"No one was supposed to know about your mother's pregnancy, even other staff members. Just me and a doctor were assigned to her, and we were paid very handsomely to tend to her needs and keep our mouths shut. And we did. Your father would come to see her from time to time, but as her belly began to swell, he stopped. Just sent money and nothing else." Her eyes glaze over with memory. "That destroyed your mother."

The silence in the room is nearly deafening. Pieces of a puzzle click into place. The empty spaces of our childhood that didn't add up come into focus. I squeeze my eyes shut, leaning my head against the window, waiting for Rosa to continue.

"Dahlia confided in me. We spent months together, just me and her, walking the grounds of the hospital, sharing meals, learning about each other's life. Your mother was a gentle spirit, as you know. She loved your father once, but he hardened over the years. His work was all-consuming. It ate at his soul, the lives he had to take, the war he waged every day on the streets. But it ate at your mother's soul as well. The violence was a stain on your family, not just blood on your father's hands.

"That's why she tried to remain innocent. She didn't know your father's rivals, and didn't want to know bratva business. She kept herself naïve to protect her heart, but in the end, well, it might be what led to her death."

A creeping cold licks down my spine. Even the air in the room seems to go still as we take in her words. My father could be distant and calculating and only became more so as he fought to build his own empire on American soil. My mother was different. She was soft and lovely and cared about the world. She resented Papa after a time—but never resented us, her children, that tied her into this life.

Another labored breath as Rosa struggles for oxygen. "See, your father knew that your mother was depressed," she rasps. "She was struggling to adjust to mafia life, struggling at the loss of so much basic freedom, so he allowed her small pleasures. She took swimming lessons and an art class at the local college, little things that brightened her day. And that's where she met him. His name was Maxim. Another Russian expat, an artist in her class. He wasn't especially handsome, but he was kind, and most of all, he doted on her. She wasn't looking for trouble, never meant to betray your father, but after being neglected for so long, she craved attention and that's what Maxim gave her. He seduced her. With her bodyguards always around, it was hard for your mother to get time alone with him, but she found a way. It was a brief affair, but that's all it took."

Fuck me. I exchange looks with my brothers, communicating without uttering a word.

"Your father knew it wasn't his child, and he was furious with her. But he also loved her deeply, and couldn't bring himself to kill her, so he sent her away for the problem to be swept under the rug." I nod. In our world, an affair is grounds for murder. As hard as Papa was, I'll give him credit for that. He couldn't hurt his beloved *zhena*.

"Your mother gave birth to a baby girl in the spring—a beautiful girl named Kira with a healthy set of lungs, and a tuft of blonde hair. It was a long birth, and it took a lot out of your mother. She slept all day after, barely able to rouse and nurse her newborn." Rosa is quiet for a moment, eyes focused past Leo on something only she can see. Her voice is softer when she speaks again. "The next morning a man came to the hospital, a man who claimed to be Maxim, the baby's father. He had guards with him. Honestly, they looked like thugs. Before I could wake your mother, or do anything to stop him, he took Kira from the nursery, and left. Just like that, and not one person tried to stop him." Her eyes shine with unshed tears. "I tried to do something, to say something, but all my objections fell on deaf ears. Dahlia called your father, but it was too late. The baby was gone, and your mother was... she was destroyed."

Rosa shakes her head, devastation still shining in her eyes. Whatever happened that day continues to haunt her. Another coughing fit wracks her body, and Leo brings the cup of water up to her lips for her to take a drink. He tenderly helps Rosa lie back down. As soon as her head hits the pillow, her eyes close, and she rests, too fatigued to continue. We all sit and stare at her prone figure for a moment, each one of us blinking, absorbing what we just learned.

"Do you have any information on Maxim, the father? Where he could be?"

Rosa opens her eyes and blinks up at me. "Maxim wasn't who he said he was. Certainly not a starving artist. Maxim wasn't even his real name. He was a fraud."

My gut sinks and I fight against the nausea that roils within me. That Oleg is Kira's father isn't a surprise. But learning that he used our mother as a pawn in a dirty mafia game is gut-wrenching. Squeezing my fists, it takes every bit of strength for me not to lash out.

Our mother was never the same after she came home, taking her own life only a few months after she was discharged from the hospital. The vision of my mother hanging lifeless from the rafters in the garage still haunts my dreams years later, as I know it haunts Daniil's as well. We found her. Two kids grabbing their bikes from the garage. A moment forever etched into our brains, into our very being. My father shipped us off to boarding school shortly after, refusing to deal with the emotional fall-out. Leo was too young to understand what happened. But Daniil and I, we bear the emotional wounds. I've learned how to tamp it down, far down where it's not real. Where ugly shit gets buried.

And here we are, kicking the hornet's nest. Twisting our own insides. All in the name of finding a sister that we didn't even know we had until a few months ago. But this is what our mother would want, for us all to be together.

Rosa—a woman I will be eternally grateful to—is softly snoring, finding refuge in sleep. "We need to move her out of this shit-hole," I say to no one in particular. "She deserves better."

Leo nods. "I'll take care of it."

I know my brothers are hurting just as much as me but I can't bear to witness their pain right now. I'm too consumed with my own.

Walking out of the room, I find Yulian standing guard by the door. Reading my expression, he knows better than to ask how it went. He knows what I need.

"Boxing ring?" he asks, as we start down the stairs.

I nod. It's that or I need to find my salvation between Georgia's thighs. Slamming deep inside her, feeling her from the inside would help extinguish the fire in my veins, but I don't want to go to her until I've taken the edge off, afraid of what I'll do to her if I don't rid myself of this crazy energy first.

"Yeah, let's head to the ring. Grab your mouth guard and jockstrap. I'm gonna need a few rounds."

CHAPTER TWENTY-THREE

ANDREI

I AM SPENT. BOXING HAS THAT EFFECT ON ME. TAKES ALL THE restless energy and eats it up, funnels it, directs it like a laser into something that leaves me exhausted. Once I've worked some of the rage out of me, I'm back to feeling numb.

Numb equals logical. Cool-headed. Objective.

A good place to be.

I slump against the ropes of the boxing ring, taking a long drink of water. Yulian is long gone, having walked out of the ring half-dead an hour ago. I chuckle, thinking back to when he lifted his hands in surrender and told me I'd have to find another sparring partner for the rest of the day. When no one showed up, I hit the punching bag relentlessly until the buzz in my veins died down to a slow burn.

"You're looking sweaty." My head whips up to see Georgia step into the gym. She's wearing her raven hair down in waves that cascade over her shoulders. Skinny jeans and a t-shirt somehow still show off every curve and heat thrums under my skin.

"Did it help? Punching the shit out of that bag, I mean." She motions with her chin to the punching bag in the corner.

"For now."

She sits down beside me on the edge of the boxing ring, eyes roving over my shirtless frame. Sweat still runs down my back and neck and her eyes don't miss a single droplet as it traverses down my body.

"Your shoulder," she says, her voice raspy. "It must still hurt."

I smile at her concern. "I've felt worse. A bullet graze is a lot more pleasant than being shot. I know from personal experience."

She bites her full bottom lip and looks around. "I don't even know how to make sense of that." Georgia leans in closer, her gray eyes dark in the dimly lit underground room. "Why do you box?" I thought maybe you'd be more into Krav Maga, you know, since it's part of my training."

Lifting my hand, I tuck a shiny strand of hair behind her ear. "Growing up, I was still scrawny. Barely had any friends. My family had money, but they didn't have prestige yet. I was just another gangster's kid roaming around the streets of Brooklyn. It's still rough in lots of ways, but not like back then. At a young age, I had to learn to defend myself from the moment I struck out in the streets. One day, I was out running errands for my father when I met one of his associates, a guy known as Little Joe. He was huge by the way, nothing little about the man. Little Joe ran a boxing studio for some of the old timers. Not a mafia joint, just Eastern European émigrés that wanted to fight semi-professionally. Joe took a liking to me, especially when I walked into the studio one day with a black eye. Took one look at me and said it was time to start my training. Best skill I ever learned," I say, and I mean it.

Her tongue brushes over her soft lips, setting off my desire for her, but she's not done with the questions. "What happened today?"

"What do you mean?"

Her mouth tightens. "Something happened. I can tell."

I scrub a hand over my face, hoping she'll just drop it. "It doesn't matter."

She blinks, not dissuaded by my silence. I consider not telling her, or at least glossing over some of the harsher realities, but what's the point? It's better if Georgia knows how fucked up this world is. The farther away she stays, the better.

"It was about my mother," I concede. "About the months before she died. Well, committed suicide."

Georgia sucks in a sharp breath. Her hand settles into my own, a touch meant to comfort. My chest squeezes like a vice, but I keep on going. "I found out Oleg posed as a starving artist and tricked his way into my mother's heart and eventually into her bed. He fathered a child with her. That child is Kira. Kira Antonov is our half-sister."

"What the... did I hear that right? Your mother and Oleg?" She can't keep the shock out of her voice. "Andrei, I don't even know what to say."

I shake my head, because there are no right words. "Oleg knew a child out of wedlock would tear apart my family and weaken my father. Today I learned just how he did it. How he tricked my mother into falling for him, and practically ripped a newborn Kira from my mother's arms, raising her in secret. If he raised her at all." I sigh heavily, a hot wordless fury still burning bright inside.

Georgia's eyes are full of horror. "But why would he do that?"

"Revenge." I drum my fingers on my legs. This is not an easy story to tell. "You know my father used to be an Antonov soldier, but what I didn't tell you was how that came to be. My father was orphaned at a young age until Alek Antonov, Oleg's father, found my papa running dice games in the slums of Moscow, making big bucks for a ten-year-old. Alek saw the potential and took him under his wing.

"He raised Papa alongside Oleg, Alek's biological son, and Masha, his daughter. As they grew up, Oleg came to resent my father. My father was a better leader, a better *vor v zakone*—that's what the Russian mafia was called in those days. *Thieves in law.* Papa moved up the ranks quickly. Oleg was the opposite. Lazy and hot-headed, ruled by his vices.

"Alek didn't have faith in his son's ability to lead, which was why he was preparing to install my father as his heir when he was killed by a car bomb in the streets of Prague. Oleg was able to maintain control of the Antonov empire, and my father became enemy number one. By that time, Papa was a skilled Vor. He left his homeland, moved to Brighton Beach, where many Russians had already settled, and he built the most powerful bratva on U.S. soil."

I tap my foot and crack my knuckles. I hate this part of my history. "My father moved on with his life. He met my mother, fell in love and started a family. But Oleg was spiteful. Angry that his own father chose my papa over him. He made his way to the U.S. and set out to destroy the Kozlovs, and what better way to do that than target the heart and soul of a family? He tricked my mother, then stole her newborn baby." I choke, unable to keep the anguish out of my voice. Rage and pain ignite in my chest. I force myself to take a slow, steadying breath before I have to revisit the punching bag.

Georgia crawls into my lap. Her lips land on mine in a bruising kiss. "We'll destroy him," she murmurs. "We'll find your sister, and after that, we'll destroy him."

Her fists curl and I see a spark, a fierceness to Georgia that I've only seen glimpses of before. And it is devastating. My arm wraps around her middle, and I bury my face in her neck, her sweet smell providing comfort.

"After my mother died, Papa lost his edge, and with that, his hold on the brotherhood. My father wasn't as brutal or as aggressive as he needed to be to stay at the top. With my brothers and I still too young to step in, Oleg slowly grew a base of operations in New Jersey, and before long, he was crowding our territory in Brighton Beach. We didn't realize how bad it had gotten until

Oleg had our father assassinated, the final death-strike against my family."

She blinks and her wolf eyes search my face. "I want revenge too, you know. I want to see Oleg destroyed more than you can imagine."

"He took from both of us, krasotka, and I swear he will pay dearly." My hands are in her hair and before I know it, I've pulled her face towards mine. Desire blazes in her eyes, a hunger that is mirrored in my own. "I'm not in a good place. If I take you now, it won't be gentle."

She watches me for a long moment, her eyes flicking back and forth between mine. She sees the fire, the turbulence, the hurt underneath it all, but she doesn't turn away. Her lips brush against my own, her breath mingling with mine. "I want you too."

I don't want to use her body to chase away my dark shadows, but my resistance is breaking. I'm a weak man when it comes to her. Without further thought, I push her down and pin her back against the mat, hands braced on either side of her. "I warned you."

I palm her breast over her thin t-shirt, my thumb flicking over her nipple. Our heavy breaths intermingle when I slant my lips over hers in a searing kiss, a clash of tongues and teeth. I usually avoid kissing on the mouth. It gives the wrong impression to the temporary woman in my bed, but none of that matters now. I'm overtaken by a kind of delirium and I can't get enough of Georgia's mouth. I suck her tongue, consuming her like she is my last meal on earth.

On a ragged breath, I lean over her, grabbing both of her ass cheeks in my hands, molding her supple flesh and pulling her in towards me, my very pronounced hard-on pressing against her belly like a pulsating brand.

"Take your clothes off so I can fuck you." My command is a harsh whisper. Tonight, I need her to soothe the darkness that threatens to overtake me.

She shivers at my words and releases a whimper, confirming what I've suspected. She is a dirty, dirty girl at heart and I am going to enjoy every inch of her.

Georgia's hands shake as she obeys my command to get naked. She sits up, pulling her top off before reaching for the zipper of her jeans. My heart pounds in a fast, rough rhythm as I help her lift her hips and wiggle her panties down her legs. Her bra is one of those fancy numbers that unclips in the front. I reach down and open it in one motion, sucking in a sharp breath as her breasts are exposed to me. They are all kinds of perfect. I drag my lips from the tender skin of her neck, down her collarbone until my mouth closes over her right nipple. She moans and arches underneath me, her hips rising off the cold floor of the ring.

With a low growl in my throat, I turn my attention to her other breast, sucking hard, scraping my teeth over her tender flesh, her moans growing in volume.

"Please," Georgia begs as I restrain her roaming hands above her head, her body writhing against mine.

Releasing her nipple from my teeth, I smirk down at her. "Please what?"

"I need you."

"You need me to make you come, huh, krasotka? I promise, I am going to make you come so hard, and fast, you'll see stars. But first I need to bury my face in that sweet pussy of yours."

I seize her ankle and drag her towards my mouth. The need to taste her is nearly overwhelming. My harsh breath warms her clit and swollen lips moments before I plunge my tongue deep inside her folds. I'm devouring her from the inside out, lapping up everything she has to give me. She squirms against me, her pleasure building. While it's glorious to watch, I'm not going to let her off the hook that easily.

"You greedy little slut." A harsh slap to her pussy. "You don't get to decide when you come. I do." She whimpers, and I take pleasure in her pain. I lash her with my tongue, focusing all my energy on her clit. "Ask permission to come on my face."

"Please, Andrei. Can I come..." She sounds so fucking needy I almost take pity on her. *Almost*.

I pinch her clit between two fingers. "Say it."

"Can I," she sobs, "can I come on your face?"

"Fuck yes, krasotka. Come all over my tongue." Her head thrashes side to side, as I lap at her hungrily, and bury my fingers in her wet cunt, wrenching a near-painful orgasm from deep within her. I love how her hoarse cry echoes through the room, how her pussy contracts in a delicious rhythm against my tongue.

Afterwards, she collapses against me, her body still reeling from the high of that intense orgasm. "I've never come like that," she admits. "Not even with a toy."

I kiss her forehead reverently, giving her space to float down from heaven. I'd make her come like that every night of my life if I could.

CHAPTER TWENTY-FOUR

GEORGIA

The moment I found Andrei in here, leaning forward with his head in his hands, sweat dripping down his body, I wanted to soothe the darkness that surrounded him.

I want to bring him into the light. And that might just be my downfall.

More than that, I want to take away his pain. I know more than anyone the pain of losing a mother. Cancer is a bitch, one of the worst ways to see a loved one go, but knowing your mother took her own life after being mistreated so horribly. That, I couldn't imagine.

And then there is the pain of being separated from your own flesh and blood. I nearly collapsed in surprise when he told me the truth of Kira's identity. That's a bitter pill to swallow.

I want to offer him distraction in the way I know he needs it right now.

Inching my fingers towards his groin, I cup him through his shorts, relishing the feel of him heavy in my palm. After eating me out like an animal, he's still hard, and my hand curls over his impressive length.

"Still hungry for more?" Andrei's eyes darken and he sucks in a sharp breath.

"I'm ravenous," I admit. "Starved." Tonight, I want everything. Everything he has to give.

His eyes are heavy with lust, savagely beautiful as I move to peel his shorts off of him, but he stops me with a hand on my arm.

"Not like this. Not here." He moves in and nips at my neck. "I need you spread wide for me in my bed."

My mouth goes instantly dry at the thought of me, Andrei, no clothes and an enormous bed at our disposal all night long.

Hell, yes.

ANDREI'S ROOM is not at all what I imagined. It's softer, somehow more inviting than I expected, while still being undeniably masculine. The bed is huge, with dark silk sheets that smell just like him. It makes my mouth water.

"I'll give you the grand tour later. Now I need to fuck your mouth."

Laying me on the bed, his eyes never leave mine as he strips out of the athletic shorts he was boxing in. His naked body makes me lose my mind. There's not an ounce of fat on him, all hard muscles and ridges, and a manly spattering of hair on his chest. His upper torso is covered in ink, making him that much more sexy. He kneels on the bed beside me, his cock rigid between his legs, beckoning me to taste him.

What I lack in sexual experience I hope I make up for in sheer enthusiasm. I didn't know what it really meant to need someone inside of you until now.

I can't stop myself from running my hands up and down the muscular planes back, indulging in the hard lines of his torso, even the scars and imperfections. Propping myself up on my elbows, I rub my cheek against his bare dick, and he trembles beneath me. But it's his smell that gets me. I inhale him: musk and sandalwood and perfection.

Before I can go any further, he tangles his fingers in my hair and stops my exploration. A pained noise escapes from my throat. Doesn't he know how much I need to take him in my mouth? He laughs.

"As much as I'd love to fuck your mouth, I need your pussy first. Spread your legs for me."

His voice is rough with restraint as he settles above me, caging me in with both arms. It's clear he's feeling as crazed at this moment as I am. He drags his mouth between my breasts, grazing his teeth over each stiff nipple, while he grinds his erection through my soaked pussy lips. He tweaks one of my nipples hard, and in one fast and brutal movement, he shoves inside of me.

Holy Mother of all that is sacred, Andrei moving deep inside of me is heaven on earth. He is hitting all the right places and then some. Instinctively, he seems to know how I need him, pulling all the way out and slamming back inside.

His ass muscles tighten beneath my hands as he thrusts up, pounding into me at a relentless pace that is pure perfection. Every strike of his balls against my thighs has me gasping for air, pleading with him for release, as my body rolls and twists beneath him.

"Tell me who owns this beautiful pussy."

"You do. Just you."

"Good." His hand slides down to the crack of my ass, circling the puckered ring of muscle with a fingertip. "And this?"

Oh no. No, no, no.

I clench my muscles before he can push in any further. "I've never..." I start to say.

He looks down at me with quiet intensity. A warning. "This ass is mine too. Let me in."

My body tenses at the intrusion of his finger, but he's quick to soothe me with shushing sounds whispered against my neck. A moment later, it actually feels good.

As my body relaxes into his touch, he picks up the pace, skewering me with his cock. Hitting the perfect place, over and over again until I can't hold back anymore. "Milk me good, krasotka. Come all over my fucking cock."

My thighs tremble and I scream as my pussy contracts violently around his hard length. "Fuck," is the last thing he says, before jerking himself inside of me, flooding my insides with warmth. He buries his face in my hair, and breathing hard, collapses against me. We stay locked in each other's arms for a long moment. My body is putty against his. All the tension drained with one glorious orgasm.

But reality intrudes before long.

"We didn't use a condom... again." I blurt out.

Still inside of me, he pulls back and looks into my eyes, a hand still fisted in my hair. "I'm clean. I've never gone bare with anyone."

I swallow hard, trying not to read too much into what that means. "Me neither. And I have an IUD." It's to help with period cramps, but it sure is coming in handy right now.

"Good." He draws lazy circles with his finger on my collarbone. "I never want a barrier with you."

It scares me how good it feels to have Andrei say these things, to feel him closer than I've ever felt to anyone, but I can't lose my head over this sexy man. We made a deal, nothing more. And when the time comes, he'll send me away.

Andrei must sense the shift in my thoughts, because he quietly pulls out of me and settles on his back, hands behind his head. I shudder, already missing the warmth he provided.

"What are you thinking?"

"Nothing, really. Okay, not nothing," I concede, flipping on to my stomach, so I can better look at him. "If you weren't born into this life, what would you want to be?"

He grins. "Like for a job?"

"Yeah."

His brows draw together and he stares up at the ceiling for a minute. "I'm not sure I've given it any thought."

"What!" I raise my head to rest on one hand. "How is that possible? There must be something that interests you, that you're passionate about."

He chuckles and wraps a lock of my hair around his finger. "It's different when you grow up knowing your path is set in stone. I am the Kozlov heir. There would never be another direction for me. Just ask Prince William. I mean not to put the guy down, but he graduated university with a master of arts degree in geography. He clearly wasn't thinking about his future career options."

I grin. "You are being ridiculous."

"Am I?" I narrow my eyes, shooting him my best dirty look. "Fine," he concedes. "I'd own an art gallery or something like that. Maybe a gallery showing only works by women artists, since they're usually underrepresented in the arts."

Shit. I did not expect him to say that. Who is this man? One part mafia tough guy, one part secret feminist... except for the stuff in bed.

"What about you?" He turns on his side to face me. "You dropped out of college."

The familiar burn of shame wells up inside of me. I watched my friends and schoolmates move on to college, and careers, and here I am. No closer to a life of my own.

"I had to help my father," I say, a touch defensively. "What choice did I have?"

He nods in understanding, but continues to regard me. "But what do you really want? When you imagine your life beyond this. What do you see?"

I blow out a breath. "That is as pointless as talking about your future as something other than a pakhan."

"You're wrong. Your life won't be this way forever."

His statement catches me off-guard and I don't know why,

but I'm compelled to tell him the truth. A truth I've never told another person, but somehow, I want to share with him.

"I'd teach art to kids. Maybe art history too."

He nods as if I make perfect sense. "You'll make a great art teacher someday."

"Whatever." I flop on my back and stare at the ceiling. I can't think about my future right now. All I can think about is tomorrow. The day after that. Making good on my promise to Andrei. Reuniting with my father. Figuring out how to move forward.

"I have to go out of town for a few days," he says softly. "But I have something special to show you when I'm back."

"Special how?" I ask.

His lips tilt up at the corners as he runs a hand over my shoulder. "Good special. A surprise. You'll have to wait and see."

"Okay," I say, feeling confused. I don't know what's happening here. The sex is one thing, but it doesn't feel like this is just about sex anymore.

He sighs, and his hand comes back to my face, his fingers brushing over my skin as if he could read my mind. How can his touch alone make me feel so much?

"We have now. Until Oleg is back in play." It seems like he wants to say something more, but he can't find the words.

"We have now." I echo.

CHAPTER TWENTY-FIVE

GEORGIA

Days pass by in a blur of training and sleep—the sleep I need mostly because I'm so damn worn-out from training. Guns, fighting, acting, computer hacking. I'm learning skills I would never have dreamed I'd possess, or even need, but it's oddly rewarding when I become a sure-shot or when I flip one of Andrei's big burly guards on his back as he attempts to overpower me.

Natalia joins me for dinner most nights, which is strangely comforting. I sense that she's actually joining me to make sure that I am following along with the plan, but we fall into an easy routine together, discussing my day, and barely discussing hers. I wonder where Andrei and his brothers are and what they are doing, but I don't bother asking, knowing she won't share anything with me.

Like everyone else in the Kozlov employ, she's tight-lipped. Well, everyone except for Piper. Though she lives off-site, she often pops by my room in the evening and offers to do my hair. It's pointless. I have nowhere to go, but I don't mind the company and the feeling of being spoiled.

Piper and I talk about everything, and nothing—the weather, music, our favorite movies and TV shows. What we don't talk about is our personal life. Occasionally she'll reveal a snippet of her world beyond the Kozlov estate, but she's guarded about her upbringing. That's fine. We all have our secrets and I'm happy to avoid difficult subjects. There's much about my own life I'd prefer not to talk about.

Tonight, she's helping me do my hair and make-up before dinner with Andrei. After three long days away, he's back tonight, and has requested I join him for dinner. Alone.

I'm more nervous than I've been in a long time. We've already shared so much, but something about tonight feels more real. Like a date. Which is absolutely insane. I need to get a grip and remember why I'm doing this—for my freedom. I cannot catch feelings for Andrei, no matter how easy it feels sometimes.

"All right, open your eyes," Piper says with a flourish of a brush against my cheekbones. The face staring back at me in the mirror is one I barely recognize. I somehow look both seductive and understated with smokey eyes, glossy lips and my hair pulled back into a low bun at the nape of my neck.

"Wow, Piper. You certainly have a gift."

"Please, it's all you." She waves her hand at me. "Andrei is going to freak."

"No, it's not like that. It's just dinner. Like a business dinner."

Her eyes narrow, and she purses her lips. "Uh-huh. Sure it is. I see the way he looks at you."

My face becomes hot and I fight the urge to fidget. "And how does he look at me?"

"Definitely not like you're a business associate."

Jesus, is it hot in here?

"You have a great imagination," I say, but there's not much force behind my words. Whatever is going on between us, and as far as I can tell, it's just sex, we have probably done a lousy job of hiding it from those around us.

I can't muster up the energy to care, though. I've already

agreed to his terms, and I might as well go all in. No holds barred.

DINNER IS ROMANTIC. There's no mistaking that this is a date, not a business dinner, as I attempted—but failed—to convince Piper. Mikhail escorts me by car to a secret location. After a ten-minute drive on winding, private roads, we emerge onto a section of pristine beach bordered by jagged rocks.

Andrei meets me as I step out of the car. He's dressed as casually as I've ever seen him, in perfectly worn-in jeans, and a black t-shirt, looking every bit as devastating in casual clothes as he does in his form-fitting suits.

His dark gold hair is brushed back and hangs just past his ears. High, slanted cheekbones give way to a hint of a five-o'clock shadow. As he steers me to a picnic on the beach, his deeply masculine scent surrounds me and my nipples pebble in response. I'm like Pavlov's dog when he's near, salivating for a taste of him. Maybe he feels the same way because his lips meet my own for a gentle kiss.

"It's nice to see you, krasotka."

I smile up at him, a cool breeze blowing over my skin. "The ocean," I say. "I knew we were on Long Island."

We both take a seat on the blanket that he's laid out, laden with delectable looking sushi. Handing me a glass of wine, he shrugs. "It was never a secret."

"I'd beg to differ." I raise my eyebrows at him. "Remember the library."

"All the time," he smirks. "I remember you coming on my face. That was fucking hot."

He loads up a plate with food, and hands it to me, before preparing his own plate.

"If we're past being secretive, why don't you tell me where we are?"

"You already figured it out, smart girl. This spot is called Barcelona Point. It's at the very northern end of East Hampton. We're surrounded by seven hundred acres of nature preserves."

"Shit," I smile, looking out over the calm water. "I had no chance of escaping."

"None whatsoever."

"Then why did you chase me? You could have just let me wander the woods for a while and freak out."

"Where's the fun in that?" He holds out a piece of sashimi with chopsticks for me. Raw fish is not usually my thing, but I choose to be open-minded. Opening my mouth, I'm not disappointed when I taste the most buttery piece of fish imaginable.

"Mmm," I moan, washing it down with a crisp white wine. "So, why is it called Barcelona Point?"

"It's thought to have been named by sailors in the eighteen hundreds for its likeness to the bluffs of the Spanish city."

"My parents went to Barcelona when they were pregnant with me. There are pictures of my mother out to here," I say, gesturing as if I had an enormous belly, "and looking so happy. Eating, and walking and enjoying everything that the city had to offer." I swallow back a suspicious lump in my throat. "I wish I could see her like that," I tell him, because somehow I think Andrei would understand.

"I know." He leans in and kisses my neck. "I get it."

We're both still for a moment, chasing our own thoughts. Finally, I turn to him and ask the one question I've been dying to know. "What does krasotka mean?"

He barks out a laugh. "You're telling me in all your time snooping in my home you didn't figure it out."

"If I had access to a computer, and could google it, it would be much easier." I feign irritation, swatting Andrei on the arm.

"Is that a subtle hint, krasotka," he says, dragging out the syllables.

"Nah, I don't even care about that anymore. But I am curious."

"It means beautiful woman. Quite fitting for you I think."

After we're both stuffed full of sushi and buzzed on fine wine, we take a walk on the beach, enjoying a sunset for the ages. We come together like no time has passed. Conversation flowing easily between us. We talk about the progress I've made training, and I am grateful for this halter dress which lets me show off my increasingly toned arms. Andrei laughs as I flex my muscles, impressed at the results of my Krav Maga training.

I know better than to ask Andrei why he was away on business—he's made it clear the less I know about bratva the better—but we talk in generalities about his work, and he seems more relaxed and at ease than he's been in a long-time.

When we're back in the car, he turns to me. "I have something for you back at the house. Also, have I told you how fucking sexy you look tonight?" His eyes leave the road to rake over my body with unrestrained heat.

"You may have mentioned it once or thrice."

"Because it's true." He takes my hand in his and presses a kiss to my open palm as he parks in the circular driveway. Before he leaves the car, I stop him with a hand on his arm. If Piper has picked up on our relationship, that means Andrei's brothers have as well.

"What do your brothers think?" When Andrei raises his eyebrows, I add, "About us. They seem wary of me."

He shakes his head. "My brothers know better than to stick their nose in my business."

"But isn't this their business too? I mean, I'm here to help you find Kira. It concerns them as well."

"I don't care what they think. What anyone thinks," he says more forcefully, before gentling his tone. "I just want to enjoy this, being with you. I trust you. I know who you are and what you are capable of. I may not see eye to eye with my brothers all the time, but they have my back and they trust my judgment."

God, this man. He always knows the right things to say. Maybe it's a mob boss thing.

Andrei reaches for my hand, and we go into the house, heading towards a back staircase that takes us straight to the third floor. With my hand tucked firmly into his, Andrei leads me down a long hallway to a far wing of the house I've never been to. Finally, he pauses before a door. The naughty smile he flashes me is enough to make butterflies erupt in my stomach.

"What is this about?" I blurt, but he puts a finger to my lips and draws me inside the room.

It takes me a moment to register what I am seeing. It's a cozy room, small by the standards of this mansion, but it has an enormous bay window facing the faraway beach. The light is fading fast outside, but I can imagine how spectacular the view is during the day.

My heart drums in my chest as I look around. Two separate easels are set up in front of a window, different sized canvases stacked up along one wall, while a table on the far side of the room is loaded with all the paints, brushes and painting supplies one could ever want for.

Andrei comes up behind me, his lips graze my neck as he murmurs against my skin, "It's for you. A painting studio."

Emotion clogs in my throat, and to my horror, I have to stifle a sob. I swallow hard before I can speak. "Why?" I ask him. Why would he give me this when my time here is so limited? The moment Oleg comes out of hiding, I'll be packing my bags, so this just feels like a tease. A taste of a life I can never have.

Andrei spins me around to face him. "So you can finally learn how to paint. I want to give you that—a gift—before you move on."

Sadness unfurls inside me even though I try to school my features. "Of course," I say, wiggling out of Andrei's hold. I need to put space between us before I mistake this gesture for something it's not.

"I didn't mean to upset you, krasotka." Andrei runs an agitated hand through his hair.

I've gotten ahead of myself. I've let him under my skin.

Inside of me. Allowed the excitement of the last few days to make me forget what this really is. Business. And it will end soon.

Sitting down at the stool in front of the easel, I allow myself the pleasure of picking up a brush and running it over the blank canvas in front of me. "Thank you," I say, composing myself. "This is the sweetest gift anyone has ever given me."

He sits on the stool opposite me—legs spread wide, elbows resting on his knees. Regret tinges his expression. "I should have thought it through, I didn't think—"

I shake my head. "I'll enjoy it while I'm here, for however long that is." My arms loop around his neck as I pull myself onto his lap.

"Georgia..." his eyes plead with me for something, but I'm not sure what.

"No." I capture his mouth with mine. "I want this. All of it." My hands run up and down his powerful arms to his shoulders. "For however long we have."

I stand and let my dress drop to the ground. I'm sick of talking. I want to lose myself in his touch.

I strip down to nothing but a black strapless bra with delicate lace fabric, and a thong. His eyes rake over me with blatant appreciation. Feeling brazen, I lower myself onto his lap so my back is to him and my ass lands directly over his straining erection.

It's an incredible turn-on to feel how hard he is for me, and I take great pleasure in grinding on him, teasing him with my body, until he's had enough and grabs me firmly by my hips, pulling me down on him as he rocks his pelvis upwards.

"You think you are in charge here?" His voice is a gentle touch in my ear, deceptively soothing, but lined with steel. "You're not."

He reaches up and squeezes my breasts hard through the lace at the same time he bites my neck. I yelp, but he's quick to soothe the hurt with little licks and kisses. His mouth is pure magic and I squirm on his erection, digging into my ass.

"You know better than that, don't you, baby?" His tongue flicks out to lick along the rim of my ear. "I own this body. I allow you to feel good. I allow you to come. Just me. Because you're mine."

His words absolutely shatter me. I'd give anything to him right now.

Andrei stands, taking me with him. Then he picks me up and throws me over his shoulder, slapping my ass as I'm exposed to him. "Now let me show just how much I am in charge." With that, he walks out of the room, and I am truly his little captive, vulnerable to whatever ministrations he has in store for me.

And I can't fucking wait.

CHAPTER TWENTY-SIX

GEORGIA

He doesn't take me to his bedroom as I expected he would. He takes me to the room across the hall from this one. As he places me down on my feet, I take in the tall vaulted ceilings and dim lighting. It takes me a few moments to realize where we are. Some sort of art gallery.

Andrei pulls my back against the front of his body and whispers in my ear, "This is my special collection. As soon as I'm done fucking you, I'll show you my favorite pieces." His words send a jagged shiver down my spine. It seems I'm forever in a perpetual state of wanting with this man.

He pushes me down on a large chaise lounge in the middle of the room. It's a long, cushy bench, with plenty of room for me to spread out. His eyes don't leave mine as he reaches for his belt. The slide of leather is audible in the cavernous space. He's quick to lose the rest of his clothes. My eyes feast on his fully naked form, my stomach fluttering at the sight of his perfection. Boxing must be a hell of a workout, because he is as close to a cutout of a marble statue as I've ever seen.

Lying on my belly, with my arms under my head, the cool

white leather of the lounge only heightens my senses. Approaching me, Andrei hikes my hips upwards. I am completely open and vulnerable to his perusal.

"Beautiful," he breathes, spreading the moisture all around. I seem to lose all thought as Andrei continues stroking me, teasing me all over my body. "Keep your hands on the bench. Don't move a muscle." I whimper at his forceful command. His filthy words and fingers make me lose control.

And then another sensation. Something I've never quite felt before.

A low moan travels up my throat, and I bite down on my bottom lip as I take in the strangely erotic sensation of little balls rubbing over my most private parts.

"What is that?" I ask, turning my head to the side. Through tunnel vision I make out a very long strand of pearls wound around one of his hands.

"Question period is over," he says, his voice rough in my ear. "Now I just want you to feel."

A harsh sting to my backside makes me howl. It's the pearls. *Fuck me*! He rubs his hand over the area he just hit, the bite of pain soothed with his hand rubbing in little circles. Just as my body relaxes into his touch, another slap with the pearls. This one is sharp and brutal.

I cry out, but again the pain is muted by the pleasure. This time he pulls the necklace taut between the folds of my sex, up between my ass cheeks, like the most erotic thong on the planet. And then he rubs the balls hard between my folds, up and down, sawing in a back-and-forth motion until my brain can't register anything else but how good this feels.

"So wet, krasotka," he purrs, his fingers brushing over my sex. But this tenderness is but a moment's reprieve before his thumb and forefinger capture my clit in a brutal pinch. I cry out, tears springing into my eyes, but his tongue soothes the pain with little licks, the pearls shoved to the side.

I don't know up from down, pain from pleasure—the only

tangible sensation that I can grab hold of is my need for release. Andrei must sense it because he sits up and shoves three fingers into my pussy while grinding the pearls roughly into my clit. My legs become slippery with wetness. I grit my teeth and arch into his thrusts as his fingers become more insistent, sliding in deeper, his cut body pinning me down as I writhe at his intrusion.

Just when I can't take the sensation of his fingers stretching my tight channel, his broad crown nudges my entrance. My body zings with pleasure.

"Please," I beg.

He flips me onto my back, his powerful frame resting between my thighs. My left leg is thrown over one of his massive shoulders. I'm spread wide for him, ready for the taking.

"Open your mouth, krasotka. You are going to take my spit and then you are going to take my cum." I do as he says, opening my mouth to drink his spit, as he rubs the head of his cock up and down between my pussy, spreading the wetness all over. I'm shaking for it, clutching his shoulders, begging him with the tilt of my hips.

Finally, one forceful pump and he's fully seated inside me. The feeling of fullness is almost too much to bear, but absolute perfection at the same time. Eyes shut, head thrown back in ecstasy, he stills, allowing me time to adjust to his girth, the full feeling only intensified by my leg slung over his shoulder. I've never felt as full as I do right now, desperate for our bodies to meld into one.

"You'll never understand what you do to me, sweet girl." Warmth floods my body at his words. "You've broken me. Do you know how weak I am for you?" An anguished grunt as he thrusts, pulling his hips back, then rocking deep inside me. Eyes glued to my own.

I want to tell him it's like that for me too, but I bite my lip, holding the words inside. My admission would only make everything that will come after this that much harder. Instead, I focus on the pleasure pulsing through my body. My back arches, my nipples chafing against his dampened chest, the intensity nearly too much to bear.

"Andrei, please..." Words are beyond me now. I'm just a bright light of need and desire.

Sweat drops from his forehead onto my breasts, and I lock my legs around his waist, wanting him as close as possible.

"I want to feel your sweet little pussy milk me so hard. Can you do that for me?"

It's not just his words that coax my orgasm, it's everything. How he looks at me, how he holds me. His massive body rests between my thighs, pistoning his cock inside me, from root to tip.

My head thrashes back and forth, as a scream bursts from my lungs, my body singing in sweet relief. As I shatter beneath him, he sits up and slams back inside me, pushing the backs of my knees up against my stomach, my core clenching him

"What are you doing to me?" His voice is tortured, as he stares down at the place we're connected. He's slamming in and out of me at a frenzied pace, the sounds of skin slapping taking up the entire room. Another tortured growl and then his body freezes. Hot spurts of his cum fill me, his hips jerking as he presses his face into my neck.

It occurs to me how utterly screwed I am. I feel connected to Andrei in a way that I've never felt before, and I'm sure this is a one way-street to getting my heart broken.

CHAPTER TWENTY-SEVEN

GEORGIA

I WAKE UP AS ANDREI GENTLY UNTANGLES HIS BODY FROM mine. We're in his bed now. I couldn't have been asleep for more than ten minutes. My limbs are heavy and sated after another round of mind-blowing sex.

After going at it like animals in his private gallery, Andrei made good on his promise and allied me to fan-girl over every piece in his personal collection. He really does love art as much as I do and that makes me even more wild for him. This last round in his bed was more intimate, more like making love.

"Where are you going?" I moan, as Andrei sits up.

A soft laugh. "To get you a glass of water and Tylenol. You're going to be sore tomorrow after how I used you tonight."

"I'm fine," I assure him. "Stay with me."

His enormous frame envelops me as we lie on our sides spooning, his warmth seeping deep in my bones. "Do you always walk around with a mile of pearls stashed in your pocket?"

"No," he whispers in my ear, his powerful chest pressed flush against my back. "But I had a feeling I might need them tonight. Or maybe I just hoped I could see you tortured by pearls. I ordered it from my jeweler the day after we met." He chuckles at his admission, and my heart skips a beat. He knew we would come together, eventually. Maybe on some level, I knew we would as well.

"They are certainly effective." I admit, stretching my arms out above me, needing to move my body again and allow blood to flow back into my limbs. He rolls me onto my back, taking my mouth in a possessive kiss, his tongue dancing with my own. When he finally pulls back to look into my eyes, I am awed by the intensity that meets me. My gaze drifts down his body, landing on his powerful chest.

"What does this mean?" I breathe, tracing my finger over a tattoo of a hummingbird over his heart, and a beautiful constellation of stars hovering below the bird.

A deep sigh, as he pulls me closer, kissing my forehead. "It's for my mother. Hummingbirds are beautiful and fragile like her, like life itself. The stars are my brothers and me, always close. Wherever she is."

"What was she like, your mother?" I ask gently, tracing the intricate art with my fingers. I'm pushing him and I know there is a chance he'll pull away. But for now, he sighs and rolls onto his back, his hands under his head.

"She was full of life. Loved art, like you. My father and her met at a charity event when he bought a piece of her art that was being auctioned off. He says he fell in love with her painting, even before he met her, although once he set eyes on her, all bets were off. He was smitten."

"So your parents were a love match?" I know that's not always the case in the world of the mafia. Like royalty long ago, marriages are arranged to unite powerful families and create alliances.

"They were," he confirms. "For a while, at least. My mother struggled in the world of the bratva—the need for protection, the constant danger—it's not a peaceful world, krasotka."

"I know," I whisper, twining his fingers with my own.

"Outsiders tend to think it's exciting at first—until they realize the shit never ends. The violence, the bloodshed, the treachery. You can't ever walk away from it. My mother loved my father when she married him, but every mark of blood eroded that love. Love isn't enough once you glimpse the ugliness."

His warning rings in my ear, a reminder that we will never be more than this.

Pulling me closer to him, he continues. "But for all the darkness, I remember a mother who loved us, who would try to lose our protection detail and take us to art galleries, who would sneak us chocolate chip cookies and warm milk in our bed at night, or pile us all into her car and drive us to Jersey shore, just so we could splash around and experience a normal childhood. But the life got to her. I was young, but I knew something wasn't right. I just couldn't help her."

"I'm so sorry," I whisper, trailing my hand down his biceps.

"You lost your mother, too." He acknowledges, pulling back so he can look at me.

"Yeah." I sigh, a hollow ache blooming in my chest. "It was hard, but I was so young. Just turned four years old when my mom got sick. That's why my dad is so important to me. He's the only family I have."

"I know, and I'm going to make sure you get back to him."

"Will you let me design a tattoo for you? One representing Kira?" Anticipation buzzes in my veins. He's quiet for a moment, looking past me into the shadows of the room. "If I find her, that is."

"If you find her, I'll give you the world." He lowers his face, meeting my eyes. It's almost too much, too intense, like staring into the sun. His lashes are spiked with moisture, his thick hair tousled and sexy looking. He traces his thumb over my bottom lip and kisses me softly. I don't know what any of this means, but I know I've never felt safer or more protected in my life.

Maybe it's foolish, but I do trust him. I trust him with my life.

"Please promise me something?" I ask. "No matter what happens, you'll look after my dad."

"Nothing bad will happen to you, krasotka. I swear it." His voice is hard as nails. Conviction seeped into every word. Andrei seems to believe he has the power to control the moon and stars, but I know that anything in life is possible.

"Fine, I believe you. But still, I need to know before I go back to Oleg. No matter what—"

"You have my word." He curves his big palm around my jaw, his thumb brushing over my cheek as he gazes down at me. "I will take care of everything, including your father. But you can't be worrying about this right now." His voice is nearly a whisper—an erotic caress over my skin. "Now it's time you slept. I used your body hard, and I intend to do it again before the sun is up."

I yawn and stretch out, feeling deliciously satisfied. "I look forward to it," I say, as I drift to sleep secure in his arms.

CHAPTER TWENTY-EIGHT

ANDREI

Trailing behind Leo, I keep my gun at my side, alert for any sounds or movements around us. We are creeping along the perimeters of a long-forgotten industrial warehouse close to the Newark airport, where Oleg has stowed his latest shipment of illegal weapons.

My family doesn't deal in arms trafficking, preferring white collar cybercrime that comes with way less red tape and political machinations, and much more profit. But I'm not fucking around anymore. Taking over this shipment is the first of many injustices I have planned to make sure Oleg's legacy dies with him. Which is going to be very fucking soon if I have my way.

I am out to destroy Oleg Antonov anyway I can. And that means taking over each and every racket that he controls. When we walk away today, this warehouse and everything in it will be ours. Moving forward, my organization will be the primary contact for arms into the U.S. I've met with the Nigerians and the Saudis and we've come to an understanding that I now control arms trafficking all along the east coast.

Today is both payback, and a message tied up with one bloody bow.

"Exterior guards have been taken out," Leo murmurs. He pulls the Glock out of his holster, checks the chamber, and keeps it in hand. "We're good to go in."

"Let's move," I say, ready for action. Craving it. With the Antonovs, revenge is personal and I *want* to get my hands dirty.

The warehouse is a wide-open cavernous space. I didn't expect the goods to be displayed so prominently, but aisles of metal racks are piled high with smuggled submachine guns, assault rifles, and heavy machine guns—whatever goodies the latest shipment brought in from Liberia. Crouching low, we take cover in the dark outer edges of the room. It's the center that's lit up, a dangling light fixture shining down on the brigadiers like a spotlight.

Weapons are spread out on the table in front of the three bozos, all of them smoking and talking in rapid fire Russian, excited about something or other. They're relaxed, no sense that danger is imminent, no prickle on the back of their neck to alert them that predators lie in wait. Even the four guards—one in each corner of the room—look bored.

I stay behind Leo as we army crawl deeper into the room, still bathed in the shadows. Daniil and Yulian are positioned on the roof, providing intel and cover. The rest of my men are fanned out in a tactical position around the premises, including on the opposite end of this room. We have the warehouse surrounded, though Oleg's men don't know it yet.

Leo holds up three fingers, then two, then one. It's showtime.

Chaos erupts around me as my men step out of the shadows and into the light, each one focused on a different target. My elbow meets the nose of the guard beside me. He's practically a kid, but that doesn't stop me from slamming bone into his brain. He goes slack in my arms, but I hold his body tight to mine, using his girth as a shield as gunfire explodes around me.

With a tortured cry, another guard lunges towards me, but I don't give him time to do any damage. Tossing the dead guard, I pull a gun from behind my back, shooting my attacker in his right shoulder. He drops his gun, grabbing his arm and howling in pain as I tower over him.

"Not so fast, my friend." Fear flashes in his eyes as he looks straight at me. "I just want to make sure that you send our regards to your bratva friends. Oh wait, you won't be around long enough to do that. Too fucking bad," I say, pulling the trigger. This time, I hit him square between his eyes.

Leo is at my side, head tilted towards the door as I drop this idiot like a sack of potatoes. "The room is clear. Let's go."

"That's all?" I frown. It was barely two-minutes of fun, but we sure accomplished a hell of a lot in those two minutes. Bodies litter the room, all of them loyal to Oleg. At least there's that.

We step out into the cover of night, Leo next to me, gun at the ready for any surprises. I quickly reload my pistol, not wanting to take any chances. Someone hiding in wait is entirely possible. But all remains quiet.

I've left my best soldiers in charge of seizing the building and confiscating the arms on-site. The Kozlovs are now officially arms dealers.

"Oleg is losing his touch. That job was child's play," Leo says, disappointment coating his words as he slides behind the steering wheel of the armored Land Rover. Moments later Daniil opens the backdoor and joins us in the vehicle.

"Well, that was fun." He leans between the two front-seats with a feral smile on his face.

Leo screeches out into the night as I take one final look back at the warehouse that is now ours. Kozlov property.

Perverse satisfaction fills me. I'm one step closer to seeing Oleg Antonov and his empire burn.

Back in our office, we're still hopped up on the high that comes with a successful mission, even one as dead easy as taking over the Antonovs' arms warehouse.

Leo lifts his shot glass and clinks it against my own. "*Za zdarovie*," he says. "To Papa's memory."

"To rebuilding his empire," Daniil adds, downing the shot.

"Fuck that. To building our own empire." I relish the burn as the liquid slips down my throat, slamming down the glass on the table. "What did Papa do for us?" Bitterness tinges my words, an old wound opened after learning the circumstances around our mother's death.

Leo sighs into his drink, and Daniil shakes his head, but proceeds with his shot. I won't leave the issue alone.

"Are you just going to ignore what we learned? He didn't protect her, not like he should have." A knife twists as the memory of my mother's listless body swaying on the rope. It's a vision that will haunt me till the end of my days.

"There's no mercy in this world, Andrei. You should know that better than anyone." Daniil spins the empty glass in his hand. "Papa did what he had to do, but he was hurting just as much as we all were. If you need to direct your anger anywhere, look no further than Oleg Antonov."

A growl escapes my throat. "Papa could have told us earlier about Kira. He could have helped find her. He kept the secret for over twenty years and did nothing, didn't tell us we have a sister being raised by our enemy." I throw my glass against the wall, anger bubbling inside of me.

The irony isn't lost on me. The day Oleg killed our father, we learned he sired and raised our sister. Now tell me that's not fucked up.

It has meant leaving Oleg alive while we try to untangle the twisted web of our family tree. We've spent every day since this revelation trying to hunt down our sister. All we know is that she's twenty-one and was raised in Russia until the age of five. After that, the trail goes cold. No matter who her father is, Kira shares our blood, and she deserves a place in the Kozlov family fold, if that's what she wants.

"He buried the truth with our mother and continued to live a lie. He should have obliterated Oleg years earlier. Instead, he just pretended it never happened."

Silence hangs heavily between us like an anvil. They know I'm right, no matter how quick they are to defend our father. He didn't kill Oleg when he had the chance, and in the end, Oleg killed him. Simply because he could.

Daniil curses under his breath, a frown pulling at his lips. "It would have meant a full on mafia war, one I don't think the American authorities would have taken too kindly to. Papa didn't want war. By the end he just wanted peace. He was tired, Andrei, tired of this life. We are finishing the job now."

"He's right, *brat*. The past is the past." Leo stands and wanders over to the grimy window overlooking desolate railway tracks. "The only thing we can control is what comes next. And that is something we need to discuss." Leo flicks a serious look in my direction. "Word is Oleg is rallying his troops, bringing in allies from Russia. He'll soon crawl up from the sewer he is hiding under, and rumors are that he'll want his trusted people back under his command. I'm sure Oleg's plotting his revenge against us, especially after tonight. This is the time to send Georgia back to him."

The floor falls out from under me. The plan was always to send Georgia in to help us find Kira before killing Oleg once and for all. I knew this day was coming, but now that it's real, the idea sends bile into my throat.

I can feel my jaw clenching hard. "What do you suggest?"

"Talk to her. She needs to know that she'll be put into play in the next few days."

My brothers eye me keenly. They know what's been going on with Georgia; we haven't been hiding it. For the last two weeks, she's been mine day and night. She's leached into my soul, burrowed deep into my very being. I never asked for this connection, this desperate need and wanting, but I can't let it distract me from the ultimate goal.

In the end, I hope she's strong enough to walk away from me and this dark world. She deserves her freedom more than anything.

Daniil tilts his head, his mouth tightening. "I know this isn't easy for you, but you know as well as we do that this is our best chance at finding Kira. We have the perfect pawn. Now we have to play the game."

"Don't fucking call her a pawn." The harsh words are out of my mouth before I can think better of it. "For chrissake, maybe for once we can rise above what's expected of us." The fires of hell await the Kozlov brothers in the afterlife; we've done things, seen things, committed deeds that there is no seeking redemption from. But the overwhelming possession I feel towards Georgia makes me pause when it comes to offering her up on a platter to Satan himself. "There has to be another way."

"Not to do everything we want to accomplish." Leo looks at me. Assessing. Weighing. "If this was just about burning Oleg's empire to the ground, we'd do that without help. But this is more delicate than that. We need access, information that only someone on the inside could provide."

A volatile energy bounces between us, my heart slamming in my throat. She's my weakness. I know it and they know it, but it doesn't mean I have to give into it. This is about learning the truth of our mother's death and reconnecting with family. Our blood.

Nothing is as important as finding Kira, I remind myself. Nothing. Even Georgia.

"I'll prepare Georgia to get into play over the next few days," I assure them. My brothers nod solemnly, as if they know what this is costing me—but they know shit, because giving up Georgia feels like fire burning under my skin.

CHAPTER TWENTY-NINE

ANDREI

I head back to the estate hours later. Just as the sun is rising.

My head throbs and my limbs ache from a restless night of sitting in the offices after my brothers left, drinking myself into a stupor. A few hours of sleep is all I could allow myself before it was time to come back here and face Georgia. Like me, she's known this day was coming, but that doesn't make it any easier. We haven't spoken about it for the last while, just enjoyed being wrapped in each other before the real world crashed down around us.

I track down Georgia in the painting studio. Her back is to me, sheets of dark hair pouring down her back. She tilts her head and focuses on the canvas in front of her, buttery sunlight pouring through the window in front of her.

Transfixed, I stand in the doorway watching Georgia dab and swirl a brush across the canvas, hypnotized by each elegant brushstroke and the way the colors on the canvas blend beautifully. She's painting a swirling constellation of color; it's the tattoo she offered to design for me. It represents Kira.

She doesn't turn around to greet me, but she knows I'm here.

"What do you think?" Her voice is light and playful.

"It's perfect." I approach, running a finger down a silky lock of her hair.

She puts down her brush and turns to face me, vulnerability flashing in her eyes. If I let myself, I'll go places with her I've never gone with anybody before. I've lost my head, but I could easily lose my heart. And this is why I have to let her go now. In the only way I can.

I roughly grab her chin and angle her face up to mine. "You're mine, Georgia. Always remember that. Promise me, baby. You won't forget that you belong to me."

Her face drops, and her eyes search my own. "What is this about?"

I nuzzle my face into her neck and breathe in her earthy scent before it's ripped from me much too soon. "Oleg." I don't have to say anything more than that. She understands.

"I see." The warm glow through the window highlights the steel gray of her eyes as she blinks. A tremor in the hand holding her paintbrush is the only indication that she is just as affected by this news. When she speaks again, her voice is flat, devoid of emotion. "We always knew this day was coming."

I reach for her, but she recoils. Pain radiates through my chest, wrapping around my lungs and squeezing. The urge to close the distance between us, to feel her against me, is nearly overwhelming, but she's shutting me out.

She turns back to her painting, picking up where she left off, as if I didn't just drop a nuclear bomb in her lap. "Don't freeze me out."

Her back stiffens at the bite in my tone, but I don't care. I'm mad as hell. Not at Georgia, but at everything else, because right now, everything except this moment is out of my control. My hand finds its way to her pulse, my thumb pressing down gently on that delicate point. She holds her breath as I stand over her.

My eyes must convey the carnal direction of my thoughts because a shiver runs through her.

"Do I need to teach you a lesson?" I stand over her, one rough fist tangling in her hair, angling her neck back so her throat is exposed to me. I breathe her in, repeating the word I may never get out of my head: "Mine. *Moya dusha.*"

My soul.

Her eyes fly open, locked on mine as if she understands what I just said. But she doesn't—what she understands is the intensity behind the words. The feeling. What I need from her.

"Get up." My tone leaves no room for compromise. When she does as I ask, I stand back. My eyes travel down her body, and her nipples bead under her flimsy top. Her pulse flutters at the base of her throat and the need to dominate her overwhelms me.

"Take off your clothes and go stand facing the wall."

"Andr—" I stop her with a slap on her beautiful ass.

"Don't fucking argue," I growl, pointing towards an empty wall on the far side of the room. "Hands above you, and don't move a muscle. I will not be gentle, krasotka."

She strips bare for me, exposed to me, ripe for the taking. My leather clad foot pushes her legs apart, as I crowd her from behind. I'm close to her, but not touching her yet. Building anticipation in the most cruel way—a cat toying with a mouse.

Her limbs shake. An electric charge fills the air with the promise of all the delicious ways I'll use her. Defile her in the best possible way.

"You're so vulnerable." My words are a whisper against her throat. "Look at you. Spread open for me, just begging for my touch." I love her this way. Naked and shaking while I remain fully clothed. One of my fingers swipes over her slit, a gentle tease, while my other hand wraps around the front of her neck.

"So fucking wet," I groan in her ear.

My resistance perishes with a whimper. I pull her back forcefully against me. Her exposed nipples tighten in the cool air and

I reach a hand around her front, palming her breast, my eager fingers flicking over her nipple again and again.

I touch her like a man on the verge. Like this is our last hour on earth and she's my only salvation. And maybe there is truth to that because what happens once we leave this room is out of our control, as much as we'd like to believe differently.

"Nobody else gets this." My hushed words hold a dark promise. "Every fucking inch of you belongs to me. Say it."

Georgia rocks her lower body back over my erection, desperate for friction, desperate to feel me inside. I want it all. But I will not give it to her... yet.

Taking a step back so I'm out of her reach, I grab her ass, molding it with my palm. "No, you don't, filthy girl. You get nothing from me until you say the words I need to hear. You. Are. All. Mine."

She resists my command for one long moment, refusing to give in, fighting what she knows is true, but doesn't want to give voice to. Delivering a stinging slap to her ass cheek, I let her know that she's running out of time. Moisture dribbles down her leg, her body revealing what her mouth won't.

I can wait all day. I want her to admit it to herself as much as to me.

Closing her eyes, she seems to have some sort of inner debate before she finally surrenders. "I'm yours," she gasps, and the truth of her words sinks deep into my bones. I want her ruined for anyone that comes after me. Forever branded by my touch.

There's nothing gentle about the way my fingers shove inside her—two thick fingers thrust deep inside her. It's filthy and so hot. She inhales sharply as I remove my fingers, drenched in her juices and lightly dance over her clit—her entire body clenches in response.

"More," she pants.

One hand folds over her breast as I slam three fingers inside of her. My raw touch nearly knocks her off her feet, and I have to hold her up. I'm filling her up to bursting, stretching her cunt in the most delicious way. My fingers move deep inside of her, jacking them against a secret spot. I keep up my merciless pace as she tumbles over the edge; her head falling back on my shoulder, eyelids fluttering closed. She shakes as pleasure spirals up through her body. She's a quivering mass of sensation in my arms and I'm so damn turned on.

My heart is pounding insanely fast, and I'm not prepared for the shock of arousal that hits me when she takes my fingers covered in her juices and licks them clean.

"Krasotka," I growl. She barely has time to recover before I undo my belt and lower my zipper. With one arm wrapped around her waist, I bend her forward, my hard cock pressed between us.

In one swift motion, I thrust until I'm seated to the hilt. I hope my fingers stretched her enough that she can adjust to my size because I can't find it in me to be gentle right now. I fuck her hard and fast, my hips repeatedly crashing into her ass.

"You feel so good," she hisses through gritted teeth, one hand against the wall to keep us steady.

My lips lower to the back of her neck, sucking and biting a path to her ear, taking my pleasure as I rail her into oblivion. Her legs are shaking so hard I have to hold her up. I want nothing more than to have her come with me, so I reach around her body, pressing my thumb hard into her clit. She releases a string of curse words that let me know she's as close to the edge as I am.

"Come all over my cock. Drench me." The brutal sounds of our bodies slapping together is my undoing. My vision becomes a blur of white dots as my body tightens with tension, her cunt pulsing around me. Georgia screams her release as my thrusts become faster, more desperate. Her name is a prayer on my tongue as I jerk inside of her, jets of my cum filling her womb.

This is what I imagine heaven must feel like.

GEORGIA

Minutes pass, my head resting on his shoulder as I fight to catch my breath. He's still deep inside of me, one arm hugging me close to his chest. Part of me just wants to stay this way forever, but reality is already crashing in—the reality that this little bubble of lust we're in is about to burst.

I pull away from him, eyes glued to the floor, as I retrieve my clothes and get dressed. Andrei clears his throat and does up his pants. Both of us are still not speaking. A wave of unease ripples through the room. Lingering awareness of what we just shared—and the cold hard reality that we can never be more than this moment.

As my gaze coasts to Andrei's, the dark storm that looks back at me suggests he can read my thoughts and he knows how disoriented I feel. He reaches for me, but I pull away in the name of self-preservation. I can't give more of my heart to him and survive.

Sex already bonded us. Hot and palpable, it was too strong of a force between us. I could never deny him my body, but now I have to deny him my heart. Walk out of his life and never turn back. Finding Kira has to take place with military precision. My final gift to him.

He stalks up to me, his movements deceptively smooth. "You wanna shut me out, fine. Play that game, see where it gets you." His lips thin and he rises to his full height.

"It's better this way. For you and for me. You said so yourself right from the start."

His jaw held so tight I'm worried he'll break his teeth. "Suit yourself. Be ready early tomorrow morning. We have something to take care of."

He gives me one final heavy look before turning on his feet

and leaving me here, alone. An errand? I haven't left his compound in weeks and now I'm running errands with him.

Hurt weighs me down, pressing on my chest like a thousand pound boulder, making it impossible to breathe. I don't know what burns more—the fact that I'm willing to put my life on the line for him, or the fact that he's letting me.

CHAPTER THIRTY

GEORGIA

"Are you going to tell me where we're headed?"

Andrei looks my way, his presence heavy and palpable, but I force myself to stare out the window instead, grateful that at least he didn't blindfold me. I huff out a breath. The tension in the Jeep is stifling, our usual zing of chemistry filling up the small space. But today it's more than that. It's how we left things last night.

Slowly, without taking his gaze off the road, he says, "I'm taking you to see your father."

"Seriously?" I'm stunned. Of all the things I thought he might say, I certainly didn't expect that. "I thought it was too risky for me to see my father right now?"

"It is. But I've figured something out." His words are sharp, but even so, he can't hide the tenderness that lies beneath.

I would ask why he's doing it, but I know why. This could be the last time I'll see my father again. No one dares voice the truth, but I'm going to be released back into the keep of a dangerous man with nothing to lose. I'm no longer afraid, just realistic.

"Thank you," I mumble. I want to tell him how much this means to me, how grateful I am, but he doesn't want my words today. He wants nothing to do with me.

I lay awake for most of last night trying to make sense of how I left things with Andrei. He was clear that he never wanted this connection between us. He fought it from the start, so I was sure he'd be grateful that I'm ending it now. A clean break. Except he's not saying that. Or anything, for that matter. He's quiet and broody and as tightly wound as a spring. His shoulders hiked up around his ears.

I don't know what to say to break the tension between us, so I say nothing, just continue to stare out the window watching rural roads giving way to long stretches of desolate highway. We're still on Long Island, but we've been in the car for over an hour.

I can't help but ask, "Are we going to my home?"

He runs a thumb over his bottom-lip, while his beautiful face remains stoic. "It's not safe for you in Brighton Beach. Oleg can't ever know that you've been with us." His voice is cool and indifferent, laced with steel. "Yulian's team will debrief you tomorrow when we have more information."

The vice around my heart squeezes tighter. I want to say more to him, but the finality in his tone brooks no room for follow-up. He's done with this conversation, with all of my pestering and really, if I am going to be honest, with me.

A half hour later, we pull up to a one-story, wood-shingled fishing cabin near the water's edge. It's a simple structure, nothing fancy. No multi-car garage, no guards patrolling, nothing that would suggest the city's most dangerous gangster spends time here. Just a cozy cabin surrounded by oak, walnut, and cherry trees.

I unbuckle my seatbelt but don't make a move. "I never really took you as the fishing type."

"Maybe you don't know me all that well," he says before getting out of the Jeep, slamming the door behind him.

His insult lands as intended—an arrow to the heart, a ball of pain expanding in my chest. Maybe he's right, and I don't know him at all. But that doesn't sit right. I know Andrei like I know the back of my hand. I know the art collector, the man who desperately wants to find his sister, the hurt little boy under all those layers who could not save his mother, try as he might.

There's the cold and calculating bratva boss that would murder, cheat and steal to get his way. The man who is using me as a means to an end. Who always intended to use me and made no bones about it.

But all of those sides make him who he is. And I know him. I fucking know him, and I want to call him mine. Even if that's impossible.

Dad hobbles into the room, looking older, more frail—his leg that the Antonovs crushed will never fully heal, but the bright smile on his face makes up for everything.

"Dad," I cry, my heart thundering in my chest. "It's been so long."

He envelops me in a strong hug, his familiar smell—a mix of Old Spice and tobacco—providing comfort. The day I was taken to Oleg's home was the last time I saw my father, and communication has been practically non-existent. I didn't have a phone or access to a computer. Oleg's men would let me email once in a while, but they closely monitored any communication. I always made it seem like everything was fine, that I was almost happy there. I'm sure Dad knew that was far from the truth, but I didn't want him to worry more than he already was. Guilt over the situation ate at his soul.

As my father hugs me and repeats my name like a mantra against my hair, I can't help the hot tears that flow down my cheeks as all the roller-coaster-like emotions built up over the last two months crash over me like a wave.

Dad holds me to him and tells me it will be all right until I calm down and focus on the fact that he's with me right now, in the flesh. Time and stress may have taken a toll on him, but he's still alive. As am I.

Andrei clears his throat behind us, and I turn to see him standing by the front door of the cabin. Dark amber eyes stare into my soul.

"I'm sorry," I say, swiping at a rogue tear. "I got a little carried away."

A fierce expression crosses his face. He takes a step towards me, then stops himself. His body is rigid as his eyes bore into mine. "Natalia organized lunch for you. It's on the back deck when you're ready. I'll leave you to catch up with your father." He gives me a meaningful look. He's already told me I can't share details with my father, just the big picture. Truthfully, I wouldn't want him to know what lies ahead for me, it would horrify him.

I mouth 'thank you', and he nods before leaving. My heart takes off at a steady gallop, overwhelmed by this gift of seeing my father again and knowing that my supposed captor has kept him safe.

I gesture for Dad to sit on one of two vintage couches set against the back wall of the lodge across from a wood-burning stove. I curl up beside him and take his frail hand in mine.

"How have you been?" My heart squeezes when I notice the deeply etched lines in his face and the gray that's mostly overtaken his hair. He looks like he's aged years since I've seen him last.

"I've been worried sick about you." He brushes my cheek with his hand. "It's so good to see you, Georgia. God, I didn't know if I would ever see you again. It's all my fault, sweetheart. If it wasn't for me—"

"No Daddy, don't. What choice did you have? If you didn't take that loan from the Antonovs, the restaurant would have gone under... and then where would we be?"

A bitter tear escapes down his cheek. "If I knew what it

would cost me, I would never have let him take you." He bows his head. "Your mother would never forgive me."

Seeing my father so bereft has my heart twisting in my chest. He's tortured himself with this, and I can tell it's eaten him up inside. "You didn't let him, Dad. It was my choice. And it hasn't all been bad," I say, quietly. The truth of my words unnerve me as my thoughts turn to Andrei. "We're under Kozlov protection now."

"I know." His lips press together. "A gentleman named Yulian came by a little while ago and we had a nice long talk. I gather you are working for them now."

I shrug one shoulder and gaze out the window towards the rocky shoreline covered in wildflowers. Such a pretty place for men that conduct such ugly business. "Not quite working for them. Working with them is more like it. We have the same goal—to take down Oleg Antonov."

"I don't know what you mean," he says, frowning. "How can you help gangsters? These men are Russian mafia, Georgia. They are just as dangerous as Oleg Antonov—maybe more so."

I shake my head, releasing a mirthless laugh. "It's not that simple. I've changed, Dad, and I want to help them. It's the only way we'll ever be free of the Antonovs. You know as well as I do Oleg will never forgive your debt. I would be his prisoner forever."

Dad winces. My news may be unwelcome, but it's not a shock. My father understands he made a deal with the devil. One he regrets, but regret won't buy back our freedom.

"Are you in danger from that man?" My father's eyes dart towards the window, where Andrei is outside, pacing and talking on his cell phone.

"No, I promise I'm not."

Just in danger of getting my heart broken.

As I watch him pace outside in the midday sun, I'm at a loss. Andrei has made me want things I have no right to want, to feel things I've never felt before. I've been trying to protect both of us from the mountain of pain that lies ahead, but I've just caused more hurt.

I want to believe that there's another option for us. I just don't know what that looks like.

It occurs to me I can't leave things with Andrei this way. This arctic chill that's settled between us is not how I want our last days together to feel. If this is all the time we have, I want to give myself to him completely.

My father's eyes coast over my face, so many questions lurking beneath the surface. I lean into his warmth, enjoying his heat and the comforting presence that I've relied on my whole life.

"I can't tell you the details of what's going on, but it'll be okay. If I'm successful, the Antonovs won't be a threat, and we can go back to our life. I can help at the restaurant and—"

My father shakes his head sadly. "No Georgia, nothing will be the same again."

I'm silent. He's right, of course, but all I can offer him is the comfort of my hand in his.

Throat thick, I say, "Maybe it's okay if things change. If life moves on from what it was."

Dad nods, and the knot in my chest loosens. "It's time for you to go back to school and focus on what you want. Your dreams. It should have never been on you to look after our little family." I'm about to argue, but my father stops me with a hand on my arm. "Promise me no matter what, you'll be careful, that you won't put yourself in danger." There's a pleading note in his voice.

My stomach hollows and I give him a weak smile. That's all I can offer; anything further out of my mouth would be a lie.

The time with my father passes by all too fast. I wish I could spend longer with him. Hell, I wish I never had to say goodbye, but after a lovely lunch and a walk outside, Yulian appears in the cabin and nods his head at me. It's time for us to say goodbye.

Once again, I fight tears as I hug Dad and promise him it will all be okay.

It's much harder to convince myself.

"I DON'T WANT it to be this way between us."

Andrei's back straightens, but he doesn't turn and look at me. He sits on an Adirondack chair with his elbows on his knees, eyes focused on the calm blue water in front of him.

When I step beside Andrei, his frosty gaze finally finds mine. He doesn't tell me to go away, nor does he invite me to get closer. He watches to see what I'll do next. The bravery that brought me here is nowhere to be found, quick to flee in Andrei's presence. But if Monsieur Coset has taught me anything, it's to fake it till you make it.

I don't wait for Andrei's permission. I step between his legs, my body eclipsing any view of the water that he was just enjoying. Although enjoying would not be the word—not with the haunted look in his eyes.

"Thank you for that," I whisper. "For the time with my father."

Warmth radiates from his body as his hands trail up the backs of my bare thighs, setting my pulse to a gallop.

"You have nothing to thank me for. You're risking everything for me, and what have I given you?" He leans forward, his forehead resting heavily on my belly. His palm continues to caress the length of my thigh, squeezing my flesh, his calloused palm stroking my sensitive skin. When he speaks again, his voice is raw. "I'm not a good man, krasotka."

"I don't want a good man." My thighs press together, needing more. Needing all of him.

Andrei has done awful things, committed crimes I don't want to know about. Darkness pulsates from him, but I also know there is another side to this man. He sees my potential; the woman hidden underneath all the layers of responsibility and family obligation. Maybe that's why he understands me so well. He carries similar burdens. He's pushed me to become a different version of me, a better version. A new woman is emerging and in her place is someone with the strength and fortitude I never imagined I'd possess. Whatever lies between us, we've only just scratched the surface of what it could be.

His anguished gaze meets mine. "You were right to push me away. Tell me you want nothing to do with me. I'm no good for you, baby."

He sounds mad—mad at me for choosing him when he's clearly not my white knight in shining armor. He's the villain who will pound me raw and let me loose into a viper's den. But I'm not a damsel in distress, and I've made my choice.

"I know, and I still want you." My words come out in a breathless moan, as his skilled fingers slip under the hem of my dress, pushing inside of me without warning. Lightning lashes in my veins as he plays me like a musical instrument, fucking me slowly, intently. His thumb dances over my clit.

"What have you done to me? You make me crazy," he growls.

One big palm curves around my jaw, pulling my head down. Our tongues slick together while his clever fingers continue brushing over my most sensitive skin, igniting every nerve ending in my body at once.

Feeling bold, I pull away and drop to my knees on the grass in front of him, mesmerized by the outline of his cock against his pants. "I want to take you in my mouth," I rasp.

His responding groan makes his hunger for me clear, but the wary way he watches me stops me in my tracks. The lines of his face grow tight as I rest my hands on his powerful thighs. I look up. He's in charge now and I'm at his mercy and command—it's beyond exhilarating. He unzips his pants and lowers them just enough to reveal his glorious manhood. God, he's big.

"Is this what you want from me?" His voice is a low growl, his amber eyes flecked with darkness. I nod, desperate to taste him.

A shining bead of moisture wells up around his crown, and I eagerly chase it with my tongue.

"Not so fast." He pulls me off him. "Hands behind your back. Keep them there, or you'll be punished."

His filthy command sparks fire inside me. Grasping my hands together behind my back, I look up at him, waiting for him to take control. Craving it. He grabs the length of my hair, wrapping it around his fist and pulls me towards him.

He goes easy on me at first, allowing me to set the pace. Running my tongue along his length, my saliva to lubes him up before I ease him into my mouth. I'm able to get to the halfway point before he rocks his hips, edging his shaft deeper with every thrust. With his head pitched back, a guttural sound escapes from his chest. His desperate response, the only encouragement I need to take him farther into my mouth, savoring his salty tang. But his gentle pace gives way to far more urgent thrusting. When his impressive length hits the back of my throat, my gag reflexes kick in, and he stills.

"Relax. Breathe through your nose... yes, that's it." He makes little sounds of encouragement as I slowly relax my throat while he continues to buck up into my mouth, holding my head still with a grasp of my hair. "You're such a good fucking girl."

With his free hand, he brushes his knuckles along my jawline, then the shell of my ear. Encouraging me. One touch so gentle, the other rough. He's showing me the two sides of his personality, the yin and yang, and I am captivated by the sum of his parts.

The muscles in his chest ripple with strain as he holds me in my place, languorously fucking my mouth. As he builds towards a steady rhythm, Andrei groans low and deep. "You are doing so well. I want to watch you take my cum down your throat."

I hum my consent. I never thought that would sound appealing to me, but Andrei makes me crave the most debased acts. The moisture pooling between my legs is proof. My acquiescence unleashes the beast in Andrei. He pistons forward, hitting the back of my throat again and again. But this time I am ready for him. I know how to relax my muscles and breathe through my nose, making the act as pleasurable for me as it is for him.

"That mouth," he snarls, his movements becoming more jagged, more insistent. "Those lips wrapped around my cock is just about the prettiest thing I ever did see."

I inwardly groan at his words, my arousal skyrocketing as he fucks my mouth in the way he needs. My scalp burns with his tight grip, but I'm also learning to swallow him down like a pro. As his thighs shake, a desperate howl emerges from his throat. I may not know much about men, but I know he's getting close to his release. For a moment, I panic. Will I be able to swallow for him?

"I am going to come for you. Swallow every last drop, krasotka." His shaft thickens between my lips, just as he spurts hot ropes of his seed into my mouth. I try to drink all of it down, but a drop of his cum dribbles down my chin. With a heated expression, he pulls out of me, and uses his thumb to swipe the moisture off my chin and feeds it back to me.

He pulls out of my mouth slowly, his breath still coming in ragged pants as he releases my hair, stroking my cheek with one long finger as the muted moonlight from the window dances over his beautiful, strong features.

I stay where I am, kneeling between his spread legs as he tucks himself back into his pants. Hands around my waist, he lifts me up so I'm standing in front of him, two feet on the ground. He burrows his head into my neck, inhaling me deeply.

"Get inside," he purrs. "I'm not done with you."

CHAPTER THIRTY-ONE

ANDREI

I DRAG HER BACK TO THE CABIN, DESPERATE TO HAVE HER ONE last time. There is no gentleness as I lead her to the dining room table, pressing her back and spreading her wide. Harder than steel, I unzip my pants and push inside of her. It's wild between us. She claws at my back and kisses my neck and murmurs things against my skin that make no sense, but still drive me insane. Her words come out in pants and sobs—telling me it's okay, that we made a deal. That this is for the best. That whatever this is between us would never last.

We knew from the start. We agreed. It has to be like this.

Then why does it feel so fucking wrong?

I squeeze her waist with both hands and barrel into her again and again, each slap of flesh echoing off the walls in the small cabin. My private sanctuary. And now she's here, ruining it with her very being. Because I'll never be able to forget her being here.

My chest collapses against hers and I bury my face in her hair, savoring her smell, her sounds, her softness underneath me. Committing all of it to memory.

Her lips find mine. Her kiss is gentle and sweet, but this tenderness only serves to destroy me. I don't want her mercy. It was easier when she hated me, and I played the part of a beast. This is all wrong.

A fever unfolds inside of me and I come inside of her with a grunt. My fingers are still working her clit, until she sobs out a cry and comes all over me, leaving me wrecked and hollow.

HOURS LATER, I'm lying in bed when my eyes snap open. A sense of foreboding intrudes my sleeping brain and lodges itself there, forcing me awake despite the exhaustion coursing through my limbs. Looking over at Georgia lying beside me, dark lashes fanned out over her cheeks, my heart scrambles in my chest.

I'm in trouble. Big fucking trouble.

The call came in last night as Georgia and I drove back from Greenpoint. Oleg is firmly back in play. He's making moves, making his presence known on the streets of Brighton Beach, meeting with his allies. Most importantly, he wants those loyal to him to show their face.

And Georgia is included in that group.

Oleg already had a few of his men scope out Georgia's father's home. He hasn't forgotten about her, but he doesn't know we have her, exactly what I hoped for. She'll tell him she's been staying with a friend out of town, laying low, and walk right back into his world with him none the wiser.

Except the idea of handing her over to my enemy feels like fire ants buried deep in my skin. Seeing her with her father today, realizing she's the only one he has left in the world, and vice versa, destroyed me. I'm disgusted by my weakness—and she truly is a weakness—but it's too late to change the course of events. What happened has happened.

A glance at the alarm clock beside her bed confirms that it's just past midnight. First thing in the morning, Georgia will meet with my men before we send her back to the nest of vipers.

I slip out of bed, retrieving my clothes from the floor of Georgia's room. She shifts in her sleep and mumbles something, but stays in dreamland.

With a pounding headache, I head towards the library. I light a cigar and pour myself two fingers of scotch before settling into an armchair, the light from the Cuban's heater the only light in the room. That's how I want it, dark, so I can stew in my own turbulent thoughts.

But that doesn't happen. Leo steps out of the shadows, silently joining me where I sit with his own glass of amber liquid.

"You can't sleep," he says simply.

I nod, then take in his full Armani suit, but note the missing cufflinks and the open buttons of his shirt. "And where were you?"

"Out." He's a man of few words, but I take this to mean he was at Dark Side, relieving tension. "What's on your mind?"

I shrug. "Uncovering family secrets is dirty business. I just hope it's worth it."

"You're having second thoughts about sending Georgia to Oleg?" Leo studies me quietly, taking the cigar from my hands for a puff. If Daniil was here, with all his swagger and cockiness, I doubt I would admit the truth, but it's hard to deny Leo. He can see right through my lies anyhow.

"I fucked up." A sharp stab works its way through my chest, hollowing out my insides. How could I expect Georgia to have her head on straight when mine is all over the place?

"You sure did." He sighs. His lazy gaze travels over me as he takes a sip of his drink.

"You don't sound surprised."

"Nah. I saw this coming a mile away." Leo hisses out a breath, his eyes boring into my own. "Are you sure?"

"The only thing I am sure of is that she's mine and the thought of Oleg laying a finger on her..." I bite out a curse word.

The thought is revolting. "There's another way to get to him. I know there is. I lead this family for a reason, and fuck me if I can't take down Oleg and find my sister without the help of someone that we should have never dragged into this in the first-place."

A blanket of tension covers the room. If Leo isn't with me, he's against me. But when I look up into his eyes, I see what looks a lot like pride gleaming there, as if he always knew I'd make this decision.

A bitter breath passes over my lips. "You're not going to tell me I'm making a mistake?" My brothers respect me but they also have no problem pushing back if they think I am in the wrong.

Leo puffs out a smoke ring from my pilfered cigar, eyes sparkling with dry amusement. "Oh, you're making a mistake. It's just one you have to make."

I shake my head. "You're wrong. I can't have her. I know I can't. But neither can Oleg."

A grunt of amusement. "Funny that you think you can let her go."

"I have no choice."

A woman in this world is a liability. A weakness my enemies will exploit, just like Oleg exploited my mother. The best thing I can do for Georgia is to let her go and figure out another way to find Kira.

"There is always a choice." He leans back in his chair, directing his gaze upward. "Georgia isn't Mama, her eyes are wide open. History doesn't always repeat itself, *brat*."

I hold my hand up, having had enough of this conversation. But Leo's words are enough to create tiny splinters in my resolve to push her away. Is there a world where I get to keep Georgia, where she wants to be with me? Could she ever be happy in this life, or will the dark underworld I inhabit eventually destroy her from the inside?

"I'll let the others know I am calling it off," I tell Leo roughly. "Tomorrow we will send Georgia and her father into hiding. I'm working on another idea to find Kira, one that doesn't include using an innocent."

Leo gulps the last of his drink and brings the glass down on a side-table. "That innocent, as you say, developed quite the impressive set of skills under our roof. She may not be so innocent anymore. She may even be disappointed that we're taking her out of play."

An ache in my chest blooms so intense it steals the breath from my lungs. Georgia will argue with me. She won't be happy that I'm giving up on her and giving up Kira, for now.

"Maybe. But my decision is final." I wasn't able to protect my mother, but I will protect Georgia. She's mine even if we can't be together.

I got her into this goddamn mess, and now I need to get her out of it.

CHAPTER THIRTY-TWO

ANDREI

"ANDREI, WAKE UP." I OPEN MY EYES TO FIND NATALIA IN front of me, wringing her hands. There's urgency in her voice. "It's Georgia... she's missing."

I jolt straight up from the armchair as if an electric shock was applied to my feet.

"What are you talking about?" I say, trying to clear the sleep from my brain.

Natalia looks like she's about to jump out of her skin. "She's not in her room, not in the kitchen, not on the grounds. I can't find her anywhere. It doesn't make sense—"

Potent fear sends me into overdrive. I head to the library desk, where I retrieve my 9mm from the top drawer. "Alert Yulian. Every man on this property needs to be searching for her. And gather my brothers."

Natalia moves at my command, and I head straight to Georgia's room. I need to see for myself that she's actually gone.

The room is exactly how I left it last night. Her bed is messy, the sheets tangled up, our clothes on the ground except my white dress shirt which Georgia wore to bed.

I am checking her room for signs of forced entry when my brothers and Mikhail rush in. The air in the room shifts violently, the calm before a tornado. No one looks me in the eye.

"How did this happen?" I grit out, waves of panic roll over me and I fight to rein in my temper. Mikhail hangs his head. He knows he's a dead man if Georgia disappeared on his watch.

"There's reason to believe that she escaped," Mikhail mumbles. "That she wasn't abducted."

"Explain," I bite out.

Mikhail clears his throat and straightens his tie. It seems to take all of his courage to look me in the eye. "There is no sign of forced entry or exit. None of the guards saw anything out of the ordinary. We captured nothing alarming on the cameras. The dogs didn't pick up an unfamiliar scent. The only unusual thing is that a member of the domestic staff, a new hire named Piper Bennett, left shortly after arriving for her shift at five thirty this morning. According to Natalia, she felt unwell and asked to go home early rather than work her shift. The strange thing is no one saw her leave the estate. And when I checked the cameras to see when she left, there was some sort of blip. About five minutes when none of the cameras were recording."

Dread snakes through my gut. While there's nothing inherently suspicious about the story, something feels off, especially the cameras being down for a short but critical time.

"Track down Piper and question her. Make sure everyone even remotely affiliated with our brotherhood is out looking for Georgia."

A sickly feeling crawls up my spine. I try not to think of worst case-scenarios—I am trained to act more like a robot than a human, just get the job done at all costs—but something about this feels terribly personal.

"Leo," I say, turning to address my brother. His face is unmoving, as if etched from stone. "Call in every favor owed to us. We need intel on Oleg and his men. If they're making any moves, I want to know about it. Now go."

Everyone scatters at my word, everyone except Daniil, who hangs back, his expression bleak. "We have to consider that she wasn't abducted, that she left of her own free-will."

"Are you fucking serious?" I snarl at him. He's not wrong. The thought had occurred to me. I just hadn't wanted to face it as a real possibility.

"There's no sign of forced entry," he continues, grim-faced. "It would be much easier for her to leave without a trace than be kidnapped without one. She's been here long enough. She likely knows the guards patrolling times. She figured out the camera angles. Did you blindfold her when you took her off the property yesterday?"

Son of a bitch.

My heart wrenches inside my chest, and the heat of this room threatens to choke me. Daniil's words hold truth and perhaps that is the worst fucking irony of all. There is only one of two options here, and both of them leave my blood cold. Either Piper abducted Georgia, or Georgia convinced Piper to help her escape. Escape from me.

"I know she put on a brave face, *brat*, but in the end, being released into Oleg's clutches was too much for her to bear." There's sympathy in his tone, even kindness. My asshole of a brother is showing me a scrap of humanity, and it's enough to make me lose my mind.

"*Zatknis*," I say, warning him to shut the hell up. I squeeze my eyes closed, needing to block out all sounds, all thoughts, all possibilities. An agitated hand tugs at my hair as I pace the room. "All that matters now is that we find Georgia before Oleg does." If Georgia shows her face on the streets of Brighton Beach, it's only a matter of time before Oleg hears about it and scoops her up. That's assuming he's not behind her disappearance and he already has her.

The possibilities are endless and all of them fucking terrifying.

Daniil nods, weariness etched on his face. "I'll check in on her father. If she escaped, she'd go straight to see him."

"There's no way she could get through the guards posted outside his building without being discovered, unless—"

Unless I've been played.

In the sober light of morning, I see my mistake. How much I trusted her, how short-sighted I've been because of my obsession with her. I left her alone with her father. I didn't even bother to listen in on their conversation. She could have made a plan to escape—she's certainly cunning enough. All the training I provided her paid off in dividends.

Bitterness singes my lungs. Freedom was her ultimate goal and when she wasn't successful with a gun in her hand, she used her body to gain my trust... to gain my love. She played me like a fool and I fell for it hook, line and sinker.

Grabbing a table top clock, I heave it against the wall. The heavy smash of glass and gears falling apart is strangely satisfying, but does little to quell the fire pumping through my veins. I rip down the curtains with my hands, and then move on to hurling a decanter against the wall, watching it smash into a million pieces. The destructive urge doesn't end until I see the familiar bloom of red on my hands.

I will blow up this world or burn it down. Whatever I have to do to find her.

HOURS GO BY ACHINGLY SLOWLY. I'm still in the house. Leo convinced me that my value is staying right here at headquarters as my men hunt down Georgia.

My hands tremble as I pour myself another shot of vodka. Somewhere inside, I know that I'm not sane or sober enough to be of use, a feeling I've never had in my life.

One woman with no money. No weapon. How far could she have gotten?

Rage is an easy feeling to conjure, but fear, fearing for her safety, wreaks havoc inside me. She's been gone for hours, and each tick of the clock tightens an invisible noose around my neck. I can't shake the feeling that I'm drowning, that nothing will be the same after this.

"I have an update—"

I barely notice someone walking through the door of my office until the barrel of my gun is trained on them, my finger hovering over the trigger.

"Andrei?" Yulian's voice registers in some distant recess of my mind. Lowering the pistol, I glare at him. He should know better than to sneak up on a man in the throes of despair.

"You have news. I'm listening," I say.

"Piper Bennett is gone without a trace."

"The new employee?" I rub my tired eyes. "What do you mean, she's gone?"

"She's disappeared into thin air," he says, his expression unyielding. "The home address she provided us with is an empty apartment. Her neighbors say she moved out last week. There's no trace of her in Brighton Beach, or all of Brooklyn for that matter."

"Are you fucking serious?" I roar. "How did this happen?"

The shadows beneath his eyes tell me he's just as troubled as I am by the turn of events. "Despite our very thorough background check, I don't believe she is who she says she is, and it's likely she is related to Georgia's disappearance."

Icy fingers stroke down my spine. Nothing makes sense. My life has taken off like a runaway train and there's nothing I can do to get it back on track. For a man who craves ultimate control, the helplessness only adds to the tension twisting up my insides.

Without me uttering a word, Yulian understands the downward spiral of my thoughts. "I promise you, *bratan*, we will have answers soon. We'll work around the clock. If it was Rowan, I would tear apart the world looking for her, and I will do the same for you."

I sag forward; the fight drained from my body. As a man in love, Yulian might be the only person close to me that understands my pain. "I know you would. I just hope that we're not too late."

Yulian stays rooted in place. "She didn't turn on you."

"What?" I shake my head, not understanding his point.

"Georgia did not betray you. We have no facts right now, but the one thing I do know is that she cares for you greatly, and I don't think she left willingly. As much as it pains me to admit that our security was breached."

Pain grabs at me, familiar and sharp. I might be in a fucked-up place right now, but I know Yulian's words are true, and I don't know why I ever doubted her.

CHAPTER THIRTY-THREE

GEORGIA

My mouth is dry, my head hurts, and the bed is suspiciously empty of the warm body that I fell asleep beside. These are my thoughts as I slowly wake from a dead sleep. More than that—something feels off.

I open my eyes to find myself in a stark white modern bedroom, a different room than the one I fell asleep in. Try as I might, I can't place it as a room in Andrei's home. It's cold and modern with none of the architectural charm of the Kozlov mansion.

Holy shit. Where am I?

Cold fear pierces my lungs, stealing my breath. I make a move to stand, but quickly realize I can't. My wrists are secured to the bed. I struggle against the ropes, attempting to twist out of their hold, but it's useless. Someone wanted to ensure I could not get away. Now the only question is who.

And why?

That's when it all comes rushing back.

Piper's vivid blue eyes flash through my mind. She was the last person I remember seeing. She roused me early this morning to tell me that Andrei had been shot, and that I needed to come quickly. I didn't think, I just followed her blindly, too distraught to question why she was leading me through the back stairwell of the house, or why she took me out a service door into a waiting car driven by a man I didn't know. My memory goes hazy the moment we sped away from the estate. A sharp prick to my neck, then the world went dark.

My chest pumps like wildfire, panic clawing up my throat. *Andrei*. Was he actually hurt or have I been played? Something tells me it's the latter. Moments that we spent together pierce through my memory like shards of glass. Whoever she is, Piper played me and she's the reason I'm here, that I'm sure of.

But where is she, and where is here?

Even with my arms secured, I have just enough slack to lift my head and gaze out the window. We're high above ground level. That's the only thing I can tell by looking out the window at the dusky sky. No other buildings or landmarks are in sight. I don't even know how long I've been unconscious, though my dry mouth and full bladder suggest it's been many hours.

Moments later, I hear the twist of a lock, and then the door opens, bringing me face to face with Piper.

A *blonde* Piper.

My mind spins in a million different directions, unable to latch onto a single coherent thought.

She grins at me, coming farther into the room. "Well, well. Look who is finally awake. Took you long enough. You've been passed out for hours."

I scramble to sit up more fully, but can't. "Who are you?" My eyes turn to slits as she takes a seat in an armchair beside the bed.

She rests her chin in her hands, observing me without a hint of emotion on her face. "You know me as Piper, but most people call me Kira." Her lips curl up at my shocked expression. "Do you know who I am?"

Shock paralyzes my vocal cords for a moment. *This is Kira?*

When I'm finally able to speak, my voice comes out thin and scratchy. "Kira, as in Oleg's daughter." I'm unsure what I find more incredible; that the transformed creature in front of me is the very person we've been searching for, or that she was under our nose the whole time.

"Very good. I guess the Kozlov brothers are actually paying attention."

The Kozlov brothers—her own flesh and blood. But does she know that? It occurs to me I'm on perilous ground. I don't know what she knows, what her intentions are and who she is working with. I can't trust her. Chills run down my spine when I realize her father is most likely behind all of this.

I blow out a heavy breath, recalling Monsieur Coset's lessons about getting others to open up while keeping my cards close to my chest. First thing is to keep her talking.

"Why are you doing this?" I say, tugging on my bound wrists. "I thought we were friends."

She rolls her eyes in a decidedly non-Piper like gesture. Kira has a lot more edge than her brunette counterpart. "It's not personal." She shrugs.

"It kind of is seeing that you abducted me and have me tied to a bed." I release a deep breath, dread coiling low in my belly. "Is your father here? Is he part of all this?"

She smirks. "Don't worry about my father. He thinks I'm minding my own business, gallivanting around Europe spending his money like a good little mafia princess." She grins at me like the cat that ate the canary. "Unfortunately, I'm no longer interested in hiding away."

"What do you mean?" I ask as a sense of foreboding trails down my spine.

"It means, I am here to reclaim my birthright. The Antonov Bratva."

My eyes widen in surprise. This is not what I was expecting her to say.

"So you're not working with your father? You want to take over from him?"

"Exactly." One elegant finger taps her temple. "I knew you were smart. I'm sick of sitting idly by and watching my father run the Antonov empire into the ground. I've spent enough time in the shadows waiting for my chance to reclaim my birthright. Now that my father is distracted by the Kozlovs, this is the perfect time for me to make a move."

Confusion must be etched on my face, because Kira just gives me a small smile. "I can see you have questions," she observes.

"I do," I admit. "Starting with—why did you abduct me?"

"It's not you I need so much as the Kozlovs' support. We have the same goal—they want to destroy my father and so do I. There's a world where the two brotherhoods could work together, not against each other. You're here to guarantee their cooperation."

"I am definitely not following."

She huffs out a breath. "When I infiltrated the Kozlov's home it was to learn what was important to Andrei. Something I could use as leverage to guarantee his support. I admit, it was hard at first. Andrei runs a tight-ship and seems to have few weaknesses. Imagine my stroke of luck when you came around, and I realized Andrei was falling for his little spy." She narrows her eyes to slits. "They were training you to spy on my father, were they not?"

I nod. "If you want to destroy your enemy, it's best to learn their secrets." She's unaware that I was searching for her, which is for the best while I try to understand her motives.

"Exactly what I suspected." She may have finagled a job with the Kozlovs, but she certainly didn't learn all their secrets. "Anyhow, it became clear to me that you were the best way to get Andrei to comply. If he wants you back, he'll need to agree to my terms."

I release a bitter laugh. She's obviously unhinged. Sure,

Andrei enjoyed my body, but he's not going to risk his life and his men's life to rescue me. That I'm sure of.

"Posing as an employee and then abducting me will not win you any favor with the Kozlovs. And I'm afraid Andrei doesn't value me that highly. I'm not sure why you think I'd make a good bargaining chip, but you're out of luck."

She tilts her head with a small smile. "You don't get it, do you? Andrei would do anything for you."

I turn my head away from her, hardly convinced. "You're going to be sorely disappointed."

"Earlier I sent Andrei pictures of you unconscious and chained to the bed. He's agreed to meet with me tomorrow."

"What!?" My head snaps back to face her. "He's meeting with you?"

"I threatened to kill you if he didn't." Her face brightens. "I guess he values you more than you think."

Great. I'm not sure if I should be flattered or horrified.

"Good luck, Kira." I tell her, and a little part of me actually means it. "You're obviously very brave, but you have no idea who you're up against. The Kozlovs are trained killers, hardened bratva. You might be Oleg's heir, but you clearly weren't brought up in this world." I hold her gaze, hoping she'll listen to reason. "Why don't you tell them who you are before you meet in person? Like you said, they hate your father, not you. Andrei is a reasonable man, or at least reasonable by bratva standards, but you won't get very far backing him into a corner."

She fixes me with a sharp look. "Revealing my identity before the meeting makes no sense. Anyhow, he won't hurt me while I have you squirreled away. If he wants you back, he'll have to work with me." Her words are heavy with disdain, her lip curling in bitterness. "This also allows him to see what I am made of. If I can infiltrate his tight as hell organization and abduct his lover from right under his nose, it shows that I at least deserve a seat at the table."

"If you say so." Her logic doesn't add up in my mind, but the determined lines etched in her face tell me she won't be dissuaded. She certainly has the Kozlov gutsiness, and looking at her flaxen hair and sharp cheekbones, the physical resemblance is also clear. My heart squeezes with a powerful emotion. The long-lost sister that the brothers have been searching for is right under their noses—except this won't be the reunion they were hoping for.

"Listen to me, Kira." There's a note of desperation in my voice, and I truly hope it gets through to her. "Nothing will help you when the Kozlovs come at you with their full force. Do you even have back-up?" Jesus, I can't believe I'm worried about my kidnapper, but I am. Not only because of our tenuous friendship, but because if Andrei hurts her, or worse, he'd never forgive himself.

Kira looks pale and tired all of a sudden. She stands, placing her hands on her hips. "My friend Jake is helping me. This is his place. For now, he's the only one I can trust." I wonder what that means but I get the sense question time is over. She's already moving toward the door, and right now, the only thing I can focus on is my bladder.

"Wait! You need to untie me." I yell at her retreating form. "I have to pee."

She sighs and returns to my side. "No can do. But I can loosen the rope enough for you to take care of business. Just don't do anything silly. I have a gun on me, and I'll use it if I have to."

I shake my head sadly. "I hope you know what you're doing, Kira. I truly hope so."

CHAPTER THIRTY-FOUR

ANDREI

THE SPEEDBOAT CUTS THROUGH THE CHOPPY WATERS OF Newark Bay, as the setting sun casts a pink glow over the water. We're waiting for the cover of dark before approaching the derelict building on the outskirts of Port Newark. This is where our meeting with Georgia's abductor is planned for tomorrow—hence, tonight's reconnaissance mission.

The now abandoned container terminal is exactly the kind of place where you'd expect to be ambushed. And yet, I'm willing to walk into my grave.

Hours after we discovered her missing, Georgia's mysterious abductor sent me a message. Not asking for ransom, but asking for an in person meeting with me and my brothers. No weapons, no back-up. Without the meeting, Georgia dies.

My organs recoil at the image that was sent to me. Georgia unconscious, shackled to a bed, still wearing my white dress shirt. She appeared to be unharmed, but for how long? Whoever has her is going to want something from me, something I may or may not be able to give them. I don't allow myself to go down that rabbit hole. It's a dark, dark place.

When night falls, Daniil kills the engine of the boat.

"Ready to do this?" he asks, voice low.

When I nod, Yulian reaches down for a small briefcase at his feet and begins assembling a high-tech pair of night-vision binoculars. Geared up, he begins surveilling the building and its surrounding areas. "No guards in place. No vehicles in the area." He continues to scan the location as Daniil maneuvers the boat around the port wall. "Three ground level exits," he continues, "overall low to no security."

Yulian lowers the binoculars and sits heavily in his seat. "I don't know what the fuck is going on, but this place is a joke. Either you're being set-up and they are going to blow it to smithereens the moment you walk in there, or this is an amateur job."

A better man might consider his options, weighing the cost of his life, and others. But I am not a better man. "We go."

My brothers—the loyal fucks they are—voice their agreement, willing to follow me into a situation that may very well end badly.

Yulian's mouth snaps into a straight line. "Walking into this meeting is a death trap—no back-up, no weapons. My team will surveil with a drone, and we'll be on standby, but we can't do much once you enter the building. You'll be sitting ducks. And if Oleg is behind this—"

"But he's not." I say decisively. "This isn't his MO. If he took Georgia from her bed in my house, he wouldn't hide that fact. He'd be gloating, flaunting our failure in our faces, especially after what we did to him." On top of that, we have acquired the best intel money can buy, and all of our sources confirm Oleg is still laying low, waiting to gather his team before striking. Whoever is behind Georgia's disappearance, they're not a known entity.

Yulian sighs heavily, bracing his arms on his knees. "Even old dogs learn new tricks."

He's frustrated, and I can't blame him. I'm leading my whole family into a dangerous situation, but I have no choice. Allowing harm to come to Georgia would destroy me in ways I can't even fathom. Even though she'll never be mine, knowing she is free and happy will be enough. It has to be.

I consider Yulian's concerns. If this job was a bunch of amateurs, we would have found them by now. The only lead we have is Piper. The fact that she disappeared without a trace means she's working for someone powerful—powerful enough to place her in our employ after passing rigorous screening tests and background checks.

"I hope she's worth it," Daniil says, lighting a cigarette and blowing lazy rings just to annoy me, which he's remarkably successful at.

"You know she is," I insist. "But this isn't about making her mine." As much as I'd like to do that. What could I offer Georgia? A life of danger. Violence. Death at every turn.

I want to offer her more than that. I want to give her the world, just not the world I inhabit.

Leo eyes me carefully. "Seems like an awful lot of trouble for a woman that you're not going to keep."

"Haven't we been through this?" I snap. "If you love someone, you keep them away from the brotherhood. Those are the rules. My rules."

Shit, I just said love.

CHAPTER THIRTY-FIVE

GEORGIA

THE NEXT DAY, I SEE LITTLE OF KIRA. I KNOW SHE'S WITH Jake, the friend that's helping her pull off this audacious mission, but I have no idea what they are actually doing. My only saving grace is that she's untied me from the bed. I'm still locked in this bedroom, but at least I have space to move around, or more accurately pace the room like a madwoman.

Kira also lent me jeans and a hoodie which I'm grateful for. I couldn't bear to wear Andrei's dress shirt any longer. It smells like him, the scent both comforting and upsetting. I'm worried about him, about Kira, about everyone. I can only hope that everything will go smoothly, because the alternative is too much to imagine.

Goddamnit, when did Andrei get under my skin? I didn't want to feel anything for him. I still don't, and yet I fucking feel so much. Moments of our time together flood my mind. Our ill-fated shooting lesson when he offered me freedom and gave me the most delicious orgasm of my life, when he gifted me the studio and our picnic dinner on the beach. The way he held me.

His smell, his taste. It was all so real just a minute ago, and now it's gone.

The room echoes with the click of a lock and a moment later, Kira enters the room carrying a takeout bag in one hand and a gun in the other hand. A gun that's pointed straight at me.

"Seriously?" I exclaim, more surprised than I ought to be.

She tosses a set of handcuffs my way. "Secure one hand to the bed frame. You can leave your other hand free."

"Is this really necessary?" I roll my eyes, but take the cuffs and do what she asks.

"Yeah, it is," she says, still standing by the door. "I hear you have lethal Krav Maga skills."

"That's true," I admit, feeling an odd sense of pride.

When she's happy I can't get away or hurt her, she settles into the same chair as yesterday and tosses me a greasy bag of tacos. We both tear into the food. She's quiet, and I can tell she has a lot on her mind, but I'm desperate to know what's going on.

"Have you heard anything more from Andrei?" I blurt.

She studies my face, not saying anything for a few moments. "No, but he's scoped out the meeting location, so he's taking this seriously."

Unease hovers over me like a black cloud.

The temptation to tell Kira the truth about her family is overwhelming, but why would she believe me? As cozy as we are right now curled up together eating fish tacos, she must be somewhat unhinged to have put this plan into action. And who knows, maybe she is working with her father and this whole thing is a set-up. I can't take a chance.

Before I can reply, she turns to me, frowning. "Did he hurt you?"

"Andrei?"

"No."

Our gazes meet and a muscle feathers in her jaw. She's talking about Oleg, her father.

"No, but it was only a matter of time." Her face falls, and it's obvious she knows more about her father than she cares to. "I'm taking it you and your father are not close."

She shakes her head, the corners of her mouth drawn downwards. "Never. I barely saw him growing up. I was basically raised in boarding schools all over Europe. The only person in this world who ever loved me was my aunt, Masha. My father's sister." Emotion clogs her throat. "And he killed her."

"I'm so sorry," I say, the food souring in my stomach thinking of everything Oleg stole from his own flesh and blood. "Why would he kill his sister?"

Her teeth clench so tightly her molars must ache. "Masha was leading an uprising against him. Some of the older members of the brotherhood still reported to her, unhappy with how my father was running things. My aunt couldn't sit idle anymore. She put this plan in motion to overthrow my father. Now I have to finish the job."

"So your aunt helped to plan all of this, but now... who is helping you to execute it?"

"Jake."

I gulp. "Is that it?"

She shrugs defensively. "He's the only person I trust. The only person willing to help me."

A stone fist squeezes my chest. "If your father found out about your aunt's plan, you might be in danger."

She waves her hand dismissively. "He knows nothing about my involvement. He thinks I'm a stupid party girl with no idea that he killed my aunt. It serves me for him to believe that. Now I have the element of surprise."

Bravado is clearly a family trait. For a five-foot nothing slip of a woman, she's got balls of steel. Or she's truly unhinged. Because she's in a sharing mood, I push her further. "What about your mother?"

"Died during childbirth."

I nod, anguished over the lie she's been fed her whole life.

Kira shrugs. "It's life, right?" She rises from the bed, collecting our food wrappers. After a moment, she glances up at me. "We need to leave soon for the meeting. We'll hold you in the same building as the place we're meeting with the Kozlovs, but on a different floor."

A chill slithers down my spine. "Will you return me to Andrei?"

"If he agrees to my terms."

"And if he doesn't?"

"I don't know," she says, a hint of sadness in her voice, "I really don't know."

CHAPTER THIRTY-SIX

ANDREI

THE CONTAINER TERMINAL IS EMPTY AFTER DARK. LITERALLY, there's not a person to be seen as we drive between stacked shipping containers, large cranes standing tall in the distance. The occasional cry of a seagull punctuates the silence.

Yulian maneuvers our armor-plated Humvee with Daniil in the front seat, and Leo and me in the back—eagle eyes scanning for anything that stands out as a threat. You could hear a pin-prick in this car. We're so silent, attuned to any movement or sound that signals trouble.

"This is it," Yulian announces, his face like stone. A derelict building rises in front of us, looking as empty as I feel inside.

"We leave the weapons in the car," I remind my brothers, "but we take these." I pass out some real James Bond shit—a basic ink pen that turns into a switchblade knife with a flick of the wrist.

"Fucking brilliant," Daniil breathes, as he tucks the so-called pen into a side pocket of his fatigues. It's innocuous enough that if we get patted down on our way inside, most of the basic level soldiers won't be any the wiser.

I haven't been without some sort of weapon on me since I was a boy, and it feels odd to be so exposed, even wearing the best ballistic body armor money could buy.

Stepping out of the car, we nod to Yulian. He'll park out of sight and communicate with our team hidden around the port area. We have drones in play, sending a live feed back to our security teams. It's the best we can do. Try to anticipate everything in advance. And hope like hell this isn't an ambush designed to wipe our family from the face of the earth.

My brothers follow closely behind me as I lead the way into the building. I expect to be frisked by security, but there is no one to greet us. I tamp down my better instinct that screams for me to turn back. As instructed, we head right, following a narrow hallway to the very back of the building, where we enter a cavernous room. It's dark when we step in, but the lights soon flicker on. There are no tables and chairs, nothing, except for a few wooden shipping crates and a large television screen set-up on the far-side of the room.

The vision on the screen chills me to the bone. It's a close-up of Georgia—she's blindfolded and gagged with a gun to her head. I can't see who is holding the gun, just the fear in the way Georgia holds herself pin straight, not moving a muscle, barely daring to breathe.

It takes everything in me not to call out to her, though I doubt she'd be able to hear me. I catch my brothers' expressions. Both of them look about as tense as I feel. Someone is watching us. This whole set-up is meant to unsettle us, and give them the upper hand. I school my expression, deep breaths calming my frayed nerves. And then a voice booms from behind us.

"Good evening, gentlemen. Thank you for coming."

All three of us spin around, only to be confronted by a familiar face smiling back at us. Except the woman standing here is no longer a brunette. Instead, she has a stylish blonde bob. Piper. The woman who somehow bluffed her way into a job in our home. I still haven't figured out how that happened, but when I do get to the bottom of it, there will be hell to pay. For now, getting Georgia back is my only focus.

"It wasn't exactly an invitation we could ignore." Daniil says tightly, his eyes trained on the gun she has pointed at us.

"No, I suppose not," she says, a hint of smug satisfaction bleeding into her tone. She gestures to the television. "This is a livestream of Georgia. A show of good faith on my part so you know she is alive and well. If you make a move to hurt me, she'll be killed, and you'll get to watch it on-screen. Keep that in mind."

"If Georgia is harmed, I will rain down a world of hurt on you." I snarl, pointing at the screen. Piper holds her ground, cold steel flashing in her eyes. Whoever she is, she's tough; she doesn't even flinch at my threat. "Why are we here?" I demand.

She crosses her arms and meets each of our eyes with her own cool gaze. "I'd like to suggest an alliance, one that's mutually beneficial," she says silkily. "My name is not Piper, although you've probably already figured that out. I'm the daughter of your sworn enemy. Our families share a history of violence, a history of hate, but I want to change that."

My stomach drops. Beside me, Leo and Daniil remain still, as if we're all holding our breath to see what comes next, to see if this moment is real.

"What's your name?" I ask. I need to hear it from her mouth.

"Kira Antonov." Shock punches the breath from my lungs. My sister stands before me, but there is no spark of recognition. Nothing to suggest that she knows we're related or that she's brought us here for a family reunion, so I test the waters.

"What exactly do you have in mind?"

"We have the same objective, you and I. We both want to destroy my father, and avoid an all-out mafia war. Help me take down Oleg and install me as the new head of the Antonov Bratva. I know I'm young, but now you've seen what I'm capable of. Together, we can move forward with our brotherhoods aligned, rather than opposing."

I'm momentarily struck dumb by what she has revealed. Kira wants to overthrow her father? It's either an act of sheer stupidity, or the ultimate example of bravery—likely somewhere in between.

I don't need to look at my brothers to know they feel as I do. It's time to get it all out in the open.

"Kira, there is something you need to know first."

My words are cut off by rapid gunfire exploding just beyond the room. The noise is deafening as a hail of bullets splinter through the thick wooden door, sending all of us scattering for cover.

Kira releases a blood-curdling scream and dives for cover.

Ice travels through my veins. I can't lose her too.

CHAPTER THIRTY-SEVEN

ANDREI

My brothers and I army crawl towards Kira quivering behind an overturned crate. Even with the gun in her hand, she's now looking much less sure of herself. Her youth and inexperience are clear.

Before we can get to her, the door is kicked in, banging against the cement walls with a heavy thud, as men dressed all in black and armed with AK-47s file into the space, one after another, surrounding us in a semicircle. Plumes of smoke follow behind them, the noxious gas seeping into our eyes and nose, obscuring our vision.

And then, through the smoke, a familiar form appears. He stops just inside the room, surveying it carefully. Ice-blue eyes land on Kira.

Oleg Antonov stands in the center of the room, a gun aimed at his own daughter's head.

"Kira, come here," he barks. A brutal command.

"Don't move a muscle," I instruct her. And then to Oleg, I say, "Leave her. She had nothing to do with any of this. If you want someone, take me."

Despite my outward bravado, my stomach is in knots. Without weapons, we can't protect her. We're surrounded. There must be at least a dozen men in this room armed to the teeth, with all their attention focused on us. Except for Oleg, who is staring at Kira, his face red and pinched as he looks ready to murder his only child.

She slowly unfolds her body and approaches him.

"Did you think I would be so easy to fool?" he sneers at his daughter. "Did you think I wouldn't find out about your elaborate plans?"

Kira fights to remain calm, but a layer of sweat forms on her upper lip, and her hands tremble. In one swift motion, he rips the gun from her, and uses it to strike her in the face. Bleeding and hurt, she crumples to the cement floor, hugging her knees into her chest.

The need to pummel Oleg into the ground is nearly overwhelming, but Leo's hand on my back serves as a reminder that we'll only make things worse for her if we try to fight. It'll surely end with our death. Whatever we do, we need to be smart.

It's not only our own lives in the balance, but Kira's too, and possibly Georgia's. A quick glance confirms the TV screen has gone blank. I can only hope that Georgia is far from here and safe.

"To betray me like this. My own child." He spits at her feet. "Did you have a chance to tell them your brilliant plan, or did I interrupt your cozy little meeting too early?" A single tear falls down Kira's cheek; the only emotion she betrays as Oleg shakes with anger.

"Leave her, Oleg," I command. "This meeting was my idea. She had nothing to do—"

"Shut up," he barks, eyes narrowed, a sneer on his lips. "I know everything. How my daughter wanted you to help her overthrow me, to join forces with her as the head of the Antonov family." He laughs, and it's a cruel, hollow sound. "As if a stupid little girl could lead the Antonov Bratva. As if my men would take her seriously."

He roughly pulls her up by the arm, a gun pressed firmly into her ribs. She looks terrified, her right eye swelling where he hit her, but she doesn't respond to his taunts.

I don't have high hopes that we'll make it out of here alive today. But I refuse to go to our graves without the truth coming out.

"Why don't you tell her the truth, Oleg? Kira clearly doesn't know who her mother is—or that we are her brothers."

Kira's eyes are wide, confusion replacing the fear that was on her face a moment ago. "What's going on?"

Oleg bares his teeth in a menacing smile. The air pulses with tension. "You don't know shit," he taunts. "Your father was a moron who I took great pleasure in wiping off this earth, and you've proved yourself no better. You couldn't even kill me when you had the chance. And now, you never will."

I block out his insults and focus on Kira. "Your father seduced our mother. She gave birth to you shortly before she died, but by that time Oleg had taken you far away. We only learned about you six months ago—we've been searching ever since."

Kira turns towards her father, devastation written all over her face. "How could you keep this from me?"

Oleg's lips twist in distaste, and he pushes the gun farther into her side. "You're lucky I bothered to keep you alive. The only thing you were good for was destroying the sanity of Dahlia Kozlov, and by extension, the rest of her family. I never had a need for a daughter, and I still don't."

Fire flashes in her eyes and with a yelp, she twists from his hold and knees Oleg between his legs. He doubles over, crying out in pain.

My brothers and I move in unison. In the blink of an eye, I tackle the soldier closest to me. We land on the concrete ground with a heavy thud. His gun flies out of his hands and skids several feet away as he roars in outrage. Around me, all hell breaks loose, but I focus on one task—killing this man.

Straddling his torso, I reach into the inner pocket of my jacket and remove the pen. With a flick of my wrist, a four-inch razor-sharp blade emerges. Without hesitation, I plunge it straight into the side of his neck. It's a bloody fucking mess, straight out of a Monty Python skit, but it has the intended effect—he's dead within seconds.

Shots ring out and a soldier to my right drops like a ton of bricks. Daniil kicks the fallen man's weapon my way as Leo drop kicks the soldier behind him. It all happens in a flash, years of training kick in and my body just reacts to what's happening around me. It's chaos. We don't notice Oleg until it's too late.

"Drop your weapons or I shoot her in the head." He has Kira's back pressed roughly against his front, the barrel of a gun pressed to her temple.

"Fuck me," mumbles Leo. I catch his eye, and he gives me a nearly imperceptible nod. We don't doubt Oleg would kill his own daughter.

Daniil, Leo, and I drop the weapons in front of us and raise our hands in surrender. We've done some damage. At least half of the soldiers are dead, though I don't doubt that there are more of them outside of this room. We're outnumbered and without weapons.

"Leave her, Oleg." I implore him. "I'll give you whatever you want. Just don't hurt her."

His cruel laughter rings out. "I'm getting exactly what I want today. The pleasure of ending the Kozlov bloodline. I've made it my life's mission to destroy your family, just as your father destroyed mine. But first, I thought you could watch me have a little fun." Evil glints in his eye and I have a terrible feeling that I won't like what's coming next. Oleg turns to one of his men. "What's taking them so long? Go bring the girl to me."

His words slice through the air like lethal shards of ice, as I realize who he means. I exchange a look with Kira, who appears as alarmed as I am. Shit, that means Georgia is on the property, and not being held off-site like I hoped.

I've never felt so helpless in my whole damn life.

CHAPTER THIRTY-EIGHT

GEORGIA

"OH, FUCK." JAKE'S VOICE IS BARELY AUDIBLE, BUT I HEAR THE unmistakable note of panic.

"What?" I say, though it's hard to speak with the rag in my mouth.

"Shit, this is really fucking bad," Jake repeats, panic rising in his voice.

His words kick my pulse into high-gear and I spit the rag out of my mouth.

"Jake, what's happening?" My voice is cold and commanding. Kira's school friend is nice enough, but he's in way over his head. Something bad is happening, and I have to deal with it, judging by Jake's level of hysteria.

"I... I don't know. A bunch of black SUVs have pulled up to the back of the building, and guys in dark military fatigues are entering the building."

Fuck me. Black army fatigues are the Antonov guards' signature uniform. "Jake, you need to untie me right now. These are Oleg's guys, and shit is about to get serious."

Jake slips the blindfold off of me and releases my arms and legs.

I join Jake by the window, our backs flush to the wall as we spy the action below. Just like he said, several black SUVs are parked haphazardly around the back entrance, as if creating a barricade, and a few armed men stand outside as guards.

"Oh shit, oh shit, oh shit." Jake paces the room, his breaths coming out in heavy pants.

Fear claws up my throat. How did this all go so wrong?

My mind races with all the various scenarios and possibilities that may present themselves. All of them are bad. But still, I need to do something.

"Jake," I say sternly. When he doesn't settle, I grab him by the arm. "Listen to me," I hiss. "This is really serious. We need to warn Kira. You need to radio her about what's happening." From what Jake told me earlier, we are on the third floor of the building and Kira and the Kozlovs are on the main floor.

He stares at me blankly. "Radio?"

"How are you communicating with Kira?" I ask, my nerves steadily rising.

He sighs and buries his face in his hands. "We weren't supposed to need a radio. I can text her—"

Gunfire pierces the air, chilling my bones.

"No. Don't do that," I say, dropping to my knees and pulling the video feed out of the wall. "We don't want anyone to know we're here. We need to move now," I say, grabbing Jake by his shoulder.

"What? Where would we go?"

"You will hide, and I will find a way to help them."

Before we can move, the sound of heavy boots thumping over concrete carries towards us. Jake and I exchange a look, his expression one of frozen horror.

"Give me your gun," I demand, palm splayed open. "Please tell me it's actually loaded."

"I don't know. I've never used a gun before."

I guess I'll find out soon enough because our time is up. The door is kicked open and two hulking men dressed in all black appear.

Adrenaline charges through my veins. It's us vs them. Either they die, or we will, that I am sure of. I take a chance on the gun in my hand and shoot. In front of me, a soldier's body jerks as if electrocuted. His face is frozen as he falls to the floor, clutching his chest.

Holy shit, I've just killed someone.

More shots erupt around me. A movement in my peripheral vision catches my attention. Beside me, Jake is sprawled on the ground, his lifeless eyes staring up at the ceiling.

I'm nearly sick to my stomach, but I don't have time to process the insanity of the moment because the remaining thug lunges for me. I don't think, I just react. My fist flies and I knock him in the teeth. His bald head reels back, his mouth bloody as I scramble to lift my gun, but I'm not fast enough. In a flash, he's back in front of me, knocking the weapon from my hand.

"You little bitch," he snarls. The ugly fucker comes at me with all his wrath. He grabs me by my hair and wrenches my head back, so I'm staring at his crooked teeth and snarling features. "If Oleg didn't want you alive, I would choke the shit out of you with my bare hands."

Despite his words, his hands rise and clamp around my throat. He squeezes, and my vision goes dark around the edges. Panic washes over me. My last thought is that I may never see Andrei again, and the pain of that realization is worse than being stabbed a thousand times.

"Enough, Rodrigo." A familiar voice breaks into my consciousness.

No.

Oh hell, no.

"Hello again, Georgia." Kristian's gaunt face swims into my vision as Rodrigo roughly releases me. I choke and cough, fighting to draw in air.

Besides Oleg, Kristian—Oleg's right-hand man—is the last person I ever wanted to see again. He gave me the creeps when I worked at the Antonov estate, and I heard just as many stories about Kristian's blood-lust as I heard about Oleg's sexual depravity.

"Funny meeting like this." Kristian's voice slithers down my spine. "We lost track of you for a time, but now I see you're just fine. Have you been hiding out with the Kozlovs?" He shakes his head, tsking dramatically. "Oleg will be very displeased to learn of the company you've been keeping."

Anger erupts under my skin, and I spit in his face. It costs me, as I knew it would. He backhands me hard, and my body flies back. I struggle to keep my footing as blood fills my mouth. Still, it was worth it.

"If that's how you want to do this, we can play rough." Darkness seeps into his eyes, and he grabs me roughly by the neck, forcing me to stand. "I'll make sure Oleg knows you want it rough and dirty, too. After we slaughter your friends downstairs, you'll come with us. And we're going to have so much fun with you."

My stomach roils, but I fight to keep my head clear. I try to come up with a plan. A solution. A way out. Kristian remembers the weak, submissive girl from before. He doesn't know what I am capable of now, and I can use the element of surprise to my advantage.

I take a deep breath and push all the fear in my body deep down, putting on a bland smile. "All right Kristian, let's do this your way. The Kozlovs weren't as much fun as I hoped. Let's see what you got."

A sneer twists his lips. He's suspicious, no doubt, but my acquiescence is easier to deal with than my resistance.

"Time to join the fun downstairs." His lips pull back in a sinister smile and his yellow teeth nearly make me gag. But I just shrug as if I'm not bothered by any of this.

Kristian leads the way, walking in front of me, while Rodrigo brings up the rear. His gun is pressed into my back, lodged between my shoulder blades. They don't bother tying me up, the gun a potent reminder that if I make one wrong move, I'm dead.

I take a last look at Jake's prone body, making him a silent promise that if I survive today, he'll get the proper burial he deserves.

They march me out of the abandoned upstairs office, through a byzantine maze of corridors and sharp turns. Every step of the way, my eyes scan the space, looking for something, anything, I could use to attack them. I'm well aware I don't have the advantage here. But that's what my hours of training were all about—how to get the advantage when there isn't one. However, the gun pressed into my back makes this all the more complicated.

We come to a stop in front of an ancient-looking freight elevator. Kristian pulls up the steel doors and then lifts the gate, ushering us inside. Fuckwad keeps the gun pressed hard against my back.

"Going down," Kristian whispers in my ear like the creepy fuck he is. The elevator starts its slow, rickety descent, but he doesn't take his eyes off of me. "I can't wait to see the bloodbath that awaits us downstairs." I nearly lose my lunch, but school my features into a neutral expression. He doesn't deserve my misery.

A loud bang, followed by a jarring screech, rings out as the elevator comes to a sudden stop. "What the hell?" Kristian spits. "Don't move a muscle," he tells me, turning around to check the rudimentary control panel.

It's the opening I've been looking for.

With Kristian distracted, I turn around and face the ogre Rodrigo behind me. "What the hell do you think you're doing?" he barks at me, as he raises the gun and points it right at my forehead.

"Just you see." I grab the gun with two hands, pushing it as high into the air as I can manage, while I duck out of the line of fire. The gun goes off. My hands feel like burning coals, but I push through, delivering a swift kick to his balls before I attack inward, bringing the gun towards his belly. The speed and power of my movements destabilizes him, and before he realizes it, the gun is mine. I throw a fresh round into the empty chamber and shoot him in the head. Shards of bone and brain matter spray my face, but I feel nothing right now except relief. But that doesn't last long.

Kristian is on me in seconds—tackling me like a linebacker, slamming my back into the wall of the elevator. I gasp as the wind is knocked out of me, and in that moment of weakness, Kristian wrestles the gun from my hand. My fist shoots out and connects with his nose. He roars as his head is thrown back, blood shooting everywhere, but it's not enough to knock him out. He grabs my hair, violently jerking my head back, the razor-sharp blade of a knife pressed against my neck.

"Big fucking mistake." His breath is hot against my ear as he grinds his pelvis into me, rotating his hips. I go motionless as terror becomes a live wire shooting through my body. "Oleg was so looking forward to having you, and to be honest, so was I. But your behavior has been appalling and, frankly, you are not worth the headache."

Another thrust of his erection to drive the point home, as the blade sinks into my flesh. I know this will be my last breath unless I strike now. Crocodile tears spring readily to my eyes, offering him the fear and panic that he craves.

"Please, don't hurt me," I beg, my voice comically desperate. "I never meant to make you mad. What can I do to make it up to you?"

He snarls, anger rippling from him. But also lust. When he pauses, I strike like a rattlesnake, my right hand pushing the knife away from my throat, as I knee him hard in the groin. When he's doubled over hissing in pain, I follow-up with another kick to his face and twist the knife out of his hand. He scrambles after me, grabbing onto my leg, but I don't give him time to do any more damage. With a tortured cry, I plunge the knife into the back of his neck, quickly pulling the blade out and plunging it in again and again. He releases a sickening gurgling sound and falls to the floor.

Never in my life could I imagine I would kill a man without thinking twice, but the proof of my actions lies in a pool of blood in front of me, twitching as his life slowly leaks out of him.

Shock nearly brings me to my knees, but I don't have time to freak out over the fact that I'm in a jammed freight elevator with two dead men that I single-handedly killed.

I have bigger problems. Much bigger problems.

The man I love might be hurt, or worse, and I may be the only one who can save him.

At that moment, I hear a commotion below and the elevator restarts its slow journey downward. The disturbance must have alerted the guards.

Retrieving Rodrigo's gun off the floor, I shove it down the front of my pants and lower my baggy hoodie over my body so the outline of the weapon isn't visible. As soon as we hit the ground floor, the doors to the elevator open, and a mean-looking guard lunges for me.

"You little bitch, we've been waiting for you. Now you can answer Oleg."

Good.

He's playing right into my plan.

CHAPTER THIRTY-NINE

ANDREI

With every second that ticks by, Oleg's irritation seems to increase a hundredfold, the air in the room thick with violence. His right-hand has been gone a really fucking long-time, and Oleg is antsy as shit, texting and calling his men, pacing the room and swearing when he gets no response.

Something has gone wrong, that much is clear.

Anxiety skitters down my spine. My brothers and I are cuffed with our hands behind our backs and forced against the wall as two of Oleg's goons loom over us with guns. Kira remains at Oleg's feet, hugging her knees, while Oleg barks commands at his men. She throws me an apologetic look, and I shake my head. She doesn't need to apologize, not for this.

Kira is brave, I'll give her that, but also reckless. Hard to fault her for something baked into her DNA.

A sharp cry rings through the air as a soldier roughly shoves Georgia into the room. Her hands are bound in front of her, and blood splatters her face.

A fresh wave of pain shoots through me. She's the last person I wanted to pull into this nightmare.

Georgia's gaze sweeps over the room—from the dead bodies on the ground, to Kira huddled by her father's feet. Finally, her eyes collide with mine. Alarm, confusion, anger—so much expressed in those wolf-like eyes of hers. Her gaze is steady, and I subtly shake my head, letting her know that I'm unharmed. She blinks slowly—once, then twice. It's a message, but I don't know what she's trying to tell me. Regardless, I hold still, waiting to see what she has planned.

"Ah, my little dove." Oleg's face lights up at her entrance.

The soldier leading Georgia towards Oleg speaks up. "She killed Kristian and Rodrigo. I found their bodies in the elevator."

Oleg looks much more pleased than one should at this news. "My little Georgia! I always knew you had the killer instinct buried under that innocent virgin routine. Still, I'll have to punish you for killing my best men. But don't worry." He winks. "I'll make sure you have fun."

She scowls at him, but otherwise doesn't move a muscle.

Kira jumps up and grabs her father's arm. "She has nothing to do with this. Please, just let her go. She shouldn't even be here."

"Shut-up." Oleg slaps Kira across the face. She cries out and crumples to the ground, holding a hand to her face.

Georgia's lips thin into a grim line.

"You motherfucker," I snarl. "I will fucking hunt you down and kill you if it's the last thing I do." I get to my feet, but a soldier steps into my path, knocking me hard in the stomach with the butt of his rifle. The air whooshes out of my lungs and I dry heave when I hit the ground.

Oleg roars with laughter. "The last thing that you will do is rot away in my dungeon, your body flayed open. Maybe we'll try feeding you your own liver. I don't believe I've tried that before."

The glee in his tone confirms that nothing brings him greater pleasure than torture, but I'll never give him the satisfaction of touching me or anyone else in the room, and I know my brothers feel the same. We are all primed and angry, waiting for the right moment to strike. Even if we die today, if Kira and Georgia survive, it'll be worth it.

"Come closer, my dove." Oleg waves Georgia forward, so she's standing directly in front of him. My insides retreat as he reaches up a hand and trails his palm down Georgia's cheek. She recoils at his touch, but that only seems to excite him, his eyes shining like onyx orbs.

"My beauty. I never imagined this is how we would meet again. Have the Kozlov devils been hiding you?" His voice is soft, almost sympathetic, but barely contained fury lies beneath the surface. "I hope not, I hope you haven't been keeping company with these *podonok*, because if so..." He roughly grabs her chin, smearing the blood on her face grotesquely. "I'll have to kill you, too. Well, not before I fuck you in every hole while your friends watch. Maybe my guards deserve a turn too, since you killed three of our own. Would you like that?"

"No, please no," she whispers, in a voice barely above a whisper. She falls in on herself, sobs wracking her lithe frame. My body hums with the need to attack, and I prepare to spring up, but Leo stops me with a low-whistle. He's watching Georgia, his eyes narrowed on something, something that holds his attention. I look to where Georgia is crumpled forward, and that's when I see the glint of metal.

It happens lightning fast. Georgia pulls something from the front of her pants. A soft click is the only warning. Oleg's mouth pulls back into a terrifying snarl as he registers what is about to happen, but she doesn't give him time to cry out. Georgia holds a pistol between her bound hands and shoots Oleg square between the eyes.

Shock registers on his face even as the life is sucked out of him and he collapses, his expression frozen in a ghoulish death mask.

Before I can warn her, Oleg's soldiers strike. A shot goes off, but she drops in time to avoid being hit. The problem is, it puts her in the line of fire of another guard, who kicks out a leg, his boot catching her face. There's a sickening thud as her head flies back against the cold cement floor.

Everything around me slows down as I watch in horror.

"No." My howls echo through the large space. In a flash, I'm on my feet running to her, tackling her assaulter like a linebacker with my full body-weight, before a piercing explosion causes the ground to tremble and shake. Acrid smoke fills my nose as debris flies through the air.

Yulian and my men have arrived.

GEORGIA

Thwop thwop thwop.

A whirring sound like the spinning of helicopter blades fills my ears and pulls me from the sweet oblivion I am floating in.

And then something else. My name. A desperate plea on Andrei's lips.

"Georgia. Georgia. Stay with me."

Drawing in a labored breath, I struggle to open my eyes as splintering pain whips through me. But I push that aside to look up at Andrei, his face inches from my own as he cradles me in his arms. I want to tell him I'm okay. This will all be okay because he looks so distraught, but I can't form words, my tongue thick and heavy in my mouth.

A jagged cut runs along his right cheek, and there's dried blood around his nose, but it's the intensity of his eyes that scares me. They shine with the intensity of a thousand suns.

"Don't fucking die on me, baby, I need you. Do you hear me, krasotka?" His hands tighten on the nape of my neck, as if he can somehow force life back into me. "I love you. I'll fucking die without you. Don't leave me."

His words reverberate through my skull, echoing in the distant recess of my mind.

Andrei loves me.

I want to tell him I love him too. That I'll come back. I want to stay awake for him so badly; I want to be with him forever, but the darkness beckons, luring me into its sweet embrace. I can't fight it anymore.

I stay underwater and melt into the void.

CHAPTER FORTY

ANDREI

I stare at Georgia's face in its tranquil state of unconsciousness and wonder what she's dreaming of, what world she is in while I keep vigil by her bed. It's been two days, two of the longest days of my life. She suffered a massive concussion when she bashed her head on the concrete floor, moments before my men blasted through part of the building's wall.

The medically induced coma she is in is the only way to protect her brain from swelling. Right now she looks so vulnerable and helpless—the only sign of life is the shallow rise and fall of her chest—but she's proved that she's anything but weak. When put to the test, she was an absolute demon, and I'd be lying if I said I wasn't proud of how hard she kicked-ass.

Not that I needed her to prove it. I knew what she was capable of the moment I met her. Maybe that's what drew me to her.

My fierce girl with a kind heart had somehow turned my world inside out in the best possible way. She's wrecked me, burrowed into my veins like no one else. I risked my kingdom for her, and would do it again. I'll tell her this, if I ever see her awake again—if she can stand to see my face. I've only rained down a shit-storm on her.

The door to my bedroom opens and closes, but I don't bother to look up. This room has been a revolving door of visitors—Natalia, my brothers, Yulian and Rowan and Georgia's father, who we have moved on to the estate—have been constantly by her side.

The only person who hasn't shown her face yet is Kira, and I know why. Guilt, overwhelm, shock—it's been a tremendous amount for a twenty-one-year-old to process. There may have been no love lost between Kira and Oleg, but his cruel words and violent demeanor in that abandoned warehouse will stay with her forever. It was painful to watch.

All of that has had her holed up in a room on our estate. We've let her have the time to process everything in her own way. Having her here with us is the only ray of sunshine during the bleak days of wondering if Georgia will ever be herself again.

"I'm sorry." Kira's voice carries over the quiet room. I look up to find her bathed in the moonlight leaking in through the heavy drapes. She's speaking to me, but her red-rimmed eyes are on Georgia. The black eye Oleg gave her stands in sharp contrast to her alabaster skin, and I wish I could kill her father all over again.

"Kira." I jump up and make a move towards her, but she holds up her hand.

"No, don't." She looks away, like she can't bear to see any softness in my expression. "I nearly killed her, and you. I nearly got us all killed. And Jake..." Her breath catches in her throat, and a fresh wave of tears makes its way down her cheeks.

"The only person to blame is your father. He's responsible for these deaths, not you." When she doesn't look at me or respond, I grab her hand and lead the way through the open balcony doors onto a small terrace. We are overdue for a talk. "Sit," I tell her gently.

She does as I say, but makes a face while dropping into the

gray lounge chair. "I knew older brothers were supposed to be bossy, but somehow I think you're a bit extra."

I smile at that. "Georgia would definitely agree. Now that I think about it, so would Yulian, Daniil and Leo. But they're bossy as hell, too. You'll see." I say with a wink. She remains quiet, and I can see the gears of self-loathing churning in her head. "Listen, Kira, no one blames you, and I know Georgia doesn't either."

Kira inhales the warm night air, gazing off into the distance. "She tried to warn me, you know. Georgia kept on telling me to just talk to you, that you'd listen to reason." Kira sighs, her shoulders slumping forward. "I was such an ass thinking I could play with the big boys."

I get up and grab bottles of water from the outdoor fridge, offering her one as I sit back down. "You come by it honestly," I say, giving her a little punch on the shoulder. "You've got the Kozlov genes. We're an audacious bunch." She flashes me a lopsided grin and her smile reminds me so much of my mother's that my heart threatens to crumble in my chest. "You have no idea how much we've wanted to find you. The efforts we've gone to. We were even going to send Georgia into Oleg's home to track you down."

Kira's head snaps up at my admission. "Why didn't you?"

I hang my head for a brief moment and let the shame of my actions wash through me. Not that Georgia was not capable of doing what we asked of her—she proved herself more than capable—but I should never have put her in that impossible position.

"At the last minute, I realized I could not go through with it. Georgia still doesn't know that. She was gone before I could tell her."

"You mean I abducted her before you could tell her?"

"You did," I admit. "And one day you're going to have to tell me how you pulled that shit off. Either our security is really lacking or you are just that good."

"I'm pretty good." She smiles shyly and sits back in her seat, fiddling with the water bottle in her lap. "But I still have lots to learn."

I rest my hand over hers. "Other than Georgia being hurt, this is the outcome we wanted. You, here with us, and Oleg, dead. This is what Georgia wanted as well—so much that she was willing to do whatever it took to help us find you."

"For you," Kira says quietly. "She was willing to do that because she loves you. I hope you can see it."

My heart stutters in my chest, but I tamp down any hope that threatens to bloom prematurely.

We're both quiet for a moment, lost in our own thoughts.

"I only wanted you to hear me out. All of this was just so you'd take me seriously enough to help me take down my father and then install me as the new leader."

"It was a bold plan," I admit, shaking my head in admiration. I pause for a minute and cock an ear towards Georgia, lying in the bedroom. The familiar sound of the machines helping her lungs fill with air. It's one part reassuring and one part gut-wrenching. When I look up, Kira seems lost in thought.

"There is something I've been wondering about," I say. "How did you know your father was a problem if he kept you far from his empire?"

She sighs and turns towards me. "Members of his brotherhood, the old-guard, weren't happy with how my father was leading the organization. He was destroying everything with his vices, becoming increasingly unstable and erratic. It was too dangerous to overthrow him from the inside, so they approached my Aunt Masha to help bring me into the fold. She was reluctant, but knew things would only get worse. Once we talked about it, I wanted to do my part." Kira's face settles into a grim line, her shoulders hang loose, all the fight drained out of her. "My father killed Masha and his men before we could put a plan in motion. So I moved forward on my own. He never thought I had it in me."

"He never deserved you," I say and mean it. The moment Georgia put a bullet between Oleg's eyes might be one of the most satisfying moments of my life. It was payback for everyone I love that he took from me. My mother, my father, my sister.

"Oleg's assets are yours now." I point out. "You rule the Antonov Bratva, whether you like it or not."

She shakes her head. "There is no more Antonov empire. I don't want to lead with that name."

"What do you want?" I ask her.

"We combine forces under the Kozlov name. My mother was a Kozlov after all." She looks wistful. The night of the attack, Kira asked us to tell her about our mother. It was hard to recount, but we sat up until the wee hours of the morning sipping scotch and telling Kira about the good times—what we loved about her, her kindness, her joy, her realness. But we also shared with Kira the tragic circumstances of her death. It wasn't an easy conversation, lots of raw emotions surfacing over what we lost, but the truth had to be aired.

"Nothing would make me happier," I tell her honestly. I stand up and lift my shirt so she can see the newest ink addition to my body. It's still healing, but it's a stunning constellation—a swirl of stars exploding with color.

"Beautiful," she says, her eyes roving over the design.

"It's us," I admit. "Georgia designed it for when we finally found you and we were all together. Except I added one more surprise. This is Georgia," I say, pointing to a bright star beside my own. "And this hummingbird floating above it all is Mama."

"This is so surreal. I never had a family, and then to discover you were here all along." She smiles, tears shining in her eyes.

"You won't be able to get rid of us," I say. We stand and I hug her, holding her close to my chest. Where I hope she stays for a long time.

CHAPTER FORTY-ONE

GEORGIA

They say people can hear everything around them when they're in a coma, but that was not my experience. I heard nothing, felt nothing, experienced nothing, but the yawning black void I was locked in. One moment I was floating through a sea of darkness, and the next moment I'm staring into Andrei's troubled amber eyes.

"Andrei," I croak. My body is clammy with sweat, my mouth dry and fuzzy.

"I'm here." He's sitting on the edge of the bed, leaning in close, emotion etched on his handsome features. "I'm here for you."

Staying very still so as not to jostle my throbbing skull, I blink rapidly, my eyes still adjusting to the bright room. Andrei is quick to jump up and draw the curtains. I'm surprised to find I'm in Andrei's bedroom and not a hospital room. There are machines and medical gear everywhere.

"How long have I been out for?"

"Three days." He holds up a glass of water with a straw for me and I drink thirstily. "Can you remember anything?"

I wince. "I remember all of it." Memories flood my brain, from Andrei finding me quivering on the floor of a closet, to the victorious moment I shot Oleg between the eyes. All of it is seared into my brain—the bad and the good—crystal clear.

His eyes go soft. It's then that I notice the scruff on his usually clean-shaven face, the dark circles under his eyes, and the cuts and scrapes on his face.

"You were a serious bad-ass. I knew you were amazing, but that was some next level shit." He shakes his head, turmoil flaring in his eyes. "God, you nearly died, and all because of me. I should have never—"

"Stop." I say, gently placing a hand on his chest. "I don't regret anything. None of it. From the moment you took me from Oleg's house to right now, being here with you."

His chest expands with a deep breath, his expression turning bleak as he says quietly, "It was pure torture sitting here these last few days, helpless. Unsure what it would be like when you woke up. Not even sure if you'd remember me or if you'd still be the same person after all of this."

"I'm here, and I'm all right, I promise." I reach out, my fingers tangling with his. The sight of him fills me with a heavy longing. I am dying for him to touch me, hold me, to show me that our love is enough to take on this world together.

"I should call the doctor."

"In a moment. Is everyone okay? Where is Kira?" I need to know that she made it out of that hellish warehouse alive.

"We're okay. No critical injuries to report. Kira is banged up but alive. She's here with us." His lips curl up into a sweet smile. "Where she belongs."

Breath whooshes out of me in relief. "I was so scared that it was going to end badly. That you'd hurt her and never forgive yourself."

He brushes his hand down my cheek, capturing my chin with his finger and thumb. "It was never on you to tell her. Or to find her. None of this was on you." His eyes sear into mine—his devastation clear. "I need you to know something. I was not going to let you go to Oleg. When the time came, I couldn't go through with it."

I blink and swallow hard, my chest tightening as I absorb his words. He was willing to sacrifice the most important thing to him in the world—finding Kira—for me, for my happiness. My mind echoes back to the helicopter when I was in and out of consciousness.

When he said *I love you.*

"You have your freedom, krasotka. You and your father are free to go anywhere, no strings attached."

What!? My heart slams against my ribs. "You think I'm going to leave you?"

He stills, swiping a frustrated hand along the back of his neck. "This is not the world for you. It's ugly and cruel. I want better for you, I want only good things for you, and there's nothing good to be found in my life."

My gut twists. After everything, he's letting me go without a fight?

"Oh, so you've decided what's best for me." I wish I had the strength to sit up straight and cross my arms to show my displeasure, but I don't. Instead, I glare daggers at him. Tears spring to my eyes, but I swallow them back down, refusing to let them fall.

His entire body is tense, and I can see how much it costs him to turn me away. It's more than desire between us. Much more. And Jesus, I want to be with him more than anything in this world. I won't let him go, even if he fights me on this.

"We both know this is how it has to be." His stare burns through me, imploring me to see reason. "You're not from this life... this world. It destroys people."

I reach up and stroke his face, and his eyes close beneath my touch. "I'm not your mother." He flinches at my blunt statement, but it's something he has to hear. "What happened to your mother is terrible, and I'm so sorry. I hate that you and your siblings have to live with that, but history doesn't always repeat. My eyes are wide open, and you are the man I want."

He stands up and paces the room, his face anguished. The trauma of losing his mother as a little boy is still buried deep in his soul. "I wish life was that simple. If not Oleg, there will be someone else. Another vicious enemy willing to hurt you to get to me." His hands curl into fists as he stops at the edge of the bed. "Seeing you hurt like that, not knowing if you were going to live, it fucking wrecked me. If something ever happened to you, especially because of me, I wouldn't survive it. I'd rather set you free and never see you again, than put you in danger."

The energy between us expands and contracts, like a shockwave. It has its own force that we're both caught up in, twisting and turning in its wild depths. My only choice is to surrender.

"Then protect me. You have the money and resources to keep me safe."

He swallows, his shoulders settling in resignation. "You are not in any shape to decide what's best right now." He holds up a hand. "I won't make that decision for you, but I will give you time and space. When you decide, it needs to be with a clear mind, when you're stronger. Rest now." He leans in and kisses my forehead—once, then twice—his feelings communicated through the touch of his lips to my skin. "I'll send your father in to see you after the doctor."

He turns away from me, taking three steps towards the door before pausing. He doesn't turn around to look at me before he speaks again. "And *krasotka*, don't make a rash decision, because next time, I won't have the strength to turn you away."

He leaves the room. As the door closes behind him, I rest my head against the soft pillow and refuse to acknowledge the raw ache in my chest at the possibility that Andrei may still choose to protect me in his own misguided way.

CHAPTER FORTY-TWO

GEORGIA

It takes weeks for me to recover. Weeks lying in Andrei's bed, his smell permeating the room, his presence everywhere, though I never see him. As promised, he gives me space. I feel him though. In the dead of night, he comes to me. Through the veil of sleep, I feel his touch, hear my name on his lips, feel him beside me. Knowing he can't stay away is a balm for my soul.

Finally, days spent bedridden turn into days punctuated with short walks down the hall. With time, I gain enough strength to walk outside and sit in the sunshine with my father or Kira, my two constant companions. Natalia joins me for a game of gin rummy daily at four o'clock, and even the Kozlov brothers check-in once in a while, arms laden with magazines, books, and various snacks. Daniil even sneaks me some vodka, but when Kira discovers my little stash, she nearly loses her mind.

No one's been as dedicated to my recovery as Kira. She's apologized more times than I can count until I finally told her I wouldn't allow her to visit me if she kept on apologizing. Guilt still fills her eyes occasionally, like when I wince getting out of bed, but I assure her, as I've assured Andrei, everything turned out as it was supposed to.

And it brought me immense pleasure to kill Oleg, and to know that he won't be able to hurt anyone ever again. Especially after all the devastation he caused.

Kira, as the Antonov heir, gave my father back the lease to the restaurant, refusing anything in return. Claiming it was the least she could do after all we had been through at her father's hands. The Kozlovs are even helping my father with the restaurant, renovating it back to its former glory.

When she's not with me, Kira spends her time dismantling the rotten bits of the Antonov empire and merging the parts she wants to keep with the Kozlovs. She got more than her heart's desire—a seat at the table and a family—and nothing makes me happier.

I'm nearly one hundred percent recovered, feeling stronger than ever. Even though the Kozlovs' personal physician has already given me a clean bill of health to take up everyday activities, everyone is encouraging me to take more time to recover. I promised to take it easy, but I let them know in no uncertain terms that I would start up regular life activities soon.

I am clear about one thing: moving forward, I need to put my passion first. I'll always be there for my dad, and help him through whatever comes next, but now I have to pursue what makes me happy. I am going to continue chasing the joy I've found living here with Andrei. I've decided to go back to college, but this time focus on drawing and painting with the hope of one day becoming an art teacher. I also plan to keep up Krav Maga lessons, because, damn my ass is looking fine if I may say so myself.

Tonight, Kira has organized a celebratory dinner for my last night as a patient. Tomorrow, I am free to do as I please, and go where I please. Even if that means leaving the Kozlov estate and never turning back.

As I step into the grand dining room, tears threaten to fall down my face. Everyone I hold near and dear is gathered in one room. And sitting at the head of the table is Andrei, his eyes trained on me, flashing with an intensity I haven't seen before.

Breathlessly, I walk towards him. He's devastating as he pulls out the chair beside him and motions for me to sit down. Dressed in a tailored dark suit, as if he knows his bespoke suits are my weakness. His inked hands grip the back of my chair, pulling it out for me to take a seat. His nearness, after all this time, shakes me to my very core, and causes delicious shivers to run up my spine.

My father sits across from me with Natalia beside him, Kira on my left, the Kozlov brothers at the far end of the table with Yulian, and his wife, Rowan, who I am meeting for the first time tonight. It's a strangely thrilling sight; my father is at the table with my onetime captors. Kira, once known as Piper, breaking bread with her former employers, now her family. My stomach bubbles with joy, because somehow, everything seems to have worked out.

Andrei takes his seat after tucking me in, and the energy between us is on fire. Weeks of not seeing this man and my panties may self-combust. A host of servers enters the room, carrying platters laden with delicious smelling food. Even with the commotion, it's impossible to tear my eyes away from Andrei. Was he always so damn fine? This man, with his impossibly handsome face and protected heart, is my undoing.

Daniil clears his throat loudly from the other end of the table. "We can leave you two alone if you prefer."

My cheeks flame, but I playfully narrow my eyes at him. "Hilarious," I say, just as Andrei says, "Please do."

He leans back in his seat and raises his eyebrows at us, while Kira gives him a playful slap on the arm—a warning to behave. "As if that's any fun," he drawls.

Leo, looking more at ease than I've ever seen him, rests his eyes on his sister. The spark of affection in his gaze tugs at my heart. "Kira, one thing you will learn about Daniil here is that behaving is not his strong-suit. In fact, he much prefers to misbehave. Best to ignore him. It's like feeding ducks. If you start, they'll chase you around looking for scraps of food."

Kira, glowing in the candlelight, rests a finger on her lips. "I'll keep that in mind. Although it's really hard to ignore him when he brings me all that baklava he keeps on making."

My father laughs heartily. "I'm afraid that is my fault. I taught Daniil how to make it at the restaurant, and he's become quite the little pastry chef. After you master the Greek pastries, we may have to move on to Russian sweets."

Rowan, a pastry chef herself, perks up at Dad's comment. "Count me in. I'd love to make *pastila* for Yulian. It's his favorite, right?"

Yulian smiles indulgently at his wife. "Anything you make is my favorite," he says, leaning in for a lingering kiss.

Natalia sighs. "I never thought I'd live to see the day. A Kozlov man in the kitchen."

"Hey." Andrei grins. "I made scrambled eggs and toast once."

"Yeah," Natalia rolls her eyes. "Nearly burned down the kitchen, if I recall."

"I never said I was successful."

Beside me, Kira digs into her steak, humming happily. "Luckily, you employ the best Russian chef this side of the Atlantic. I could certainly get used to life under this roof."

The air is sucked out of the room for a moment, all three brothers shifting their attention to their younger sister.

"I hope so," Andrei says gently. "You are our family. You belong here, if you can stand us."

Kira dabs her mouth with her napkin and sits back, a smirk playing on her lips. "I'm sorry. Was I not clear enough when I said I could get used to living here? As in, I have no plans to leave for the foreseeable future." Her eyes sparkle with mischief. "Well, until I meet a man that sweeps me off my feet."

Leo puts his hands over his ears. "Please, no mention of

boyfriends just yet. I'm still adjusting to this whole little sister thing." His comment garners chuckles from around the table.

"Damn right," Daniil leans over and rubs her head playfully. "We have a lot of time to make up for, sis."

"Uh, watch the hair, D," she says, in her best bratty voice, smoothing down her short blonde locks.

The rest of the night is pretty raucous. We eat like kings and drink like frat boys, but the whole time I am aware of a volatile energy rolling off of Andrei, one that dances around me and threatens to consume me. And damn, I want him to consume me. Judging by the need pulsing deep in my core, I will not make it much longer without Andrei Kozlov's hands all over me.

I'm ready to tell him how I feel, but he beats me to the punch.

"I propose a toast," Andrei says, rising to his feet and raising a glass of champagne. Composed as ever, despite the round of vodka shots that Daniil just insisted we all do. "To Georgia, and her amazing recovery. Za zdarovie."

We all take a sip as Andrei stays standing. He clears his throat, the smallest of nervous gestures. He's about to say more, but I stop him by standing up beside him. It's my turn to say something.

"I'd like to offer my own toast," I say, glass in hand. I've thought long and hard about what I want to tell this group of people. The people who have somehow come to mean more to me than anyone else in the world. "To all of you. My friends and family. The day Oleg took me was the worst day of my life, second to the day my mother died." My father looks down in his lap, and I know my words have touched a chord. "But I wouldn't change any of it because it led me here—to all of you. But especially to you." My eyes land on Andrei, and I turn to face him. He's still as a statue, not moving, maybe not even breathing. "I know you want to keep me safe, and shelter me from this world —your world—but there is no place I am safer than in your arms. You've given me time and space to make my decision, and I still choose you."

Andrei nearly slumps with relief, and it feels like everyone at the table releases a breath along with him. "You're too precious for this world, but I'm not strong enough to deny you. I can't. I'll move heaven and earth for you, and anywhere in between. But I need to know something, krasotka."

Before I can register what's happening, he's down on one knee and pulling a small black velvet case out of his pocket. Oh boy. The realization of what he is about to do hits me right in the solar plexus and I can barely hold myself together, my hands shaking in anticipation. The pleased look on my father's face tells me that Andrei has his blessing.

"I never thought love was in my future, and I was fine with that. A loveless marriage seemed preferable. It was clean, no messy emotion to get in the way. But I found you, the person I want to spend the rest of my life with. Every day and always. Forever."

My heart lurches into my throat. Marriage was not top of mind, but looking up at Andrei after everything we've shared, after everything we've been through together, there's no question in my mind that he's my soulmate. My every day, always and forever, wrapped in one delicious package.

"So what do you say, krasotka? Do you want me as your husband?"

"Hell yes!" He stands and kisses me hard on the mouth while the room breaks into raucous cheers and congrats. I pull his face close to mine. "You know there is no one else for me, don't you? You're my everything."

And as our lips touch and my mouth opens for him, I know that I'm his everything too. And no one in the world could make me happier.

EPILOGUE

FOUR MONTHS LATER

ANDREI

Georgia's body shudders, and she releases a final moan before collapsing on my bare chest. Her hot pussy still spasms around me with the aftershocks of orgasm. As I look up into her gray eyes, hazy with pleasure, I wonder how I got so lucky. The gentle waves of the Indian Ocean play like a lullaby in the background, while the warm Maldives breeze dances over our naked, sweaty bodies, tangled together on a beachside chaise bed. It was more than worth the cost of renting a private island for the week of our wedding and honeymoon.

We were married yesterday on white powder sand, surrounded by our closest family and friends. Today, the island is all ours, everyone else having boarded the private charter back to the mainland this morning.

It's me and krasotka and an entire week of doing nothing but having sex, splashing in the aquamarine waters and lazing in the sun. This is my idea of paradise on earth.

I kiss her forehead and gently pull out of her, shifting her slightly so I can watch my seed leak from between her shapely legs. While we're not actively trying to get pregnant, we're not, not trying to get pregnant either. We're both open to whatever comes next. I admit, the idea of breeding Georgia makes me deliriously happy, and I'm pretty sure my beautiful bride knows that.

Georgia raises her head from my chest, and I tuck a strand of her wild, dark hair behind her ear. I don't think I'll ever get enough of looking at her. Especially when she's like this, untamed and sun-kissed, after days spent basking in the equatorial sun.

"I wish I brought paint," she says softly. "The sunsets are amazing." She gazes out towards the horizon. "I don't think I'll ever see anything quite like it."

"Hmmm, aren't you lucky you have such a thoughtful husband?" Husband. I'll never get sick of hearing that word.

Her face lights up with pleasure. "You didn't? You brought my paints."

I nod. "And canvases, and brushes, and everything else you'll need." I kiss her gently on the mouth. "I like to see you happy. And you're happiest when you're painting. Only second to when I'm inside of you."

"Mmmm," she agrees, releasing a deep sound of satisfaction. "You know me well." She traces the lines of the tattoos on my chest and closes her eyes, a blissed out expression on her face.

"What are you thinking about?"

"How freakin' happy I am. Here with you." She grins, her eyes still closed. "Is it wrong that I'm also thinking about how excited I am to start school soon? Lame, I know."

"Nothing lame about that." My fingertips skim along her arm, teasing goosebumps to erupt over her flesh. "You're going to be an amazing teacher."

Georgia is going back to college. After protracted negotiations, we finally worked out a plan that allows Georgia the freedom to go back to school and pursue her dream of painting, with the hopes of one day becoming an art teacher. The catch is that one of my men will go to school with her, posing as just another student in her class, all in the name of keeping her safe. She fought me on the idea, but I recruited her father to help plead my case. She finally saw the light and agreed to the plan. I don't know how I'll handle it when she's a teacher in a classroom full of kids, but one step at a time.

Maurice has become a fixture at our home, joining us for weekly Sunday night dinners. In turn, we're regular guests at the restaurant. Kira picks up a shift or two every week, not because she has to—she's plenty busy learning the family business—but the normalcy has been good for her. As has spending time getting to know me and my brothers.

I smile to myself, releasing a contented breath.

"You sound happy." Georgia touches my face, skimming my scruffy jaw with her finger. Emotion circles my heart, flooding my center with warmth, with love.

"I am happy, krasotka. The happiest I've been in my life." I kiss her deeply and pull her in close so she's flat against my chest. "There's perhaps only one more thing in this world which could make me happier."

She props her head up on her hand. "And what's that?"

"Hopefully, you'll find out in nine months."

She smiles, her eyes turning molten. "Maybe we will."

With that, I flip her onto her back and do my darnedest to make us both really, really happy.

Thank you so much for reading Merciless Heir!

Want more of Georgia and Andrei?
Download the bonus epilogue from my website:

https://monicakayne.com/bonuses

ALSO BY MONICA KAYNE

KOZLOV EMPIRE

Merciless Heir

Cruel Deception

Fierce Vow

Shattered Crown

BRATVA KINGS

Ruthless Reign

Savage Reign

Brutal Reign

ACKNOWLEDGMENTS

About five years ago, I caught the writing bug. Honestly, I had no aspirations other than to get my words on paper, and maybe, just maybe, one day, share them with the world. Now that it's actually happening, it's beyond surreal and also as satisfying as I hoped it would be.

So thank you to my friends and family—and I really mean everyone —I couldn't have a more supportive squad cheering me on. Even if I have forbidden some of you from ever reading my books!

Special thanks to my husband, who didn't even blink when I told him I was going to take time off work and try my hand at this writing romance thing.

And lastly, I'd like to thank each and everyone of you who picked up this book for taking a chance on me. I hope you enjoyed reading it, as much as I enjoyed writing it.

Monica

xoxo

Printed in Dunstable, United Kingdom

64134166R00150